Alibis:

Murder on Tour

Alibis:
Murder on Tour

Roger G. Baker

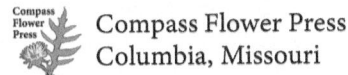
Compass Flower Press
Columbia, Missouri

Cover art by the author

Grand Canyon photo ©Roger Gene Hager

Compass
Flower
Press

Compass Flower Press
Columbia, Missouri
compassflowerpress.com

Library of Congress Control Number: 2025915233

ISBN: 978-1-951960-73-5   Trade paperback

ISBN: 978-1-951960-74-2   eBook

Dedicated to my wife Janice and all who assisted in making this novel a reality.

Special thanks to Josiah Jackson Krash, the alter ego of my dear friend and confidant Roger Gene Hager. It is a true joy to have such a friend and be allowed to have him as a major character in one of my novels.

CHAPTER 1

The name is Casper Gray. In college I was called Ghost by many of my closer friends, or I was called Spook by those with whom I was not as close. One of my history buddies said my personality was closer to John Singleton Mosby, the Gray Ghost of the Confederacy, than to Casper the Friendly Ghost of cartoon fame. He said, "Gray is able to be in a location and seems never to be noticed, and he knows almost everything about everyone in the vicinity. Either he's nosy or physic."

I really would have preferred to be thought of as curious. I enjoy people and always wanted to know what they were really about. So, I tried to stay in the background and just watched and listened as the others went about their daily routine.

Yeah...I guess I am a little bit nosy, and yeah...also a bit dippy in my sense of humor. As a child, I developed a habit of reading people, both their names and physical attributes, and then creating a funny name for them that reflected their description. But I can tell you more about that later if I need to clarify any facts.

So back to my story. I was born and reared in southern Illinois. Farming was the family industry, and I enjoyed hunting and fishing when I had any spare time. We lived near the Mississippi River, so all types of fish and game were at hand. Both of those hobbies required me to be quiet, listen, and watch. So I suppose I did learn to be a little ghostlike.

After high school I was fortunate to be able to go to a small college, Bristers, in a little town in Indiana. Since we worked the farm to make a living, it was decided that a business degree would be of great value to the family.

Sadly, late in my senior year the farm experienced a financial reversal, and my father had to sell out to keep from going bankrupt.

He and Mom were forced to move onto a tiny farm nearby to live. However, he had been a good farmer, and because of his farm knowledge he found a job field-managing a farm near our old home place. In the long term his wages amounted to more money than he was earning while running his own operation. He and Mom became very satisfied with their new endeavor.

But I'm boring you with that, so I will get back to how a spook of a common guy got involved with murder.

At the age of forty-seven, I was disappointed—my life hadn't been as rewarding as I had hoped it would be when I graduated from college. Twenty-five years ago the whole world was wide open before me, and all I needed to do was reach out and take what I wanted.

Lillian and I met while we both attended Bristers. She soon became the dream of my life. Lily was from Dayton, Ohio, and her field of expertise was writing.

Lily thought my game with names was a great gag, so she would egg me on to do it with everyone. She was the only one I could never create a name for. The only name I could ever come up with was: Lily, my beautiful love.

We married immediately after graduation and began to make great plans. She was a city girl, but my stories of life in the country inspired her interest in that style of living, so we decided we wanted a large house in the country. Then we wanted a nice car. Our biggest dream was of a child or two to make us a complete family.

Almost from the beginning things began to fray around the edges. Then, as if we were cursed, everything swiftly unraveled. No, it wasn't what you might be thinking; we loved each other and supported each other, but things just didn't evolve the way we envisioned.

First, I secured a fantastic job as office manager for a huge, financially successful business. My wages and benefits were unbelievable. But to keep the job I was required to live in New York City. We never had the chance to own a large house in the country. The nice car! Who can afford to own a car in New York City? Public transportation and rental properties became our way of life. Then almost immediately we discovered that Lily was barren. Unless we adopted, there would be no Gray children. That last revelation almost destroyed both of us.

My work eventually helped me get past that blow to our desires, but I never really discovered how it affected Lily.

Lily never held a full-time job. My job was good enough that she really didn't need to work. However, she did work off and on as a freelance writer, writing short stories and magazine articles, to keep from being bored.

The last weight to fall, the one that almost drove me crazy, was the sudden loss of Lily about five years ago. Unknown to us, she was born with a congenital heart defect, and this caused her early death. Her father had also died at a rather young age, but the doctors told us it was probably caused by his lifestyle, so we never questioned beyond that. And, of course, no autopsy was performed on him. Her mother ran away with another man when Lily was very young, so we thought that might have also shortened his life. He died at the age of fifty; Lily died at forty-one.

She didn't feel well for a couple of days, and we believed it was the onset of the flu. I came home from work one afternoon and found her on the couch, appearing to be asleep, still in her pajamas. It has taken the last five years for me to get past that horrible event. Presently I can't even describe her unless I'm looking at her picture.

For a long time after her death, making up names was the only lighthearted thing I could accomplish; that helped me to remain sane. When I created a new funny name, I was actually able to laugh a little as I conveyed my thoughts to her in my mind.

After that I decided to retire early, take the rewards my retirement offered, and try to enjoy whatever years were still left in my life.

CHAPTER 2

To honor Lily's memory, I decided to leave the city and try to make a life somewhere in the beauty of the countryside. Lily would go with me in the silver urn where her ashes dwelled.

After conferring with a financial adviser, I aligned my monetary wealth in a way that would ensure I would be able to enjoy my future in the style I desired. It was decided I could spend up to half a million dollars to buy a home and some land in the great outdoors and still be able to live a comfortable life from the remaining money I possessed and my monthly retirement check.

I began searching the internet and contacting real estate agents to find a nice place to settle, hoping I wouldn't need to spend $500,000 for what I wanted.

After living in New York, I desired to be near a larger city so I would have access to things I had become accustomed to within easy reach. The first thing on my list of wants was to locate somewhere in the middle part of the US. That way I could travel in any direction and not have to cross the entire country to get to my destination. No flights from one coast to the other or from border to border. I decided Missouri or Kansas were the best states to consider. Nebraska was also a slim possibility. I really wanted property situated near a larger water source. Since I had grown to adulthood on land near the Mississippi River and lived near the ocean in New York, I really wanted to spend my last years in the forest near a river or lake.

I finally located almost exactly what I wanted in the middle of the state of Missouri. A realtor called and stated that he had located a fifty-acre tract of land on a high bluff overlooking the Missouri River just a short distance from the capital city, Jefferson City. And he explained that from the bluff I could see for several miles across the river. To seal the deal, he described a historic old home on the apex of the bluff that had been built in the 1850s by a member of one of the first families of the county. It was one story, built of native stone, and had been well restored only a few years earlier. The realtor said the present owners would make good any defects I found during a purchaser's inspection, and I was assured I could make the purchase for $300,000 or a little less.

As soon as I could, I scheduled a flight from New York to St. Louis. There I rented a car and drove halfway across the state to Jefferson City. Having earlier made an appointment with the realtor, when I arrived he drove me from his office to the property for a prospective buyer's inspection.

About ten miles west of Jefferson City he turned right off State Road 179 into a small secluded lane. We wound our way up and around until the land leveled out toward the edge of a higher plateau, looking out over the rich river bottom land that edged the slow, rolling, muddy Missouri River. And there on the highest point, among the trees, almost hidden in its simplicity, was my historic dream home.

The house was long, low, and constructed almost entirely of native Missouri stone and beautiful black walnut timbers. Even before we entered the building, I knew Lily and I would be very happy in the solitude. After a quick, almost needless courtesy tour of the interior of the house, I agreed to place a cash retainer down for thirty days while I had two law firms investigate if everything was fair and legal. Within a short time both firms reported the same thing: The deal was legal and aboveboard.

A final price of $273,000 was agreed upon. Having almost $30,000 left out of the $300,000 I originally allotted, I would be able to also purchase a few pieces of period furniture to give the house a historic appearance. I felt five rooms would need at least three pieces each to appear historically authentic. I then hired one of the firms to complete all the necessary paperwork and the final transaction.

I was very happy with the purchase. It was not a big house, but it was what a retired widower and a lover of history would enjoy. And Lily would have a spot in the large front window to also enjoy the beautiful river and countryside. Besides this, Jefferson City was nearby, and the university town of Columbia was only about thirty miles away. Neither town was really that large, but they would do for all I needed.

After a flight back to New York, I cancelled my condo contract and paid the early withdrawal fee, sold and gave away all my excess personal property, and packed to move back to a life in the country.

When I made my permanent arrival back in Missouri, all that was left for me to do was find things to participate in to keep my life interesting.

Very quickly I discovered that my old love of hunting and fishing rushed back into my being. I thought perhaps that, still being a younger middle-aged man, there might be a younger middle-aged lady for me to spend some time with.

Since Jefferson City was the nearest of the two larger towns, I proceeded there to find a banking firm to handle my financial affairs. After a little research I finally settled on one that had been conducting business in the area for around a hundred years. I moved part of my ready cash out of my New York bank and into my local choice.

CHAPTER 3

Work I desired had already started on my new home, and I was promised it would be completed by a certain date or there would be reductions of my cost. I decided I would never find a better deal than that. Finally the day arrived when I could take ownership and move into my historic country palace. The construction was completed two weeks ahead of schedule, and the contractor included a two-year, no-questions-asked agreement on any updates or repairs that had not been done to my satisfaction. Again, I was greatly impressed.

I moved out of the apartment I had been renting and into my dream home. I hoped that Lily was excited as much as I. God! How I still missed that woman.

After a few weeks of settling in, I started looking for things to excite my interest and help me start to live again. I was doing a little fishing, and I purchased a .22-caliber rifle to allow me to hunt small game and kill a poisonous snake now and then.

One day as I was doing my regular banking, I noticed a flyer lying on the counter advertising a travel club within the bank. I asked the teller about it, and she directed me to another bank official who was in charge of that facet of their business.

Lily and I had traveled some around the eastern seaboard, but nowhere else. And I had not traveled at all after her death. So, out of curiosity I walked into the office and inquired about the travel club.

The young lady in charge was extremely excited and proud of what her office did for the bank's patrons who were interested in seeing the United States and some of the rest of the world through her program. And she also explained that day trips were offered to the theaters around the state and to professional baseball games in St. Louis and Kansas City. As a child in southern Illinois I was a rabid Cardinal fan, so that really piqued my interest.

I asked her what I had to do if I decided to participate in some of the travel her office provided. She said, "Decide which trip you desire to take, pay the fees, be prepared to leave on the appointed date, and board the bus or plane."

Then I asked her, "What trips do you have coming up in the near future?" She handed me a brochure about a trip to the desert southwest that would be leaving in about three weeks

Since I had never traveled in the western parts of the US, I quickly became interested in the possibilities. And when I discovered that one of the cashiers I did my banking business with was going to be personally involved in the tour, I felt more interest. She was a little younger than I, and I knew from our conversations that she had been divorced for a few years and was not involved with anyone else at that time. Her traveling with the tour caused me to be a little more than just interested.

I was told, "We have filled about half the slots available for this tour. If you are interested, we would love to have you join us on this adventure."

I checked my cell phone calendar and, as usual, I had nothing pressing for the next month...or two...or three, so I said, "Sign me up." With a great amount of anticipation, I signed on the dotted line, paid my fees for the tour, and then went home to enjoy the exciting thoughts of my first bus tour.

Good or bad, win or lose, Old Casper was headed on a bus tour to the desert southwest and a great adventure.

Thinking about Melody, the bank teller who would also be our tour director, caused a good feeling about the coming possibilities. She was charming, she seemed to have a sense of humor I could enjoy, and her looks were classic. She was of average height and slender build, with a nice rear, long legs, and ample breasts. Her face was oval-shaped with large hazel eyes, a narrow nose, and lips that appeared large with lipstick applied. Her hair color...hard to say because you can never be sure about a woman her age. And hair color didn't matter to me anyway, as long as it wasn't blue or green. She was simply a beautiful woman.

CHAPTER 4

June the 29th arrived, and I was at the Walmart's parking lot in Jefferson City at 6:00 a.m., ready to board the bus to see more of this great country.

I hired one of my neighbors to drive me to the meeting place so my new truck would not be left on the parking lot for the days I would be traveling.

Some of my new local friends and fellow church members told me I was being foolish for going to the southwest of the US at that time of year, as the temperature would be blazing hot in the high desert. However, I was afraid if I waited I might never have the nerve to try to travel without Lily ever again and would simply wither away of loneliness in my new environment.

As we boarded the bus I observed that just a few more than half the seats were occupied. I guessed most people didn't want to travel in the heat, but I didn't believe I would mind it as I always hated the damned cold in New York City, which arrived in late September or early October and lasted until as late as May. *Who knows,* I thought, *I just might love it blazing hot.*

We left Jefferson City and moved out onto the highway toward Kansas City. I sat back in my seat and silently studied my fellow tourists. The ghost was returning to his old college habits. See but don't be seen, listen but don't speak.

There were several couples, a young man who appeared to be alone, and another group of men and women like me—about my age and traveling as singles.

A group of about ten or fifteen appeared to be closely acquainted. That was probably not unusual, as Jefferson City, not really being that large, would lend itself to a lot of people knowing each other.

Later I learned that the group was really very well acquainted, as they all lived in the same neighborhood—most next door to each other, on the same street, or in the same block.

After a while I laid my head back, listened to the drone of small talk and the dual wheels rolling on I-70 beneath us, and slipped off into a traveler's nap.

I was afraid the first day on the road was going to be a little humdrum, as the only sightseeing mentioned was a short, off-road drive through Monument Rocks, a Kansas state tourist attraction. Being only a state park, I assumed it wouldn't amount to much.

After a fast-food lunch and potty break, we traveled on the interstate into western Kansas.

We left I-70 and took off on Old Highway 40 at Oakley, Kansas. Then we turned south on State Road 83 at Campus, toward Garden City. About twenty miles down the road I saw a sign that said, "Monument Rocks, Chalk Formations, a Kansas Natural Wonder."

I was pleasantly surprised—there were cliffs with natural windows through them and odd-shaped formations created by blowing wind and sand, all in a beautiful moonscape-like setting. We stopped a couple of times for quick picture-taking, and then it was back toward I-70.

That first night we stayed in a nice motel in the middle of nowhere and ate in its connected dining room. The fare was plain but adequate.

The next morning we arose early, had a quick continental breakfast, boarded the bus, and cruised on I-70 toward the Colorado line.

About twenty miles from the Colorado border, the bus turned south off I-70 onto Highway 27. A few miles south we turned west onto an unimproved road. I began to wonder if we were lost. My attention level heightened, and I watched closely to see where we were headed.

Shortly the intercom came on and our tour guide announced that the rise in elevation right ahead of us was Mt. Sunflower, elevation 4,039 feet. Then she laughed and said, "From now on, for the rest of your lives, you can tell people you have been to the highest mountain in Kansas."

After a short stop for pictures, we headed back north on another unimproved road to Kanorado, Kansas, and I-70.

In Kanorado we ate a quick lunch, then back on the road—Denver, Colorado, next stop.

As the bus continued its steady toil toward Denver, I continued to play the ghost as I watched and listened to the activities of my fellow travelers. I began to notice a slight ripple of social uneasiness, a sharp word in one area and an embarrassed giggle in another. Oddly, some of the people in the neighborhood group, those well acquainted, were not associating with each other on friendly terms. In fact, you could almost sense outright hostility. They did not outwardly antagonize each other, but the scent of trouble among them could be detected in the air. I hoped that whatever the problem was, it wouldn't spoil our southwestern tour.

As we crossed the state line into Colorado, I grinned and said to myself, *I guess Kansas isn't as dull as most Missourians think it is.*

But I never saw a Jayhawk on the prairie beside the interstate or flying overhead.

CHAPTER 5

In Denver we visited the Museum of Natural History. In the past, Lily and I had toured the Smithsonian so I wasn't overly impressed. But there were a few things of interest, so I still enjoyed the stop.

That night we stayed in another nice hotel in Denver. After checking in, we went directly to the dining room for dinner. There was a choice of fish or steak as the main course. I chose steak, and it was very tasty and satisfying.

As I walked back to my room, I passed the door to the bar. I didn't ordinarily drink in public, but I decided a cold beer might be a nice finish to the day, and we were beginning to get into the warmer temperatures.

Being alone, I looked for a seat out of the busier area of the bar. I located a seat in one of the darker corners and decided to visit, in my mind, with Lily as I enjoyed my beer.

The music playing from the speakers was old country and western "somebody done somebody wrong songs." And it brought back memories of my youth and Lily. With my eyes closed and Lily nearby in my thoughts, for a long while I simply listened and sipped my beer.

I finally opened my eyes, and I noticed in one of the other corners of the room, in the shadows, was a couple from our tour. I say a couple, but it was odd—the man was with a lady who I believed was the wrong woman, and the woman was with a man I didn't think was her husband.

The first night on the road, I seemed to remember, those two had gone into their motel rooms for the night with two other partners. Oh well, perhaps the beer and music had loosened my memory a little, and I was terribly mistaken. No matter—whichever couple they were, they were enjoying each other, a lot more than the beer.

Slowly and quietly I left my seat and slipped out of the bar and headed for my room. I'm not sure they even knew I was there.

As I stepped out of the elevator on my floor to get to my room, I almost walked head on into the opposite couple from the two in the bar, and again I thought, wrong husband, wrong wife. As we passed in the hall, I could see the woman appeared to be frustrated, and I believed she had tears in her eyes.

I nodded, said good night, and proceeded down the hall to my room. They disappeared around a corner, and I heard a door open and close.

With the joy of Lily in my mind and beer in my gut, I undressed and crawled into bed. I don't even recall brushing my teeth. I probably thought, *Hell, I can do that in the morning.*

Breakfast was a total delight: choice of eggs, sausage links or patties, biscuits and gravy, hash browns, pastries, coffee, milk, or hot tea.

As I started to sit down at a table with my food, the man from the bar the night before sat down across the dining room with a woman other than the one he was with about nine hours earlier. He was slender in build and sported a small Hitler-like mustache. The woman with him was light-brown to blond haired. And she was the one in the hall with the football-player type in front of my room the night before. She was the one with the hard frown and tears in her eyes. I call him the football-player type because he was muscular and square built. Then I was absolutely sure: wrong man, wrong wife.

I enjoyed my breakfast and put aside the men and women and their problems—not my business anyway.

After breakfast, our luggage was collected and loaded under the bus. Next stop would be ski country and Vail, Colorado. We would see the fabulous hotels and the scenic ski slopes. There would be no snow, but the ski runs would be a real sight for a New Yorker.

I gathered my small personal belongings from the room, turned in my key, and headed for the bus.

As I walked onto the bus and down the aisle to my seat, the football player was seating himself next to the polished redhead who was with the slender man in the bar the night before. Now I knew the game had a smell like dead fish.

As I passed his seat he put out his hand and said, "I'm Bob Bulkowski, and this is my wife Rhonda. Boy, did you have one tied on last night—you almost stepped on us in that damned shadowy hallway." Turning to the redhead, he continued, "Remember that, Rhonda?" She kept her eyes down and grunted in agreement.

I said, "I'm sorry, I don't remember much about what happened last night after dinner—must have been the beer. Sorry again if I caused any trouble."

"No trouble; that's what these trips are for, to turn loose and enjoy life a little. Oh say, what's your name?"

Clumsily I mumbled, "I'm Casper Gray, and I'm really sorry about last night." Quickly I rushed to my seat, sat down, and looked out the window as the bus lumbered out into the traffic on the interstate.

Then a small giggle escaped my lips. I imagined the couple's name immediately: Bull and the Red Flag!

Later I scanned the passengers all around me, and in seats a few rows ahead of me was the slender man with the teary-eyed, brownish-blond-haired woman next to him.

Earlier I had checked the bus list, and he was Jeb Pinn, and the lady was his wife Bonnie: Mr. Slim and Blondie.

With Denver behind us we started climbing the slope of the Colorado Rockies toward the Eisenhower Tunnel. Our guide said we had enough time, if we cared to, to skip the tunnel and drive on up and over Loveland Pass. Many on the tour group had been through the tunnel, but some had never traveled over the pass. A vote was taken, and the majority was for a drive over the top. I hadn't been west of the range either, so I said to myself, *I'll get to see more of the country from the mountain pass.*

In the early afternoon we motored into Vail and the huge skiing center of the Rockies. I was impressed with the grandeur of the mountain ski slopes and the Alpine buildings of Vail. We exited the bus for a short potty break, then back on the bus to motor through Vail with another hour stop at some high-priced shops to purchase T-shirts and souvenirs. I found a tee that fit my situation to a T. On the back it said, "From the Rockettes to the Rockies."

Then it was once more back on the bus, headed to our next stop for dinner and another night's sleep.

As I got back on the bus, Mr. Slim and a short, portly, balding man appeared to be in a heated discussion. I heard the slender one say something to the effect of, "Let it lay until after the tour. You know I've always been good for it!"

Bald Dome, the Dude, tapped his finger on Mr. Slim's chest and said, "Or you're history!" Then he turned and moved to his seat.

Slim moved past me to his seat with an indescribable expression on his face.

I quickly retrieved my carry-on bag from the rack overhead and checked the tour list to identify the Dude if I could. As I scanned the list I became fairly certain that he was Dub Waller, a businessman and one of the neighborhood group that was traveling together.

At the time I didn't know that Waller's business was big-time illegal gambling. But I thought Pinn was probably into the Bald Dome for a lot of cash.

Then I realized the bus was moving and we were headed to our next hotel.

CHAPTER 6

As I started to relax in my seat with questions flowing through my mind concerning the other creatures I was touring with, an interesting creature by the name of Melody came down the aisle toward where I was seated. I assumed she was headed to the bathroom in the back as I closed my eyes and continued in thought.

Instinctively I sensed that someone was looking at me, so I opened my eyes. Melody was standing next to me in the aisle with her hand resting behind my head on the back of the seat. She asked, "Do you mind if I join you?"

Because the bus was not full, the seat next to me was not occupied, so I said, "No, please, I would be delighted for you to join me."

She sat down beside me and immediately whispered, "You appear to be the only man on the tour near my age and single. If we visit, I will not have to worry about a jealous wife or the others thinking I'm hitting on one of the older gentlemen."

I grinned and jokingly replied, "I thought my good looks and charm caused you to want to visit."

Almost seriously she said, "Yes, I also had already considered those two facts." Then she continued, "Seriously, when you came into the bank to do your financial business, I decided I wanted to get to know you better if I could ever figure a way to see you away from the bank. And, I thought I sensed that you were also interested in who I was."

Then it was my turn to say something, so I spoke frankly. "I'm a widower that hasn't been able to have a sincere thought about a female since my wife's death. You were friendly, and yes, I wanted to find out if I could be a man around a woman other than her. I hope this doesn't scare you away."

She dropped her head and spoke, almost in another whisper, "My husband ran away with another woman, and since that time I haven't been able to trust another man. So we both are trying to test new waters. We might prove to be good for each other, even if all we end up being are friends. Would you care to try?"

I thought for a moment and then answered, "We can't lose a lot by trying."

She reached over, touched my hand, and said, "Will you have dinner with me tonight so we can start to get to know each other?"

Of course, my answer was "Yes."

She sat back, closed her eyes, and held my hand as the big wheels continued to hum as we traveled farther into the Rockies.

At that moment I had no time to think about Bull, Slim, the Dude, or any of the others on the tour. My mind was totally filled with Melody and Lily.

As Sweet Melody and I sat there next to each other, hand in hand, the big "Seeing America" bus continued its conquest of Interstate 70, on toward our next stop for the night in Glenwood Springs, Colorado.

After a pleasant interlude holding Melody's hand and exploring my own thoughts of her, she suddenly stood up and made her way toward the front of the bus. Her sudden move caught me by surprise. But then as she turned on the intercom mic I realized we must be nearing our motel, and she was preparing us for our overnight lodging.

In a voice I was quickly beginning to enjoy, she announced that the Glenwood Suites was directly ahead and that a short time after our arrival we would go to Big Leroy's Steak House for our evening meal. All that registered in my mind was that I was going to enjoy Sweet Melody's company as I also enjoyed a huge steak at Big Leroy's!

As our luggage was moved into our rooms, I noticed that Melody's bright-pink matching pieces were moved into the room next to mine. I said to myself, *Is this a coincidence, or is there a plan I'm not aware of?*

I quickly freshened up a little before leaving the room to join the short walk to the steak house.

As I came around the corner of the hallway headed to the group meeting point at the main entry, I passed a young man from our group talking to another middle-aged couple. Loudly and angrily he almost shouted, "Can you believe that? I'm in the room right next door to that son of a bitch Pinn and his mealy-mouthed wife. I hope he chokes to death on his steak and I can spit in his dead-ass face!"

Then the man in the couple, with tears in his eyes, said, "Shane, you would be the third in line behind Wanda and me."

As I continued down the hall, I wondered what the story was that I was not privileged to.

Then I saw Melody, and my mind moved on to the more important things of the evening. She gathered our tour, and we walked out the door and down the street toward Big Leroy's.

After a short distance she fell in beside me, and we continued, as a couple, to the steak house.

CHAPTER 7

When we got to the reserved section at Big Leroy's, Melody assisted in seating all of our tour except herself and me. After all were seated, she looked at me and motioned with her head for me to follow. We went around behind a large potted plant in a corner and found a small table for two, almost out of sight of the rest of the tour. With a huge smile on her face, she asked, "Is this satisfactory, sir?"

All I could get out of my mouth was, "How?"

Again the smile. "Remember, big boy, I make all the arrangements."

As I held her chair and then seated myself a puzzled look probably crossed my face.

Before I could say anything, she said, "Please, at this time don't read anything into the room assignments. I'll explain that later."

Quickly I smiled and said, "Let's order. I'm starved, and I want the biggest steak this place will serve. Besides, you're paying for it."

Returning my smile, she answered, "Not me. It's you and your bank who's paying."

As we sat there eating and talking, my curiosity overcame me, and I asked, "Is there a story about a part of our tour group that I should know? It appears that some members of our tour really hate each other."

A dark shadow crossed her face as she started to answer. "I could get into real trouble at my job for telling you what you are asking about. But, I can tell you what appeared in the newspapers, because it is public knowledge."

She took a breath and collected her thoughts and then continued, "Some years back, just a short time after the bank started sponsoring the travel tours, a group of neighbors formed a travel group to go on the bank tours together. At that time it was great fun."

Taking a drink of her iced tea, she thought again and then continued, "Then about a year or so ago something happened, and the group fell apart as friends. However, they still travel together, for what purpose I don't know."

"What happened?" I asked as my curiosity burned in my mind.

"One of the couple's daughter committed suicide, and one of the other members was blamed for causing it."

Before I could stop myself, I blurted, "Is Old Slim the one who was blamed for the suicide?"

Melody gave me a funny look, and I quickly corrected myself. "I mean, I believe his name is Pinn. Is he the one?"

She said, "You already know the story."

"No, this evening as we were gathering for dinner, I heard an exchange between a young man and an older couple hoping that Pinn would drop dead on this tour."

Melody thoughtfully said, "Probably Shane Chance and the Parks. The girl who died was Shane's girlfriend, and the couple was probably Charles and Wanda Parks..."

Before she could finish, I said, "The dead girl's parents!"

"Yes, ZuZu was eighteen when it happened." With tears in her eyes, Melody said, "Could we talk about something else? This subject is not what I envisioned us talking about on our first...date? I know you are interested, but you can look up the story in the old newspapers on the web, and that will tell you more than I probably know."

With complete sincerity I said, "I'm really sorry I asked those questions. What would you like to talk about?"

With the big beautiful smile, she answered, "Us."

Before she could say anything else, I said, "Besides my wife, I have never said this to any other woman: Mrs. Muldune, you are a very lovely woman, and I am almost speechless, if that is possible, to be enjoying this meal and evening with you."

She replied, "And I am very pleased that you decided to take this tour, and I am honored to dine and be with you tonight."

I reached across the table and took her hand in mine and looked directly into her eyes for a long moment.

She suddenly pulled her hand back and dropped her head, looking into her plate. A tiny voice escaped her lips as she said, "I'm sorry, but suddenly I had a feeling toward you that I have not felt about a man for a long, long time. Please give me more time to sort out who and what you are, because I don't want to make a mistake or foul up something really great."

I sat back, smiled, and answered, "Sweet Melody, I have all the rest of my life to be around you. Let me know when and if the time is ever right."

She reached back across the table, took my hand, smiled, and replied, "The time may be closer than you think, and that's what scares the hell out of me."

Then our conversation continued as small talk while we enjoyed all the food Big LeRoy's had to offer. And as I enjoyed the presence of Melody just across the table.

We began to hear people moving around and realized that the tour group had finished eating and was ready to return to the hotel.

Getting up from her chair, she came around the table, took my hand once more, and said, "What the hell, I'm an adult, so who cares what the rest of them think. Come on, let's herd the troops back to the bedrooms."

I giggled and said, "We stay around each other for much longer, and we will act as silly as a couple of teenagers."

She also giggled and replied, "Being a teenager wasn't so bad."

Still holding hands, we delivered the group back to the Glenwood.

CHAPTER 8

I delivered Melody to her door, next to mine, and turned to enter my own room. As I turned she grabbed my hand, and I turned back around, looking her in the face.

With eyes lowered and a guilty smile on her face, she whispered, "I thought I might at least rate a small kiss for my evening's work."

Leaning closer to her, I whispered, "Should we be doing this in the open hallway? I don't want to have stories get back to the bank that you are involved with one of your tour people."

She quickly looked both ways up and down the hall and, seeing no one watching, pulled me into her room and closed the door. Then, placing her lips close to my ear, she whispered, "Now keep quiet and properly thank me for being your teenage date for the evening."

Feeling myself break out in a cold sweat, I put my arms around her and delivered a clumsy kiss. She softly giggled, squeezed me tight, and delivered a fantastic return. I almost melted in my shoes.

Then she quickly said, "Please don't take that as some type of invitation; it's way too soon to make a more serious move. Do you understand what I'm saying? I'm not saying no, just please wait for me to be more prepared."

Then I kissed her the way I had planned to before and answered, "Yes, I understand, because I am scared to death too. I feel like I'm cheating on my wife, and she's been gone more than five years. I also need time and preparation."

Then in her full voice she said, "Would you like to stay awhile to visit and get to know each other better?"

I took her hand and answered, "Yes, yes, and yes! I want to know all about you!"

She held up one finger as a motion for me to stop. I paused, and she said, "I put us rooming next to each other so I might have you to visit with in the evenings. As a single on these tours, I sometimes get lonely with no one to talk to. This way I won't have to run all over the hotel if I want to visit. All I'll have to do is knock on the next door. After the past couple of minutes, it looks like my plan is okay."

I nodded.

Then we sat down together on the small couch in the room and told each other a lot of our life histories.

After what seemed like only a few minutes, I looked at my watch and then realized we had chatted continuously for more than four hours. It was 1:15 in the morning, and we had to be at breakfast at 7:00. I jumped up, pecked Melody on the cheek, checked the hall for any prying eyes, then rushed next door to my room.

CHAPTER 9

The alarm sounded at 6:30, way sooner than I was prepared for. Since retiring and enjoying country living, I had developed a desire to sleep a little longer in the mornings, so I was not prepared to open my eyes at that moment. But I suddenly remembered there was a certain charming lady to have breakfast with, and I didn't plan on missing that. I hadn't shared the breakfast table with a woman for more than five years, and I wanted to start enjoying that activity once again.

It took me a grand total of twenty minutes to shave, shower, and dress. I set my suitcase outside my room and closed the door at 7:00 a.m. on the dot. Then it was time to find Sweet Melody.

When I rounded the corner and entered the breakfast room, I found that beautiful woman assisting one of the little old ladies from our tour with her tray and coffee. A small touch of jealousy formed in my mind. I wanted her to be close to me, right away, so I could again experience the warm feeling that started to return last night after having been missing from my life for so long. Then reality returned as I remembered that this was her job and I would have to wait until her work was finished before she could join me.

I located a table for two and proceeded to find the coffee pot and a cup to begin my morning ritual. I sipped my morning brew until Sweet Melody was once more free to join me.

I sensed her behind me before she came into my range of vision. Feeling her fingertips touch my shoulder, a tingling charge of energy shot through my entire being. I suddenly knew I would not need too much more time until she would become my entire reason for existing. But at the same time I also knew I could not push her, or I might lose her. Damn this game of falling in love! It certainly is a young man's game, but old farts get drawn to the bait and caught too. But damn, I knew I was really enjoying the fisherman, or woman, involved and could hardly wait for her to set the hook.

Then she smiled down at me and said in her usual voice, "Good morning."

Then in a voice just a little louder than a whisper, she added, "Love."

It was almost more than I could do to keep my hands off her as she seated herself across the table from me and commenced to eat her breakfast.

CHAPTER 10

At 8:00 a.m. sharp the bus doors closed, and we were back on the road. Melody was in her usual spot in the front seat with the intercom mic in her hand. She explained the tour plans for the day concerning places of interest, potty breaks, and snacks, and then she began joking and gearing us up for adventure.

I was totally out of the excitement of the adventure, as all my mind was involved with was the sound of a Sweet Melody. I didn't remember feeling this giddy since the first moment I met Lily. And that was so many years ago.

Then a sudden piercing thought crossed my mind, and I remembered the dark part of this tour. Slim slid back into my thoughts and then the Chance kid and the Parkses. The way I was starting to feel about Melody caused me to remember that Chance, no doubt, felt the same way about ZuZu, and then she was gone. I thought, *That kid must be in terrible pain.* Then it hit me: Shane, the One in Pain. Not a funny title but one that fits. Then I also thought of the Parkses: Two Sad for Words. Another sad title.

I promised myself that as soon as I could find time alone, I was going to check the net on my laptop to read the stories about ZuZu's suicide.

Then I heard Melody announce that we would be in Moab, Utah, by nightfall and would stay at the Moab Sands Lodge. She said it was ultramodern but had a regional appearance—whatever that meant. I hoped it had a nice steak house for our dinner; I was beginning to love those places. But, if not, I would still be close to that beautiful creature. Ain't love grand?

At about 11:45 we stopped for lunch at a little junction that proudly sported a newer McDonald's. Melody once more joined me and caused the hamburgers to taste like filet mignon. I was beginning to think I could live on her love and need nothing else.

Between a bite of hamburger and a french fry, she smiled across the table and silently mouthed, "I think I could love you."

I choked and coughed as my mind attempted to digest that. Then I silently thought the words, *Thank you, God, for putting me on this tour.*

Then it was back on the bus as Melody announced we would be driving through Arches National Park before we arrived in Moab.

As I looked at my watch it was a little past 1:00 p.m., and I saw a sign that said Arches National Park was fourteen miles ahead. Looking out the windows I saw large odd-shaped rock formations on both sides of the blacktop road we were traveling on. Shortly I saw a large rock formation with a hole through it and then understood why the area was called Arches. As we continued on, some of the holes in the rocks were large enough that if the road went in the right direction the bus could have traveled through the holes. More than a few looked like bridges, and some were definitely naturally arch-shaped.

We stopped at some of the arches that were near the pavement so those who desired to could take photographs. I had no one to show pictures to, so I was not even carrying a camera. But I got off the bus to get a closer look at the oddities of nature and to be closer to Melody. I believed she was what I wanted and needed, but the thought of a relationship after being alone for so long scared me senseless.

After several stops and foot tours, Melody said we needed to head on toward Moab to arrive for our dinner reservations. Hot damn! She announced it was another famous regional steakhouse: Reggie's of the Rocks. It was built before Arches National Park was established, so it sits directly under one of the few arches that exist outside the park. By today's laws it could never have been built under an arch.

The Moab Sands Lodge was just as Melody described it. It had a regional appearance, but I'm not exactly sure what region. From the outside, it was a monstrosity of tinted glass and steel. It could have been built on Mars, it was that modernistic.

But after we got inside, I was more than pleasantly surprised. It was nicely air-conditioned, the furnishings were modern but comfortable, and the soda and beer were ice-cold. And yes, the rooms were very pleasant also. And yes again, Melody's room and mine were next door to each other. Now if Reggie's proved out, I'd believe I was batting a thousand.

After checking in and picking up our keys, Melody announced we would meet in about forty-five minutes, as it would be necessary to ride the bus to Reggie's.

After being out of the bus and in the heat several times during the afternoon, I was happy to have time to freshen up and put on a clean shirt.

I touched Melody's hand and said I would see her in a few minutes as she was rushing to her room to freshen up also.

CHAPTER 11

At 6:56 I left my room and headed toward the front door of the motel to meet Melody and catch the bus. As I stopped in the foyer looking for her, I noticed Mr. Slim and Blondie were quietly talking to an African American couple from the tour, but I didn't know who they were. As I started past them the new couple blocked my way, and the gentleman said, "I'm Henry Chum, and this is my wife Roberta. We are trying to become acquainted with everyone on the tour."

He held out his hand to shake mine, and I replied, "Casper Gray, retired office manager. Very happy to meet you."

Then he turned back toward Slim and Blondie and said, "This is Jeb and Bonnie Pinn. I work in the same office as Jeb."

Then it was my turn to stick out my hand to shake with Mr. Slim. "Really a pleasure to meet you also." Then I shook hands with Blondie.

At that moment Melody came into view, and I excused myself from the Pinns and Chums, then walked to meet her.

Once my back was to the foursome, I felt a huge grin on my face and a laugh in my heart as I said to myself, *Henry and Roberta Chum— that would have to be just a couple of old chums, Hank and Bob.*

I guess Melody thought I was grinning at her, because she said, "It makes me feel so good that you are so happy to see me."

I allowed my amused grin to change to a smile of happiness as she took my arm and walked with me to the bus.

Reggie's was not Big Leroy's, but the food was still tasty enough that I would give it an 8 or 9.

With Melody across the table from me, I could just as easily have given it a 10.

As we ate we discussed viewing the natural wonders that the tour was visiting. Melody said the Grand Canyon or Monument Valley would be the absolute highlight of the trip. I winked and said, "For me there was one more." She dropped her eyes, and her face blushed. I said, "I was thinking of the great food."

She looked me in the eye and replied, "Uh-huh!" Then she seriously asked, "Can we visit again tonight? Or do you have something else to do?"

I smiled and said, "Being with you is all I plan to ever have to do."

She replied, "I could say the same thing to you, but one of us still has to work for a living."

I was chewing a piece of tender beef at that moment, so I couldn't immediately answer. Realizing my predicament, she waited, giving me time to compose a serious answer in my mind.

"If things work out, perhaps you won't be working, and we will be enjoying life together."

To that she gave no answer.

Like the night before, the others began to break away from the dinner to return to the bus. Melody did not immediately follow their lead, so I gave her a questioning look.

"When we get back to the lodge, I'll need a few minutes alone before you come to my room or before I come to your room. Is that okay?" she asked.

"I'll be in my room, so if you want me in your room, give me a call. If you are coming to my room, just knock."

As we left the bus and were walking back to our rooms, I wasn't sure what was happening, but I went into my room, freshened up a little, and slipped into a simple T-shirt to get cooler.

CHAPTER 12

I turned on my laptop and began to surf, looking for a news source that might give me some information about the ZuZu Parks suicide. I figured I wouldn't have much time before Melody made an appearance, but at least I could see if anything was available. The things going on between the members of our tour from that neighborhood were making me uncontrollably nosy. I was almost frantic to know what went on at the time of ZuZu's death and what was going on presently.

I had just made a hit on the archives from the Jefferson City TV station, KRCG, when my cell phone rang. It was Melody asking that I come to her room for the evening.

I closed my laptop, turning off the stream but not the power. I decided I might look into the story a little bit when I came back from Melody's room.

Then my mind clicked into another sort of nosy as I wondered what game Melody had in mind this evening.

I quietly opened my door, checked for movement in the hallway, and then stepped in front of the next door and knocked.

I barely heard Melody's voice speak out, "It's open."

I checked the hallway again, then opened her door, stepped inside, and closed the door behind me. I immediately saw a bottle of champagne on ice and two wine glasses on the tiny reading table.

From the bathroom Melody said, "Would you open the champagne and pour us each a drink?"

As I turned toward the table to pour the drinks, with my back to the bathroom door, I sensed she had come into the room and was standing directly behind me. I picked up the two half-full glasses and turned to put one into her hand. What my eyes beheld caused me to almost drop both glasses.

Melody was dressed entirely in black! If you could call it dressed.

She stood there in a Victoria's Secret string halter top and a thong with lace trim. I knew she was beautiful, but I never dreamed she was dazzling.

Holding up one finger in a signal to stop, she said, "First, I'm sorry; as I've said before, this is not an invitation. I'm still not ready to venture to the next level. I just wanted you to know that you are only the second man who has ever seen me this close to totally naked. I'm doing this to let you know you are very, very special to me. In the not-too-distant future I hope I can become completely special to you."

Then she took both glasses of the cold champagne out of my hand, set them back on the table, and without warning was in my arms with her beautiful bare flesh all over me.

Then she whispered, "Short of making sexual love, I want you to hold me and enjoy me! I want to prove I'm all yours if you want me."

Then I said something I hoped Lily would understand: "You are only the second woman in my life that I have ever wanted."

Sometime later in the evening, the champagne was gone, Melody's eyes were droopy, and I knew it was time for me to remove myself back to my room. I enjoyed one last kiss, then it was check the hall, and back into my bedroom.

The ZuZu suicide would have to wait, so I shut down my laptop and returned it to my carry-on.

I only took time for a quick shower and a tooth brushing, then it was into the sack with warm, lovely thoughts and dreams of a beautiful woman.

CHAPTER 13

It was one of those mornings. A 5:00 wake-up call and on the road at 5:45. The champagne came back to me with a vengeance. Something in it left me with one hell of a hangover. I couldn't face breakfast, so I phoned Melody to tell her I would see her on the bus. She sounded worried, but I told her I would be all right, I just couldn't drink that brand of champagne ever again.

I was the first one on the bus and had my head back and eyes closed as the others began to come on board. A couple slid into the seats behind me, and as they spoke I recognized their voices as the Chums. I smiled inwardly as I once more thought, *Hank and Bob.* They must have believed I was asleep, as they allowed their voices to creep above a whisper.

"That sucker has done it to me again," I heard Henry say.

"What?"

"Jeb stole another one of my innovations, and the company is paying him a bonus for it. The thieving bastard, this is the fourth time he has pulled something like this on me."

"But Babe, he is your boss; shouldn't he get the credit for what is developed in his department?"

"Hell no! No matter who the employee is, he or she is to be recognized and paid for any idea that increases the company's bottom line."

"How did you find out?"

"The SOB bragged to Bulkowski that he had screwed me again, and Bob told me during breakfast. I guess the company called Jeb and thanked him for *his* great idea." With what sounded like revenge in his voice, he continued, "I hope he gets his, someday, someway!"

Then the intercom came on, and I couldn't hear anything else they said.

Melody began to give the daily instructions as everyone else started discussing and asking questions.

I felt much better, so I raised my head and heard her say we would drive through Glen Canyon National Recreation Area and on into Page, Arizona, for the night.

Then she turned off the intercom and started down the aisle in my direction, stopping to talk to first one person and then another. When she got to my seat, she sat down next to me, and we talked for a short time. She asked if I had done any research on ZuZu yet. I told her I started last night before our visit but didn't get very far because I was rudely interrupted. I winked at her, and she blushed. After a few moments she reached over and squeezed my hand and then told me the bus had Wi-Fi.

She said, "It's not perfect out in this part of the country, but you might get something."

Then she excused herself, saying she had paperwork and scheduling to do as she moved back to the front of the bus.

I decided I would take her suggestion and surf for information instead of napping all day. I retrieved my laptop from my carry-on and turned it on to see if a signal could be found. I was in luck, so I reestablished a stream to the KRCG archives.

CHAPTER 14

As I returned to my research of ZuZu Parks's suicide, I was not expecting what I found. After watching the TV reports and reading the newspaper accounts, I couldn't understand how young Chance and the Parkses could be on the same bus with Pinn. And surely the others who appeared to be friendly with him had to know the story, unless they were blind and couldn't read.

The accounts told a story of probable rape and possibly other sadistic actions on the part of Pinn leading to Miss Parks's suicide.

The account basically was as follows: ZuZu Parks was a senior in high school and by all school records was very intelligent. She secured a job in the evenings and on weekends working in Jeb Pinn's office. She took the job to earn money to help out with her expenses when she entered college in the fall.

After she accomplished a very difficult task at the office that caused Pinn to get a commendation, he informed her he was throwing a party at his home to thank her for the fantastic job.

After she was raped, she told the police that she had walked to Pinn's house because it was the next house down the street from her parents' house with a small park in between. When she got there, Mrs. Pinn was not at home. But, Jeb Pinn told her that was not a problem, as the party was still being held. Then he took his cell phone out of his pocket and said it was vibrating, and he went into the next room to take the call.

When he returned, he explained that his secretary had dropped the ball and had not notified the rest of the office personnel about the party. With great apology, he said that he would reschedule the party for a later date. But, since she was already there, why not have a drink and some dessert before she returned home?

She said he seemed to be so nice, she agreed. Besides, she was eighteen and would be off to college in the fall, so she could handle one drink.

She told the officer that she took one small drink from the glass. And the next thing she knew, she was sitting on a swing in the park and her dress was badly torn. When she stood up, she realized she was not wearing any lower underclothing. And she was experiencing some pain in the genital area. She said she then made her way home and, while almost in total hysteria, told her parents she believed she had been raped.

Her father immediately called the police, and they arrived within minutes.

One of the officers was a young female, and she quietly began to question ZuZu as to what happened. In the narrative, she suddenly said, "I think Mr. Pinn must have been the one who raped me, because the last thing I remember was taking a drink from the glass."

The young female officer remained with ZuZu as they waited for an ambulance, while the other officers went down the street to question Jeb Pinn.

After all the Q and A and wading through the intrigue, Pinn's final story was that ZuZu drank like a fish and then said she would see herself home, that she did not need him to drive her. He stated he believed on her way home she ran into some trashy boys and had a good old sex party.

The police checked with Pinn's secretary, and she said Mr. Pinn had left a note at the office for her to call him at home at about 7:00 p.m. She said she called, and he asked her how many of the office personnel were coming to his house for Miss Parks's party. She said she was not aware of a party at his house. Then he berated her for not notifying the staff about the get-together.

As she burst into tears, she said, "Things have not been good with me for a few days, and I guess I forgot to forward the party invitation. But, I don't really remember being told there was to be a party at the Pinns' home."

Sadly, when ZuZu was examined, it was determined that she had been raped, but there was no DNA evidence in or on her to identify the guilty party.

As soon as Pinn was approached as a possible suspect for the rape, he sent a message telling her she was fired because he did not want a filthy little sex pervert working in his office.

Almost immediately after that, local radio talk shows began to receive calls claiming Pinn was bragging in some of the bars around town about putting the make on a good-looking little bitch, and there wasn't a thing she or anyone else could do about it.

In a short time, ZuZu was dead of an overdose on the sleeping pills she was given after the rape. She had taken them all at one time.

After my research, I was sorry I had found out about her death. I didn't know if Pinn was guilty or not, but I certainly didn't enjoy what I had learned.

CHAPTER 15

I shut off my laptop, closed it, and sat there in a state of shock. If Pinn was not a rapist, neither was he a nice man. No one should ever be treated the way that man treated the little Parks gal. Especially right after she was raped. If I were her father, I would have tried to take his head off.

I looked toward the front of the bus, and there he was. I felt ashamed to be in the same area where he was. And after what I overheard from Henry Chum, Pinn appeared to be a real piece of work. No one had a good word to say about him.

While my passion was inflamed toward Pinn, I also wondered what involvement Dub Waller and Old Slim had with each other. I remembered hearing Jeb say, "You know I've always been good for it!"

Good for what? I asked myself. *Does Pinn owe Waller money on a loan or something?*

I decided to check out Dub Waller on my laptop. I entered Dub Waller and his business affiliations in Jefferson City into my search engine and was surprised when William W. Waller popped up on the screen. A blog appeared stating William W. "Dub" Waller was a suspected associate of Giarmo Gobbie, mob gaming boss out of St. Louis. He was also suspected of mob money laundering through his business venture in Jefferson City.

Bingo! Waller was probably Old Slim's bookie, to whom Slim appeared to owe a ton of cash.

Then my mind went into a whirlwind. *Everyone from his neighborhood must hate him, but they are still traveling as a group, a club. There's just one couple from the group who I have not heard say something bad about him: the Rainses.* A light flashed across my mind. Even though I was feeling nothing but darkness at that moment, their name released the old habit as I thought, *Clyde and Thelma Rains, The Damp Pair.*

As thoughts of all kinds shot back and forth across my mind, I was stopped short as I heard Melody's hypnotic voice float from the intercom.

"We have arrived on the edge of Glen Canyon National Recreation Area. You are aware Glen Canyon runs from central Utah into northern Arizona. But, today is a very special day. If you have not been paying attention, today is the Fourth of July, Independence Day. Utah does not allow fireworks in the park, so to celebrate the holiday, for the first time this tour is including a visit to Rainbow Bridge National Monument. For you who do not know, Rainbow Bridge is another natural arch. However, it is extremely large and considered to be a very special natural wonder of the southwest. That is the reason we had to leave the motel so early this morning."

Immediately the questions and discussions about Rainbow Bridge commenced. Melody was almost consumed by the demand for all types of information.

I laid my head back and allowed myself to nap. The last I heard Melody say was, "It took a lot of planning and contracting to enable this group to go up to Rainbow Bridge. A surprise is that you will be taking a boat ride to the site."

Sometime later I became aware that someone was gently shaking my shoulder. I opened my eyes, and Melody, with a concerned look on her face, said, "Are you okay?"

I grinned and said quietly, "I am now," as I reached up and softly squeezed one of her fingers for just a moment.

She sat down next to me and asked, "Did you find out anything about ZuZu's death?"

With almost a growl I nodded and answered, "Pinn must be a sorry individual, or he is lower than an animal. If he's guilty of only half of what I've learned, he shouldn't even be living."

Then she voiced what I had been wondering all along: "Why does this group still travel together? They must all know what he was accused of. Do you suppose he could have some leverage over all of them?"

"I don't know, but we can't allow him to take our fun and happiness away, so let's put it out of our minds, if we can, and try to enjoy Rainbow Bridge."

"Yes please. I've made this tour several times, but I've never been to this arch, and I'm dying to see it. And, I'm going to get to see it with someone I love."

When she said that, a huge lump formed in my chest, and my heart began to pound. I guessed I was also in love.

She got up from the seat and moved back to her spot in front and once more turned on the intercom. "From this point on, you will need to follow all my instructions, to save time, to make connections, and to get you to Page for dinner and our lodging for the night."

And then she added a short statement I believed was directed at me. "And any other special night plans you might have."

And I was already planning some!

In a short while we left the bus and boarded the boat.

At Rainbow, as we stood there on the level stone surface, I was almost overcome by the beauty and splendor of the huge stone arch. It rose majestically into the air, dwarfing us mere mortals there below. I know I must have squeezed Melody's hand so tightly that it hurt her. But she didn't try to break my grip or make a sound. She simply stood there with her mouth open in wonder also.

The stone was worn smooth by eons of moving water and sand. Its color was a beautiful shade of pinkish orange that absorbed the sun and then cast it back out of itself into our faces to continuously hold our attention.

I've seen the Empire State Building and the Twin Towers, but they grew small in comparison to this natural wonder.

All too soon it was time to get back on the boat, return to the bus, and continue on to Page, Arizona, and another night of contemplations. And for me, perhaps a chance to touch and hold what had become very important to me.

CHAPTER 16

Must be getting old. After the boat adventure to get to Rainbow Bridge and then hiking the short distance to the viewing point, I was almost totally bushed. The fairly short ride to Page, Arizona, just seemed to add to my feeling of being all worn out.

When Melody joined me near the end of the ride, she said, "I'm ashamed to say it, but I feel like I've aged ten years today."

I grinned and replied, "If you believe you're tired, you should sit in this seat for a while, it will really let you know how worn out you are."

She changed the subject and asked, "Was all the extra energy we used worth it to see the bridge?"

I assured her it was, by far, the best part of the tour so far.

"I'm glad, because it took a lot of negotiating with the bank before they would allow me to add it to the tour. They considered the boat trip to be a huge liability."

Then she changed the subject again. "I'm so tired I'm not even hungry. Why don't we skip dinner, go for a swim in the hotel pool, then sneak away to one of our rooms and pretend we are teenagers on a date in the old man's pickup?"

It sounded a little brazen to me, but I was all for it.

"How about a beer later, if we decide we need something for our stomachs?"

She grinned and answered, "Maybe some roasted nuts or salted peanuts too?"

Since a kiss was out of the question, I played the old squeeze-her-hand trick. She squeezed back.

Then it was time for her to go up front and explain our night's lodging and the plans for our departure in the morning.

She started her commentary with a promise that the next morning's wake-up would not be as early as this morning's. For that she received loud applause. She explained that the boat ride to Rainbow Bridge was the reason for our early departure this morning.

Next, she announced that we would be staying at the Baymont by Wyndham in Page and that they had a pool and hot tub for anyone who was interested. She explained that the Baymont did not have an evening dining room, but there was a very nice smorgasbord across the street with almost anything you could imagine to eat. And it was included with the night's lodging. And oh yes, they served until 11:00 p.m.

"And," she added, "a buffet breakfast will be served in the hotel."

Last she said, "We won't need to be on the bus in the morning until 8:00 a.m. Suitcases outside doors by 7:15." Another round of applause.

I looked up the aisle and out the windshield and saw we were approaching the loading zone in front of the Baymont. The bus came to a stop, the driver kneeled the big coach, and we gathered our carry-ons and filed out the door in front.

As I passed Melody at the bus door, she whispered, "See you at the rooms."

I found room 605, tapped the electronic lock with my key card, and entered the door. I assumed Melody would occupy 603 or 607. I didn't know what this room was costing the tour, but it was swank. It had everything you could imagine and probably more. It was really sad that Melody and I were both occupying rooms that were being paid for when one room would have been more than sufficient for the two of us. But she was not my wife, so it was not the right situation yet.

I showered, freshened up, got dressed comfortably, and stretched out on the bed to wait for Melody.

Some time later I heard a light knock on my door. When I opened it, there was Melody in a pool robe, wearing rubber pool shoes. Then I shook my head and admitted that I had been so tired, I'd forgotten our swim date. Melody giggled and said, "Now I see just how important I am to you—you can't even remember when we have a hot date scheduled."

I said, "Give me five minutes," as I grabbed my suit, ran into the bathroom, and slammed the door. Five and a half minutes later, we were on the elevator headed down to the pool.

CHAPTER 17

The water in the pool was cool and refreshing. Seeing Melody remove her robe and appear in a muted black one-piece swimsuit almost caused my heart to stop. Being past her teenage years and closer to early middle age did not detract even a tiny bit from her being a very desirable woman. I was ashamed of the thoughts that kept going through my brain—no, not vulgar thoughts, only thoughts that she was more beautiful than Lily. Those thoughts almost caused me to bawl. But, no matter, she really was.

I guess she noticed I wasn't quite right, as she asked, "Are you still feeling a little ill?"

"No, just reviewing old memories from many years ago."

Then she understood as she dropped her head and, almost in a whisper, asked, "Lily?"

"Yes."

"Have I intruded into somewhere I shouldn't be?"

"No!" I replied. "She's close by telling me that you are making me happy like I used to be when she was with me. And she's very happy for both of us."

Then with big tears dripping from her eyes, she said, "Lily, if you are near, please believe, I know I can never make him as happy as you did, but I want to make him as happy as I can."

Then she was in my arms and whispered close to my ear, "Can we go to the rooms now? I don't want any beer or peanuts; I just want to be with you for a while."

We wrapped our towels around us as we slipped on our swim shoes, picked up our robes, then headed for the elevator.

Melody stepped to the door for room 603 and tapped her key card. Then she said, "Come to my room in about ten minutes."

I entered my room, quickly showered, and put on my lounge tee and shorts. Then I slipped into my loafers and checked my watch. It had been about eleven or twelve minutes, so I decided to give her a full fifteen minutes before I went next door.

When I knocked, she immediately opened the door. I could see she had been crying. Before I could say anything, she blurted, "Can you ever really love me while you're still in love with Lily?"

I didn't put my arms around her; I only touched her hand as I answered, "I know you don't understand, and I'm sorry about that. But I love you because of my love for Lily. I know it sounds crazy, but you are everything that Lily wasn't, and Lily was everything that you are not. But damn, I love every bit of both of you. You make me happy in ways she never could, and I don't miss the ways she made me happy when she was still here. All I can say is, it almost killed me when she left, and I don't ever want you to leave, because I wouldn't be able to live through that again."

Then I noticed she was wearing a soft pullover sheath robe and bunny slippers, and I couldn't stop myself from laughing.

Then she was in my arms and whispered, "I don't want to replace Lily; I just want you to want me as much as you wanted her."

Then I told her the whole truth: "My God, Melody, I've been that far with you from the first moment I touched your hand. And I don't ever intend to turn back."

I pulled away from her and walked over to the bed and retrieved two of the large stuffed pillows. I carried them over to the small couch in the corner and placed one against the back on each cushion. Next I pulled the desk chair in front of the left side of the couch with the back toward the couch. Going around the desk chair, I seated myself on the left end of the couch with my hand on the top of the back of the chair. And then I said, "Hey, are you a junior or a senior? How would you like to go for a ride with me in my dad's old pickup and maybe watch some fireworks?"

Melody wiped the tears from her eyes, and a slight smile appeared as she answered, "I should ask my mama, but I suppose it will be all right because you have a nice smile. And I hope you don't mind—I'm only a freshman, and I know you're the captain of the football team."

Then I said, "That's okay—you're the first girl I've wanted to ask, and you're prettier than any of the sophs, juniors, or seniors."

She was in my arms again before I could think and, in a little girl voice, asked, "You're going to kiss me before you take me home, ain't ya?"

I didn't answer at that moment; I just pulled her to me and then said, "Pretty little girl, I'm not waitin' till it's time to take you home, I'm a kissin' you now." And then, in all seriousness, I said, "Melody, from this moment on you are the only one I will ever want. Yes, I will always love Lily, but you are here to love me now, and that is all that matters."

As she raised her head to kiss me, she whispered, "And, I love you now and will always love you."

I realized how quickly the situation could get out of hand, so I kissed her once more and made an exit back to my own room.

Later, in bed, as I watched the headlights from the traffic passing on the highway flicker through the window blinds, I thought of all I had done in my life and all the happiness I had experienced. And then it struck me like a bolt of lightning—I believed at that moment I was happier than I had ever been, and perhaps I would experience more happiness, from now on, than I had ever experienced before. And why? One Sweet Melody!

As I lumbered off to sleep, I wondered, *What will tomorrow bring?*

CHAPTER 18

Before morning, my unconscious mind had conceived a silly but cute idea. After our meeting the night before, a whole new name came into my mind. From then on, she would be my Teen Angel.

The idea must have come from something I saw in a small historical society museum in a little town just north of Jefferson City. I believe the name was New something or other. Oh yes, New Bloomfield. During the rock-and-roll years of the 50s and 60s, a young musician by the name of Mark Dinning recorded a record, *Teen Angel*, and it became a nationwide hit. One of the old men in the museum said he was buried in a little country cemetery nearby.

There was also a second part to the idea. Since our actions had become like a couple of newly dating teenagers, I decided that, during our next...visit...I would act the part and ask her if she would like to "go steady," just to get her reaction.

After my morning ritual, I checked the overall itinerary to see where we were off to today. I was enjoying Melody's company and attention so much, I was losing track of everything else. The schedule said we would drive through the Painted Desert and the Petrified Forest, then on to the Grand Canyon this evening. When I got down to the breakfast area, Melody was getting juice from the cooler and did not notice me as I walked up behind her. I decided to start my little game right then.

"Miss Melody Madison, would you care to have breakfast with me?"

She turned and gave me a very serious, questioning look.

Perhaps she had forgotten that during one of our first evening visits she had told me what her maiden name was.

"What do you mean by that...how do you know...? Oh, of course I've already told you." Then she grinned and asked, "What is this all about? Are you off on one of your silly notions again?"

"One of the other boys told me you had your seventeenth birthday a while back, and now your parents will allow you to date. So...will you have breakfast with me?"

Almost in hysterics, she nodded and giggled out, "Cassy Gray, if I have breakfast with you, will you buy me chocolate ice cream to put on my eggs sunny-side up?"

"Why not have eggs a la mode, with whipped cream?"

She jumped up and down, clapped her hands, and then realized everyone in the breakfast area was giving us funny looks. She blushed, picked up her juice glass, and headed for her table.

As we sat down to our eggs and sausage, she looked at me in a very serious manner. "Please don't do that again. I enjoy you so much I forget who I am on this tour and fall right into enjoying your humor, and it might get me into trouble."

"I'm sorry my foolishness puts you in an undesirable situation, but I love to see you laugh and enjoy life when I act up. From now on I will save it for the times when we're alone."

She smiled a beautiful smile and answered, "I love to join you in the fun when we're alone."

We privately touched fingers and knees, then it was time to load the bus.

Melody assumed her tour director's spot and was quickly on the intercom explaining the day's activities. First she talked about the Painted Desert, then the Petrified Forest, and last she described our arrival at the Grand Canyon. She stated that the Grand Canyon of the Colorado River is one of the most visited natural wonders of the United States and that she believed we would consider it perhaps the most interesting and enjoyable attractions of the tour.

I already considered her to be the most exciting and enjoyable attraction of the tour. But, after this morning, I decided it was best not to mention it at that moment. I would wait until we were alone.

CHAPTER 19

Before lunch we drove into the Painted Desert. The colors of the earth truly looked as though someone had spilled brilliant splotches of paint and it had oozed in all directions mixing with other splotches close by. I understood how various elements combine to cause colors in substances, but I didn't claim to understand the Painted Desert.

Almost immediately we entered the Petrified Forest and began to see actual logs turned to stone, with beautiful colors formed in the stone.

Again, I understood how the wood rotted away and the areas were filled with water carrying various elements that, over a long period of time, became solid and formed into stone. Both the desert and the forest were beautiful, but not of the caliber we saw at Rainbow Bridge, and probably not what we were going to see at the Grand Canyon.

Just a few minutes after entering the Painted Desert, we stopped for our noonday lunch. Melody and I split a pizza and enjoyed a local tea made from some exotic plant. Probably a plant I would rather not know the truth about. I was familiar with stories of the peyote cactus.

As we were returning to the bus, small rodents of some type came out from under the cactus plants and begged to be fed peanuts or other junk food we might be carrying. They were cute but at the same time a little bit of a nuisance. However, we stopped to watch their antics, and some of the people gave them bits of food.

Old Slim tossed a bit of something and then tried to stomp a little fellow as he came to check the tidbit. I thought, *What an ass!*

From behind me I heard a growl and then harsh words. "We were right, the son of a bitch is a sadist. He will try to destroy anything that gives someone else pleasure."

I nosily asked, "Are you talking about the Parks girl?"

Mr. Rains said, "I could be, but I'm actually talking about our little dog. For twelve years we had a miniature toy peekapoo, then we moved into our new neighborhood, next door to the Pinn-headed bastard. We were there less than a week when Poopie died of strychnine poisoning. We let her out in the backyard to do her business. I saw Pinn throw a little something over the fence, and Poopie picked it up. She made it to the back door for a drink of water and dropped dead.

"We rushed her to the vet, but of course she was dead. I paid for an autopsy, and they found fresh bites of chicken and strychnine in her throat. I know what that devil did, but there's no way to prove it. I would love to dance on his grave!"

I thought to myself, *I don't believe I would want to be that man. If he has done all the things I've found out about to the people in this group, who else has he messed with that would cause him harm, or worse?*

As I got on the bus, I once more felt a deep darkness in my soul. Was I riding on a bus with one of Satan's own disciples?

As soon as my tail hit the seat, I heard Melody's beautiful voice, and my mood began to lighten. She proved more and more each day that she had the ability to take me to a level where life was once more a joy to live.

The only problem? Everything about her was driving me to total distraction.

She was announcing our accommodations for the next few nights. We were going to see the canyon in almost its entirety. She said we would be staying at Bright Angel Lodge in The Village, located in the center of the business section of the South Rim. Over the next few days we would travel from the lodge by bus to most of the points of interest on this side of the canyon. She explained the rooms were rustic and decorated in the style of the area.

The only interest I had on my mind was to get that young lady alone and love her until I couldn't breathe. But first, was there a fine dining room in that place?

Surprisingly I heard her voice break through my thoughts as she said, "We will dine tonight at The Hump, another fine steak house in the Market Plaza, just a short ten-minute, enjoyable, level walk from the lodge. It's named The Hump because, when it first opened many years ago, buffalo hump meat was the main item on the menu."

And then she personally recognized me: "No, Mr. Gray, buffalo hump is no longer on the menu."

In my mind, I crowed, *Hot Doggie! Melody and steak—I've hit the jackpot once again.*

I sat back and closed my eyes for the last few miles to Bright Angel Lodge.

Once more I became aware Melody was speaking.

"Your suitcases will be delivered to your rooms probably by the time I have secured your keys and room information and distributed them to you. Don't forget your carry-ons that you will need tonight."

I filed out with the rest of the group and stood by until Melody gave me my room packet. Mine was the last one, and she head-motioned for me to follow her down the hall. The rest of the group headed to the right down the hall as we turned left.

Our rooms looked out over the canyon and had a common little raised balcony with a chair outside each of our atrium doors.

As soon as I opened my door she pushed me inside, slid in behind me, and quickly pushed the door closed. Almost before I could throw my night case on the bed she was nearly off the floor in my arms. When she finished kissing me, I was afraid I was going to faint from lack of oxygen.

"Now football jock, just because I'm a freshman doesn't mean I can't handle my man. You keep your butt away from them older girls, or I'll kick yours and theirs both."

Then she let out a mock yell: "Go Jays!"

She grabbed me to kiss again, and there was a knock at the door. She let me go and then took on a look like a deer in someone's headlights, trying to find a place to hide. I shoved her into the bathroom, closed that door, and opened the room door. One of the luggage handlers set my suitcase inside the door, I handed him a couple of bucks, he left, and I closed the door.

As Melody came out of the bathroom, we heard a knock at her door. After a couple of knocks, we heard her door open, then a slight pause, then the door closed again. I whispered, "He just put your bag in your room."

Before I could move, she was back in my arms and we were lip-locked again. When she turned me loose that time, she pointed her finger at me and asked, "Well, big boy, if you want me, what are you going to do to keep me?"

It was the opening I was waiting for.

"Angel, would you want to go steady with me?"

"Can I wear your class ring around my neck?"

"Well, it's at home, and I won't be able to get it for a few days. But you better believe you'll be wearing it, and don't go flirtin' with any of the other guys on the team. You belong to the quarterback only."

Then in a serious tone she said, "Not a lineman, not an end, not even the coach or the president of the bank. Only Cassy Gray."

Then one more long kiss.

As she glanced at her watch, she stated, "Time to get the herd to the watering hole. You want a steak, love?"

"Only as long as I have the most beautiful thing on the bus eating with me."

"Then I guess I'd better go next door and at least comb my hair and straighten my clothes."

With that she peeked out my door and then disappeared into the adjoining room.

My mind immediately came up with an idea that would be one of my better schemes if I could pull it off. And I thought I could. I learned a long time ago that if you are willing to pay enough, someone will do the work. I was going to find out if I could have a special ring made for Melody to wear around her neck. One that would mean something until I could replace it with a gold band, when and if we really arrived at that special moment.

Shortly she knocked at my door, and we walked down the hall to join the rest of the group waiting to go to The Hump.

It was another unforgettable meal in the presence of absolute beauty. I was beginning to reach a point where everything and everyone seemed to sink into nothingness as Melody totally filled all my area of concentration.

She leaned as far across the table as she could and whispered, "Can we take another ride in your old man's truck tonight and maybe stop, park, and just neck awhile?"

"Whatever makes you happy thrills me to death."

CHAPTER 20

Back in my room, I quickly changed into a light pullover and knit shorts and waited for a knock at my atrium door. I had the door drapes closed so Melody's entry into my room could not be clearly seen from any of the other rooms. After what seemed like hours but was only a few minutes, I heard a light tap on the glass. I turned the lights off in my room, slightly opened the drapes, and slid the door open.

Instead of a beautiful body stepping into my room, a soft hand reached in through the door and gripped the front of my T-shirt and pulled me outside. In the muted moonlight I saw a figure in a dark-colored gown of some type. She melted into my arms and reached up and kissed me on the neck under my chin. I put my arms around her and felt thin fabric almost like gauze. And then I realized there was nothing else under the fabric except a nude body. She stood on tiptoes and whispered in my ear, "I already have the old truck warmed up and ready to drive away, or we can stay parked here and neck."

With hot sweat rolling down my body under my T-shirt and walking shorts, I croaked, "With the state I'm in right now we should probably drive somewhere for a long time, but I would love to park and neck!"

Then with a devilish giggle, she whispered, "You think necking in the nude would be great fun, don't you?"

I was so embarrassed, I couldn't make a sound.

Then she pressed against me so tight, I could feel every natural curve she possessed. Once more she whispered, "That's what I think would be great fun!"

And with that, she peeled off my T-shirt. But she did not attempt to touch my shorts. She took me by the hand and led me into the darkest corner of the tiny balcony, where she had dragged the lounge chairs together to form the truck cab and had placed four pillows for the backs and the seats of the old rattletrap.

I sat down, and she sat down beside me, and the wild necking session began. And yes, it was the greatest fun I had ever experienced. I don't remember any time, ever in my life, including my teenage years, that any girl made me feel so satisfied.

Suddenly I snapped awake and realized the sun was beginning to peek over the canyon rim. I had been awakened by Melody's curse of, "Oh crap! I hope none of the others have seen us in this position."

With that, she unwrapped herself from my arms and rushed into her room. I picked up the pillows and tossed them through the door behind her. Then I grabbed my T-shirt from the floor and ran into my room also.

CHAPTER 21

I looked at my watch, and it was just past 6:00 a.m. I took a short shower, then removed the hair from my face and put on my garb for the day. The time was 6:30, and they began serving breakfast at 6:00. My timing could not have been any better.

As I searched the way from my room to the breakfast area, I assumed Melody would be there a little later, because she would need a little time to shower and dress. In what I considered warp speed, she walked into the breakfast nook, as prepared and beautiful as I had ever seen her. She saw me and walked off in another direction. I was immediately confused—what had I done to receive an obvious brush-off? In a short time, she came back into view and slowly worked her way to the table where I was seated. Standing in front of me, she turned completely around, then looked down at me, and in a low voice said, "Last night you never told me if you liked how I was dressed. I was extremely disappointed, because it took all the courage I could muster to come to you that way."

With a little embarrassment I awkwardly tried to explain that I had been totally at a loss as to what to say. That the moment I touched her and realized she was almost totally nude, I was nearly struck mute. As she continued to stare down at me, I decided it was time to lay my cards on the table.

"To be honest, when you slipped into my arms and I realized what you were not wearing, I almost committed a criminal offence. And I thought by you being so close against me, you could feel what I was thinking."

With almost a tear-choked voice, she whispered, "I'm sorry. I truly was baiting you, and when you did not try to force me to have sex, I was afraid you had been just toying with me."

Then I decided I had to totally explain, if I could. "I may be a lot of things, but with you I have been completely honest. It has been hard for me to make any moves toward you because of my past and yours. But as I told you before, after Lily, you have been the only other woman I've ever wanted. Now, if sex is what you want, I'm ready to do whatever is necessary to make you happy."

Before I could say anything else, she grabbed my hand, slid into the seat across the table, and rapidly whispered, "No, no, no, I wasn't ready for us to make that move, but I was jealous of Lily and couldn't believe you would ever want me over her."

Then it was my turn to apologize. "My love, you never have to be jealous of Lily. She's gone, and you are here. You're beautiful, loving, and I want you. The moment you are ready, I want all of you. But, I'll wait until you decide when that moment is."

Then as I got up from my seat, I said, "Follow me."

As I started down the hall, she stepped in a half step behind me and reached forward and took my hand. When we reached the rooms, I unlocked my door, and we stepped inside. I roughly grabbed her to me and ran my hands over all parts of her body and then whispered in her ear, "This is what I have forced myself from doing until this moment. Yes, I want you in the worst way, but I could never force you to do anything you didn't want to do. When you're ready for whatever...you must let me know, and I'll try to please."

Then I kissed her and tried to release her. But, she would not let go as she said with a huge grin, "Big boy, all I ever want to do from now on is wear your ring, either around my neck or on my finger." Then she kissed me and continued in a serious tone, "If we are going to have breakfast, we'd better hurry."

We left the room and rushed back to the breakfast nook. She finished her last bite just as the bus driver excused himself and headed to his driving seat. Getting up from her seat, she said, "It looks like it's time to be on the bus to travel to our first tourist site on the canyon rim."

As Melody took her guide's seat, she picked up the intercom mic, and for her it was back to the old grind. I waited, and then the sweet music began in my ear as I heard her first words.

"Our first stop on the canyon tour will be at Desert View. I picked this spot for the first stop of the morning because the early morning sun releases shadows and colors that you will not see anywhere else in the canyon."

The sun shining through the window on her face released a feeling in me that I knew no one else in the world could cause to happen, and that made me feel satisfied. Then I picked up her words again, as she instructed, "Sit back, relax, and look at the views of the canyon as we make a twenty-five-mile drive to Desert View."

About thirty minutes later, Melody's voice once more broke the silence. "In a few minutes, a tower will come into your view. It's a natural stone tower built on the edge of the rim to mark Desert View and to give you a nice view of sites in the canyon. Also there are bathrooms nearby, with drinking water available. We'll be here for about forty-five minutes."

Desert View was impressive, and Melody's description was 100 percent correct. The sun over the landscape caused totally black shadows on the canyon floor. The light higher up on the rock formations cast dark-purple and royal-blue shadows. And in the full brightness of the sunlight, radiant reds, yellows, and greens faded into lines and crevices of tans and browns.

Our tour was a maelstrom of oohs and ahs, with a continuous click of camera shutters.

After enjoying the visual pleasures, taking a trip to the bathroom, and refilling my water bottle, it was time to head back to the bus.

During the stop, Melody was kept busy by the little old ladies wanting to know more and more about the canyon and asking what else we would be seeing over the next few days.

I was a little jealous of her total involvement with them, but she seemed to enjoy playing the authority and answering all their questions.

CHAPTER 22

Finally it was back on the big coach, waiting for the driver to ferry us farther out along the canyon rim.

Some of the views were more spectacular, in their own way, than Desert View, and some less. Melody verbally attempted to make every view of the canyon the most spectacular sight we would ever experience. I decided that later I would tease her about being just one more of my friends who were full of bull.

Soon Melody announced it was 11:00, and that at noon or a little after, we had reservations for lunch. She promised another fabulous, regional meal. We were to have Bar-B-Que at Injun Joe's.

"Now there's an original name! How many times has that moniker appeared throughout history?"

But, she explained, we would have our choice of lamb, chicken, or turkey. Or, the more adventurous on the tour could have rattlesnake if they wanted. I didn't see any hands go up to volunteer.

I sat back and cleared my mind, as I had other fish to fry, so to speak.

As soon as we were underway I fired up the old iPhone and located the number of the central office for the Jefferson City Public Schools. I placed the call, and in a few moments I reached the office operator. She asked who I would like to speak to, and I said the purchasing agent for the system. She transferred my call, and a second secretary came on the line.

She asked, "To whom am I speaking, and what can I do to assist you?"

I said, "I'm Casper Gray, and I would like to know what jewelry company makes your senior class rings."

"Are you a parent? Did we make a mistake with your graduate's ring?"

"No, I would just like to order a special ring directly from the company, if that's possible."

"Just a moment, and I'll see if I can locate that supplier."

In about three minutes, I heard, "Sir, the company we do business with is Volkens out of Chicago. They are on Lakefront. Are you on the net?"

"Yes."

"It would be much easier for you to locate them on the net than to write down all the information I would be giving you."

I thanked her for her time and help, then clicked off. I got into my carry-on and retrieved my laptop. When I turned it on, the bus Wi-Fi was loud and clear. Volkens was easy to find, and their phone number was at the top of their homepage. I closed the laptop and dialed their number.

In a few moments a young lady answered the phone with a cheery, "Good morning, you have reached Volkens of Chicago, the makers of the finest scholastic rings and awards in the continental United States. I'm Sherry, how may I help you?"

Taking her casual lead, I answered, "Sherry, you are speaking to Casper Gray, and I'm calling from the Grand Canyon. I would like to order a very special custom class ring from your company if that is a possibility."

"What school or educational facility are you associated with?"

"I'm not associated with any educational group. I just need to know if your company, for the right price, could or would create a very special, one-of-a-kind class ring."

"One moment, sir. I will connect you with our head designer, who is also one of the company partners."

I heard a buzz, and almost immediately a male voice greeted me. "Good morning, sir. My secretary said you have a question she could not answer about a special ring."

"Yes sir, I'm Casper Gray from mid-Missouri, and I would like to commission your company to create a one-of-a-kind class ring."

"Sir, that is an unusual request. First, are you prepared to pay the price for such a request?"

"If I state my desires, I assume you could quote an approximate price for such a ring."

"Probably within two or three hundred dollars."

"Oh yes, I believe I'm prepared to meet your price, if it's a fair market price."

"It will be, probably, the lowest price you will find for a scholastic item."

"I understand you do class rings for the high school in Jefferson City, Missouri."

"One moment, and I'll check my computer file."

I silently waited for a few moments, and the gentleman returned to the line.

"Yes, we do a fine business with that system, but I thought you wanted something special."

"I do. Can you use the design of the 2017 Jefferson City class ring, but make it of 14-karat gold with an actual ruby as the stone? And where it says JCHS 2017, I want it to say CSB, then a space, and then the letters SWT 2017."

"I believe I can create such a ring, but it will cost considerably more than a standard class ring."

"I understand, and I am prepared to pay, within reason."

"I can prepare a proposal and call you back in a week or ten days with the possibilities."

"Oh that's another thing—I would like to have the ring within ten days."

There was a silence on the line.

"Sir, I don't mean to sound blunt, but you are a little presumptuous with a request like that. And now you are talking quite a price."

"Sir, make me a proposal sometime today, and I will attempt, if the price is right, to convince you to deliver the ring in ten days. And, oh yes, I want it the smallest size you can make in the man's ring design. That's Casper Gray, phone 555-896-8000; it's to your company's advantage for you to call today." Without further discussion, I hung up.

I won't call Injun Joe's bad, but it was sad. However, it was filling, and the iced tea was great.

We made one last stop to view some California condors as they flew from their nest high on the rim and patrolled low into the canyon searching for food. Then they would reappear and sail like great white ships of the sky back to their nests. Melody told us they possessed wingspans of seven feet. After more oohs, ahs, and clicks, it was back on the bus. Then our Angel announced it was back to The Village for free time.

A while later my phone rang, and it was Volkens of Chicago. I looked at my watch, and it was just barely an hour and a half since my call. "Am I speaking to Casper Gray?"

"Yes sir, speaking."

"Mr. Gray, I would love to have the honor of creating a scholastic masterpiece for you, but I'm afraid the price is going to cause you a good deal of displeasure. After considering what you requested, the best price our company can propose is $3,100. And to make delivery in ten days is completely out of the question."

"Sir, to whom am I speaking?"

"I'm Saulvester Singer, quarter owner of Volkens."

"Mr. Saulvester Singer, sir. Could your company deliver the ring in ten days if I added an additional half of the price to the price?"

Again there was a silence on the line.

"You are saying you will pay $4,650 for the ring if we deliver in ten days?"

"Yes sir, and I will pay 50 percent of the price today...right now."

"Mr. Gray, we are proud to be doing business with you. Thank you. I'll reconnect you with my secretary, and she will take your credit card or however you wish to pay the first half of the price. And I will personally phone you for the balance and shipping instructions in seven days. Goodbye."

I grinned as I thought, Saulvester, Putty Tat, and his secretary, Tweety Bird.

CHAPTER 23

In a very short time we arrived back at the lodge. Then in super quick time everyone melted away to get involved in their own afternoon devices.

As Melody and I stood near the coach, we also began to make plans for the rest of the afternoon.

She asked, "Would you like to spend the next couple hours in the room and try to become reacquainted after our trouble this morning?"

I answered, "Please don't misunderstand, I'd love to, but it might appear we are shacking up if someone misses us. Maybe we should stay in sight for now. But, would you care to walk along the canyon rim at sunset or maybe later in the moonlight? By that time everyone else should either be headed to bed, to the bar, or to some other places of interest. Then if we get a little forward, no one should be around to see."

"What do you plan to do for dinner?" she said.

"How about just a nice dessert after that huge Indian Bar-B-Que we had for lunch?"

"Sounds like a plan I can live with. But right now I would like to go to my room and freshen up a little."

We turned toward the lodge and made our way to the rooms. As I opened my door, she slightly touched my hand and whispered, "I know how you must have hated yourself for your actions with me in your room this morning. But I must tell you, I didn't mind, as I expected it and perhaps wanted it to happen much sooner."

With that, she disappeared into her room.

I went into my room, stretched out on the bed, and attempted to rethink where I was in this interesting relationship. About thirty minutes passed, and my cell rang.

A sweet soft voice said, "I'm ready for our great adventure."

We left the lodge together to explore The Village and find some excitement.

A pair of ears picked up the sound of a familiar voice. A soft, almost soundless mumble escaped a pair of lips made dry by seething anger. "That son of a bitch Pinn."

Out of sight behind a thin partition, the ears listened to Jeb Pinn as he carried on a conversation with the young lady working behind the counter.

"Miss, do you know you have the facial features of a classic Native American woman?...No, you wouldn't...but I would. My name is Paul Pine, and my mother was one-third Navajo. I'm here in the area with my crew, taking pictures for the Great Southwest Magazine.*"*

Then there was the sound of a chair moving and footfalls on the hardwood floor.

"After walking around you and observing your features from several angles, I believe you are one of the types I would like to have in a picture along the canyon rim. Would you agree to pose for some magazine shots I want to take of the canyon at sunset?"

"You're kidding me," the young woman said.

"No, we will be filming along the trail on the rim, below the lodge, at sundown. Why don't you come on down, and we can try a few shots. Just come in your work clothes, as I have some classic Native American costumes in our van."

"You might really want me for pictures in a magazine?"

"Yes ma'am. Get down to the rim about 8:00 p.m., and we will make you famous."

More sounds of chairs moving and footfalls on wood.

"See you at 8:00."

"Okay."

The voice, sounding ready to scream with deadly anger, quietly spit out the words, "You bastard, you destroyed one young lady and got away with it, but may I be damned for eternity in hell if I allow you to hurt this one. Pinn, prepare to kiss your own ass goodbye."

With that, the entity arose from its seat behind the panel and ambled off into the late-afternoon haze.

It was about 7:20 when Melody and I finished our sinful dessert dinner and headed out to the canyon rim for a lovers' walk along the blacktop path. We were walking hand in hand, stopping in patches of deep-blue shadows for a quick hug or kiss. Melody was telling me she couldn't wait to get home to tell her best friend at the bank that she was in love with a very special man and he loved her in return. It sounded a little silly, like something a teenager would tell about her first love. But to be honest, I wanted to tell someone also, but the only one I had to tell it to was Lily. Lily...I knew she would be happy for me and would be there in her special place watching to see what would happen next.

Suddenly, ahead of us, out of sight around a bend in the trail, we heard a scream of pain and fear.

"Help me! Please somebody help me!"

Then I heard another voice, a voice I seemed to recognize. "Shut your mouth, you little bitch, or I'll shove you over the edge."

Melody gasped as she pushed me ahead and screeched, "That's Jeb Pinn! Go!" She ran past me in the direction of the voices.

As we rounded the next bend, side by side at a dead run, I saw Old Slim ahead on the trail, pulling a young woman's arm up behind her back with one hand as he attempted to tear her dress off with the other.

Hoarsely I shouted, "Pinn, you bastard, what are you trying to do?"

He turned his head toward me, and when he saw Melody and me, he roughly pushed the girl toward us, turned, and ran madly down the trail. I caught the young lady as she stumbled into me. As I steadied her, she pulled her bra strap back up onto her shoulder, covering one breast that had been exposed. Then she attempted to gather her torn dress and hold it together to cover other exposed body parts.

Quickly her voice returned, and she sobbed, "Why did he want to hurt me? I only came to make the pictures."

Melody tried to soothe the girl and at the same time screamed at me, "Go get that piece of trash and bring him back to the lodge, even if you have to drag him."

As I raised my head to run after Pinn, I heard a jumble of words and profanity. I looked down the trail from where I was standing, and about seventy or so yards farther on, past bushes and rocks, I could just barely see Pinn stopped at the end of the blacktop.

Beyond that point there were no chain-link fences or guardrails, only signs saying, "Do Not Venture Beyond This Point."

First, he stepped off the edge of the trail and looked down over the rim. Next, he turned and looked back away from the rim for a moment. Then, he raised his arms up in front of his face, did a dancer's pirouette on his left foot, and appeared to simply step off into space. I heard a terror-filled scream and then total silence.

Then I noticed Melody had guided the girl over to where I was standing, and they were both leaning lightly against me. Melody had a strange look on her face as she blurted, "Did Pinn just walk off the rim?"

I then realized we could only see a little of the trail and the rim edge because of all the bushes and rocks hanging over that part of the trail.

Then I answered with a question of my own. "Melody, did you hear what sounded like two voices?"

"I don't know what I heard. I only know I just saw a man die. Did he jump, fall, or what?"

Then a bolt of lightning hit me: "Or was he pushed?"

Though Casper, Melody, and the young lady were too far away to hear, from the bushes came an almost amused sound. Far less than a whisper, more like the release of a long-held breath: "Take that, you worthless sack of crap. You'll never again hurt anyone else." Then the entity turned and ambled off through the brush, toward the lodge.

CHAPTER 24

I quickly phoned the desk at the lodge and asked if there were emergency personnel available. I was asked what the emergency was. I answered that a man had fallen from the canyon rim at the western end of the blacktop lodge trail.

The gentleman at the desk said the medical and rescue team would be contacted immediately. Almost at once we could hear the sirens commence to wail, sounding closer as each second passed.

I hurried up to the rim road and waited to direct them to the accident scene.

The first vehicle in a small caravan was a brown Jeep SUV with a large Grand Canyon logo stenciled on the door. It stopped as I signaled, and a lady in a park ranger uniform got out and quickly joined me. Without a pause, she asked, "Where is the injured person?"

I led her to the rim, and she looked over the edge. For the first time, I also looked, not knowing what to expect to see.

There, about two hundred feet below us on a fairly large ledge, lay Pinn. His body displayed physical injuries, but it was not broken in the manner one would expect after a fall of that distance. He almost appeared to have simply lain down and fallen asleep.

The ranger said, "I doubt he's still alive, but we will send someone down immediately to check. As I turned to locate Melody and the girl, I saw men already gearing up to descend to the ledge and Pinn. At the same time I observed someone talking to Melody as he physically checked the young lady. A doctor or nurse I supposed.

Almost before my mind could comprehend, the female ranger came and informed me Pinn was dead.

But at the same time there was also some good news: Dora Strawflower, the young lady, was unharmed, except for being almost scared to death. Hopefully, in time, she would heal physically and mentally, but Old Slim would never compose another evil deed.

Then the ranger held out her hand and introduced herself. "I'm Florence Gomez, Grand Canyon ranger."

As I shook her hand, I returned, "Casper Gray, Grand Canyon tourist."

Then in a business tone, she asked, "Were you near when the accident happened?"

"Yes."

"Did you see him fall?"

As I answered yes, I thought it best to try to fully explain what happened, so I would not appear to be hiding any information.

"Ma'am, actually I was going to try to apprehend him after he attacked the girl. But before I could get to him, he went over the rim."

"Was he alone when he fell?"

"I could only see his frame because the rest of the area near him was obscured by rocks and brush."

"Did you hear anything?"

"Yes, I heard a jumble of words and curses, then I heard him scream as he went over the edge."

"Was he the one talking and cursing, or could someone else have been out of your field of vision?"

I answered, "I really don't know, as I was too far away and involved with the welfare of the girl."

At that moment one of the rescue team walked up, and the ranger turned to talk to him.

He said, "It will take a little while to do our investigation and retrieve the body, perhaps all night. So if it's okay with you, we'll get started." The ranger told him to get to work and then turned back to me.

"Are you staying at the lodge?"

"Yes."

"When will you be leaving the canyon?"

"When our tour leaves, and that may be a while, as the dead man is from our tour."

"Who is your director? I will need to talk to him."

I answered, "The tour director is right behind us, and he is not a him, he is a her."

I turned and motioned Melody to come over and join us.

When she arrived, I introduced the two ladies.

"Ranger Gomez, Melody Muldune, tour director for the Centrail Savings Bank's Travel Club of Jefferson City, Missouri.

"Melody, Ranger Florence Gomez, Grand Canyon ranger."

The ranger directed all her attention to Melody and said, "Ms. Muldune, in a while there will be a lot of information needed by our ranger group. How long are you scheduled to be here at The Village before your tour is to leave?"

Melody paused for a moment as she thought about the question.

"We are scheduled for five nights, and this is the beginning of the second night. So we are scheduled for three more nights after tonight."

Then Ranger Gomez dropped her eyes a little and said, "I'm second-in-command here at the canyon, and because of the magnitude of this situation, I'm sure the chief will be here in the morning to take over the investigation. Would it be possible to have your entire tour group someplace where he can interview whomever he chooses to?"

Melody answered, "I'll arrange something and have the group available if the chief ranger desires a meeting."

Gomez then asked, "What happened to the girl with the torn dress?" Directing her next comment at me, she continued, "I believe I heard you say something about the dead man attacking her."

Before Melody thought, she blurted out, "Yes, he got just what he deserved!" Then she caught herself and continued, "I guess I'm sorry I said that, but she didn't deserve to be almost raped and perhaps worse."

Though being an officer of the law, Gomez in almost a whisper replied, "He shouldn't have died, but I agree he would have deserved some kind of severe punishment." Then as her mind moved back to the present circumstance she asked, "Was he traveling with anyone else on this tour?"

Melody answered, "Yes, his wife is with him."

"She needs to be informed of her husband's death, but I will not be available until his body has been removed from the ledge."

Melody at once told Gomez, "As the tour leader, it is probably more my responsibility to inform her immediately. If that would be acceptable?"

Officer Gomez quickly gave Melody her permission.

After a few more minor details were discussed and the victim was told she might be questioned more on the morrow, Casper, Melody, and Dora Strawflower were also given permission to return to the lodge.

Melody found one of the older lodge workers, and she agreed to see Dora home and help explain to her family what had transpired.

When Melody and I reached our rooms, she asked me to come into hers for a few minutes. It was late, but I knew she was not ready to try to sleep. The moment the door was closed, she came completely apart. She was in my arms, not just crying but bawling and shaking.

Through her sobs, in broken words and sentences she began to speak. "That...poor girl, she...was so...so...so scared and hurt. And...what...what about Bonnie...Bonnie? Pinn...he...he was a...a roach, but she...she loved him. And...and now he's...gone."

As her sobs lessened, she continued, "It's my job to...to find her and...and tell her."

Quickly I broke in, "I'll go right now and tell her."

"Oh, could...could you?"

I pulled her closer to me, kissed her, and said, "You crawl up on the bed, rest, and I'll go right now."

As soon as she was settled, I went to the desk and inquired as to what room the Pinns occupied. I explained that Mrs. Muldune was indisposed, and I needed to inform Mrs. Pinn of her husband's accident.

The desk clerk asked, "Isn't he the one who was killed tonight?" I nodded, and he gave me the room number.

Then I had a thought. "Could you also give me the room number for Mr. and Mrs. Bulkowski, as Mrs. Pinn may be in their room visiting."

It took a few minutes to walk to the Pinns' door. I knocked and waited. After several more knocks and no answer, I gave up and proceeded on to the Bulkowskis' room. I knocked, and shortly a man's voice asked, "Who is it?"

I answered, "Casper Gray with a message from Melody Muldune."

A few moments passed, and the door opened just a crack.

"What's the message?"

"Is Mrs. Pinn here? I need to speak to her."

"Why in hell would you believe Bonnie is here?"

I just decided to be blunt. "Because I know if she is not in their room, she's usually with you."

Suddenly the door popped open wide, and Mrs. Pinn was standing there, covered with almost nothing.

"Why do you need to speak to me?" she asked.

"I'm very sorry, Mrs. Pinn, but your husband was killed earlier tonight."

There was a long, eerie silence, and then from deep within a den of horror came a sound of raw pain, anger, and grief. It began to rise higher and higher until the walls around us seemed to vibrate.

"NO!...NO!...NO! Damn it! No, no...o...o...o! Please, no!"

And then her legs would no longer support her as she wilted to the floor and began to sob inconsolably.

As Bulkowski attempted to be of some comfort to Bonnie, I wondered, *Where is Red Flag?*

CHAPTER 25

B ack in her room I found Melody, not awake but neither asleep. No matter what any of the people in the tour thought, I was not going to leave her alone. After removing my shoes, I sat on the bed with my back against the headboard and held her close all night.

Morning brought a pleasant calm, but it was only, as the old saying goes, the calm before the storm. Breakfast was completely out of the question.

Melody arose and disappeared into her bathroom to prepare herself for what would probably be a hell of a day.

At the same time, I returned to my room and performed my morning ritual.

In what I thought was an incredibly short time, Melody appeared at my atrium door and knocked gently. I opened the glass, and she slid inside and then into my arms and said, "Please stay close today; I will need you to help me make it through this hell."

I kissed her and assured her I would stay as close as I could.

Immediately after that she left my room and headed to the front desk to ask if there was a place for our group to meet with the chief ranger. I was right behind her. The desk clerk stated that all the meeting rooms were already scheduled, but we could meet on the lawn behind the lodge. It was not what she would have preferred, but she thought it would probably work out.

Melody asked the desk clerk to call each of our tour members and inform them that we would meet on the lawn behind the lodge after breakfast at 9:00. Then she called Ranger Gomez and told her we would be assembled behind the lodge at 9:00 a.m. Gomez told Melody that she and the chief would be there to interview the group.

We then returned to my room, sat on the couch, and held each other until it was time for the meeting.

At 8:45, we went behind the lodge to the place the meeting would be held. Our group members arrived one by one or in couples, and they began to congregate around us, asking questions and discussing among themselves.

At 9:00 to the minute, a ranger Jeep pulled into the parking lot adjacent to the back lawn. The Jeep doors opened, Gomez exited from the passenger side, and a man of about forty-five, like a lithe animal, uncoiled from behind the wheel and stepped out the driver's door onto the pavement.

As the chief ranger walked up to our group, I noticed his facial features indicated that he was of Native American birth. He was of medium-brown complexion and was narrow-faced, and his eyes were almost black as night. His body frame was rectangular in shape, about two and a half times taller than wide. There did not seem to be an ounce of weight out of place.

I stepped forward, and as he stuck out his hand to shake mine, he stated, "The name is Christjohn Gray Fox, federal ranger, assignment, Grand Canyon. Does anyone know anything about the death of your friend?"

Everyone began to mumble and shake their heads, telling the ranger and each other that they had not seen Mr. Pinn since around dinnertime last night.

Bull and the Red Flag had their arms around Mrs. Pinn, trying to console her. Between loud sobs, she was almost screaming, "Bob, you bastard, if I had not been forced to be with you last night, I would have been with Jeb, and this would have never happened."

Bull had his hand almost over Bonnie's mouth, trying to keep her from saying what she was screaming at the top of her lungs. Rhonda was also trying to whisper in her ear, loud enough that we all could hear, that she shouldn't be airing dirty laundry to the whole group.

Bonnie then started screaming, "Swapping was always your idea. Jeb and I never wanted to get involved, but you two pushed it on to us. Jeb told me he would never have agreed to it if he had not been forced too."

Then Bull roared so loud there was no question as to what he was saying. "Jeb, the lousy bastard, was the one who started it all.

He wanted to screw Rhonda so bad, he made a couple of my bad deals right so I would agree to go along with it. And besides that, Rhonda didn't want to sleep with the son of a bitch, but she went along with the deal to help get me out of the crack I was in."

Almost without thinking, Bull roared once more, "I'm glad that piece of crap is dead!"

I noticed that the ranger was taking the whole scene in, and he didn't look pleased.

CHAPTER 26

Gray Fox looked Rhonda Bulkowski over and evidently grasped the swapping situation immediately, then he directed his next observation and question at her. "It appears that your husband and Mrs. Pinn have an alibi for their whereabouts when Mr. Pinn died. What do you have to say for yourself? Can anyone vouch for where you were located or what you were doing at that time?"

The Red Flag dropped her head and took several seconds to collect her thoughts, then she replied, "I suppose what I'm about to say will end my marriage. But, when Bob and I decided the only way out of our financial difficulties was to agree to Jeb's offer of becoming swingers, our marriage was finished anyway. When Bob said I had to sleep with that jerk, I decided it was time for me to enjoy my life any way I could. So I started doing whatever I felt like."

Then Rhonda dropped her head again, and tears began to run down her face. Her flaming-red hair could not hide her total defeat. "I guess you could say I have an alibi set in stone. After Bob decided to sleep with Bonnie last night, it appeared I would be stuck spending the night with Jeb. 'Whoopee,' I said to myself. But when he saw me before dinner, he said he had other plans."

Then Rhonda lost her grip totally as she almost howled, "I went out to walk off my anger in the cool air...and in the parking lot were several bikers. They had a bottle, and I helped them kill it. Later the group began to couple up and look for a place to make out. Then Devil, who I took to be the head honcho, asked me if I would like to spend the night with him. I thought to myself, 'What the hell, Bob treats me like his whore anyway, so why not?'"

Then in a high voice, with tears gushing, she began to giggle hysterically as she spoke, "I ended up spending the night and making it with..." Then she commenced with insane laughter and quoted the title of an old 1960s teenager's biker song: "...the Leader of the Pack!"

Then she crumpled to the ground, sobbing, "Find Devil; he'll say I was damned good, all night long."

Ranger Gray Fox abruptly changed directions and made the speech I'm sure he was prepared to deliver. "The forensic team has completed its work at the rim and on the ledge where Pinn was found."

He continued, "Until the team reports its findings, I have to cover all the bases and treat this as the worst scenario, as a murder. And, because of that, everyone on your tour is a suspect. Especially all the people that live in the same neighborhood and know each other very intimately."

He also said, "If this is a murder, I have to believe that someone in this group will prove to be the killer."

As the ranger was preparing to question each of us as suspects, I noticed all of the group traveling together was there except Old Bald Dome. He wasn't anywhere to be seen.

I walked over to where Melody was standing and asked her, "What room is Waller in? He's not here in the group, and he is just as suspect as any of the others."

She replied, "He's in the hospital in Flagstaff. Yesterday he was not feeling well before we left for Desert View. He was experiencing stomach distress and thought perhaps it was a bout of minor food poisoning, so he decided to stay behind in bed and not go with us. Later in the morning he called the desk for assistance. They called me, and we decided that, to be safe, they would send him to the hospital in Flagstaff. I received a call about noon yesterday and was told by a nurse that they had performed an emergency appendectomy on Mr. Waller soon after his arrival. He'll fly directly home as soon as he is released from the hospital."

I rolled my eyes and observed, "I guess that pretty well clears him as a suspect. It would be pretty tough to have part of your gut cut out at noon in Flagstaff and push a man off a cliff at the Grand Canyon right after supper."

I observed that Ranger Gomez was interviewing the tour members that were outside the neighborhood group.

I left Melody's side and walked to the back of the gathering as Ranger Gray Fox continued his discussion with the neighborhood group.

When I looked back to where Gray Fox was, I saw he was in a small discussion with Melody. Then he came to where I was standing.

"Mr. Gray, the tour guide said you are pretty astute and may have noticed things that could make my job easier. Can you help?"

I asked, "Could we go someplace out of earshot of the rest of the group?"

He turned and headed for his SUV and motioned for me to follow. He unlocked the vehicle's doors, and we both got in. He started the engine and turned on a computer that he said would record our conversation.

Next, he said, "Tell me all you know or think. Don't leave anything out because you believe I already know about it."

Then he did something that appeared strange to me. With the air conditioner running, he produced a small wad of what I took to be some common dried grass. He placed it in a small dish and lit it on fire with a wooden match. It did not burn; it only gave off a tiny curl of smoke that circulated into the air. I did not smell anything, but something was there.

He nodded and whispered, "It will help you think and remember."

I started by telling him of my first feelings about the neighborhood group appearing hostile toward each other.

Then I told him of catching the Pinns and Bulkowskis swapping on the road.

Next, it was overhearing the Chance boy and the Parkses bad-mouthing Jeb Pinn. I spoke about my research into ZuZu Parks's death and said that Pinn looked pretty guilty of rape, in my view. I mentioned Chum and his accusation about stolen credit on the job, and the Rainses and the loss of their little dog.

I thought about not mentioning Old Bald Dome sounding suspicious, because he was not around when Pinn died. But, Gray Fox had said to tell him everything, so I relayed the discussion I had heard on the bus.

The Sly Fox replied, "Certainly didn't have many friends in that bunch! Any one of them had enough hatred to have killed him."

I said, "I don't think Bonnie would have done it. She seemed to have loved him."

"Don't kid yourself! She may have loved him, but there's a lot of hate in love sometimes. You know, you and Mrs. Muldune would also be suspects if you had not been assisting the girl at the moment he went off the rim."

Then I butted in, "Waller couldn't have done it either, because he's in the hospital and had part of his gut cut."

"Well, eliminating three is great, but that still leaves twelve as possible suspects."

In my head I counted and corrected, "Only eleven."

"Twelve! Pinn may have done himself in. Though it's not viewed as murder, it's a homicide just the same."

The chief ranger thanked me for my input and snuffed out the smoking grass, and we exited the car. I walked back to the crowd and informed Melody I was back by her side.

CHAPTER 27

After the meeting with Ranger Gray Fox, the entire tour was turned upside down. Melody and I headed back toward the rooms.

She said, "I need to phone the bank and explain all that has happened. I'm sure that the news of Pinn's death has already been broadcast nationwide and the bank is waiting for my report."

Then she asked me if I had anything planned while she was filing her report.

I assured her, "I'll be in the room whenever you need me or my help."

She quietly said, "Pinn's death has really played hell with the beginning of our relationship. I was really starting to enjoy sharing the highlight of the trip with you, and now who knows what will happen next."

Then she asked, "After I contact the bank and get as much cleared up as possible, could we go and walk along the rim of the canyon? Maybe we can reclaim some of what we were feeling last night."

I told her to file her report and I would be waiting for her, there, as I entered my room.

She unlocked her room and went inside.

I took my shoes off and lay on the bed with my back against the headboard. I wasn't sure what this tour was going to become, but it wasn't going to get any prettier. I felt bad for Melody, but no matter what transpired, I was going to come out a winner. I got to see some of the desert southwest of the US, and better than that, I gained a new love. I felt I had really hit the jackpot.

But Pinn's death had really piqued my interest. I already knew a few things, and because of that, I could not get it off my mind. Did he fall, did he jump, or...was he pushed?

Suddenly I realized it had happened again. I opened my eyes as I heard someone knocking on my door. It's crazy—I thought Pinn's death would keep me wide awake, but it seems I'd fallen asleep.

"Who is it?"

A sweet voice answered, "Are you dressed? Can I come in?"

I almost ran to the door to open it.

Before she could say anything, curiosity overcame me, and I questioned, "What did the bank say?"

She answered, "All the bigs have to discuss the situation, and they will contact me early tomorrow to tell me what to do. How about a little lunch? I'm hungry because we skipped breakfast. And after lunch, let's enjoy some of the canyon if we can."

I agreed, and we headed off to lunch.

We found a small Chinese walk-in and had dim sum and hot green tea. Then we found an ice cream shop and had a large bowl each. She had strawberry, and I had pistachio almond. We sat and talked for a while and then decided to walk part of the rim and maybe, as Melody said, recapture some of what we had started the night before.

As we walked, my love became more and more like her old self. Perhaps the beauty and grandeur of our surroundings blocked a small part of recent history from her mind.

I had just guided her off the path into the brush and put my arms around her to see if her kiss was the same then as it had been the evening before.

Our lips had barely touched when there was a wild rustling in the underbrush near where we stood.

Then out of nowhere appeared a long, gangling, bowlegged body with all types of photo equipment taped and tied to it. The body was dressed in hunting garb reminiscent of the jungle hunter in the old Robin Williams movie *Jumanji*. It sported a pair of canvas above-knee shorts, with a multi-pocketed canvas jacket. Attached to the body was a scrawny neck supporting a long face with a broad nose and what appeared to be a couple weeks' growth of whiskers over parts of his lower face. Covering the top of the head was an old, badly worn pith helmet. On its feet were mid-calf leather hunting boots. Sticking out of the boots were rough, hand-knitted, red wool socks with the ends rolled over the top of the boots. In the hands,

I was expecting to see a huge double-barreled big-game rifle. But instead there was a large-format, professional digital camera with a high-grade tripod. The camera's format was probably six by eight inches, at least.

As the creature cleared the brush, we noticed it was actually tall enough to be able to look down at Melody and me.

A human male voice sounded out as a large hand was extended toward us in handshake position. "Sorry if I startled you—just doing what I do most of the time, taking pictures of anything and everything."

Then he stammered a little as he continued, "Sorry again. The name's Krash, Jack Krash. Hopefully soon to be Krash the Fantastic, as soon as I get that one big frame, just the one big frame!"

I took his hand and answered, "I'm Casper Gray, and this is Mrs. Melody Muldune, and we're part of a bus tour."

"Glad to meet you, and welcome to the grandest canyon in the United States. I'm hoping to get that one big picture while I'm photog-ra-fatin around here."

I wished him luck in his quest. Then Melody and I excused ourselves, as it was time for us to make a reappearance in the group.

Though everything else was fouled up, my Teen Angel still had to be sure the troops were fed and billeted. So, we headed back to The Village.

So the afternoon would not be another total washout, I looked both ways on the trail, saw no one, and stole a long great kiss in the shade of some mountain pines.

CHAPTER 28

When Melody and I got back to the lodge, there was the entire tour, including the bus driver, waiting in the shade near the parking lot.

Melody immediately apologized for our absence but explained she was so confused over the events of the past twenty-some hours that she had taken a break. There was no alarm or hard words from anyone; they just wanted to know what was to happen in the next day or two.

Melody further explained that she had contacted the bank about Pinn's death and the few other things she knew. She also told them that she would be contacted as soon as the bank had come to any concrete conclusions.

Then she told them that dinner would be at The Canyon Wilds in The Village at 7:00. It would be another Native American restaurant specializing in local plants and common vegetables prepared from Native recipes. The meat dishes would be the usual—beef, lamb, turkey, and chicken—except that they would be charbroiled to order: done, well done, or charred. Beef of course could be ordered rare or medium rare. And, no hard drinks would be available.

Because it was past 5:00, the group began to break up and return to their rooms to prepare for dinner. Some were already rested and dressed, so they drifted toward the area of The Village where the restaurant was located or looked for a place to have a cocktail before dinner. Melody and I moseyed back to the rooms and freshened up for Canyon Wilds.

Needless to say, we spent a few short minutes alone together being wild.

At 7:00 we joined the rest of the tour for dinner and enjoyed most of the Native dishes. Of course I was able to make my meal of the charred steak. I usually ordered my steaks medium well, but

I decided to try the charred. It was well cooked and a little dry, but with the special sauce served alongside, it was very tasty. Melody ordered something she'd had before and enjoyed every mouthful as I enjoyed every move she made.

At about 8:30 we returned to the rooms. She stopped me at the door and said, "Cass, I'm really worn from last night and today. Could we just say good night and see each other in the morning?"

I agreed as we held hands for a moment and then went into our rooms. I had just gotten showered, shaved, and into my pajamas when my phone rang. A low sweet voice whispered, "I've changed my mind a little. Would you come over, tuck me in, and kiss me good night?"

I turned off my lights, stepped out the sliding glass door, and found her sliding glass door was unlocked. I entered the darkened room, and a small flashlight came on. I walked over to the bed, and Melody turned the light off, raised up, put her arms around my neck, and kissed me hungrily. Then she purred, "I knew I could never get to sleep without a good-night kiss."

With that she released her hug, laid her head back on the pillow, and was immediately asleep.

I turned, walked out the glass door, went into my room, got my room key, and returned to her room. I closed and locked the glass door, went to her room door, cautiously checked the hall, and returned to my room. When my head hit the pillow, I was also gone.

Since the tour had gone into a stall, I didn't set the alarm. I figured if I missed breakfast at the lodge, I could catch a brunch somewhere else, alone or with Melody if she was available.

I looked at the clock, and it was 8:30 a.m. I leisurely got out of bed and fumbled my way toward the shower. Just as I had reached the nude stage, my cell rang.

Mumbling to myself, I went back to the bed stand, picked up my cell, and answered. A dazed but sweet voice, through a yawn, asked, "Are you out of your room yet?"

"No, just headed to the shower."

Then I heard a giggle, as she this time asked, "Do you want to come and join me in mine?"

I said, "You damned little tease. I know you don't really mean that."

"Yes, you're right, but you don't know how close I might be."

I quickly changed the subject. "Do you want to go someplace for breakfast, rather than doing breakfast here?"

She answered, "They serve here until 10:00. We might as well save money and eat the lodge's eggs and mystery meat."

There was a short pause, and then she continued, "I need to work all day on this messy-assed tour. Save your money, and I'll eat up every dime you have for dinner, if I get my work completed by that time. You may as well check around The Village area and see if there's any unknown information about Pinn that you and Gray Fox are not aware of. If I need you, I'll just call you."

Then I asked a joking question: "Could I come over and get a kiss as you get into the shower?"

I received a quick, "No! But, if you hurry while I still have my jammies on, you might get lucky."

I didn't need a written invitation!

Later, slightly before 10:00, we stopped for a quick cold breakfast. Everyone else had already been served, and the kitchen staff was starting to clear away the breakfast leftovers. No problem, the coffee was still hot for me, and Melody had a yogurt and juice.

We stepped behind an ice machine in an alcove, and I kissed Melody as she prepared to get down to problem-solving, and as I prepared to do a little ghost work to see if anyone knew anything and didn't know they knew it.

I decided if Pinn was a predator of women, perhaps he had made some moves in the background that I might find out about. Then it struck me: If he did make any moves, it would not have been out in plain sight or in the busier areas of The Village. *So, Ghost, let's look behind the stage for his nasty little tricks.* I also remembered he had approached the Strawflower girl at a small lunch counter.

The first place that caught my attention was a hair salon. I opened the door and was immediately met by the odor of hair spray and the super cool of a heavy-duty air-conditioning unit.

The first was an unpleasant distraction, and the other was a very welcome sensation.

An older lady was preparing her equipment for a future client and did not know anything about Jeb Pinn. She said no one of his description had been around her shop in months, maybe years.

My next stop along the way was a little launderette just around the corner, off the main street, on the last street in The Village.

I boldly walked in and asked if a slender man with a small square mustache had left his laundry there in the past couple of days. A young woman turned around and asked, "Is he a friend of yours?"

I felt a little cool settle over me, so I answered, "No, I'm just looking for him if he's still around."

"Why?"

"It's a little private...about my wife."

"Did the bastard try to put his hands on her too?"

"How did you know that?"

"He had his hand up the leg of my shorts, from behind, when my husband literally kicked his ass out the door. And, no! Laundry was not what he was after."

To carry on the charade, I asked, "When did it happen to you?"

"A couple of days ago."

"That son of a bitch, he must have tried to bother my wife as he was coming in here, or after your husband kicked him out. Have you seen him since?"

"No, and he better not come back here, or my husband will kill his miserable ass."

Then in the meanest voice I could fake, I said, "He won't have to if I catch his miserable ass first."

As I left the launderette, I thought, *How many women did that man hurt in his life?* I also wondered, *Did that woman's husband find his miserable ass and kick it off the rim?* But no, I believed, like the Sly One, if he was murdered, it was someone from the tour. But, I still needed to forward this information to Gray Fox.

It dawned on me—Pinn evidently did not waste time. He had to have made his move at the launderette the moment he got off the bus from the tour.

CHAPTER 29

I played some more games in and around several small businesses in the area, but no one else remembered Old Slender Ass.

I went to the little lunch counter where Dora Strawflower was approached by Pinn, to see if anyone else had noticed anything.

As I pushed open the door, I saw an older Native American man working behind the counter. I asked him if he knew Dora, and he nodded. Then in slow deliberate English, he said, "She my niece... not working today...sick."

"Is she getting better?" I asked.

"Damned man! Almost scare her to death; she not know what to think. Keep ask, 'Why me?' How you know about?"

"My friend and I were the ones who found her and the man."

"I am glad he dead. Not good man."

Then I asked, "Is this your lunch counter?"

"No. My brother's. I cook. He Dora's dad."

"Did you see the man when he was talking to your niece?"

"No, in kitchen cooking, hear a little, but not see anything."

"Was there anyone else here while the man was here?"

"Yes, someone holler, 'Can I use bathroom?' I holler back, 'Yes.'"

"Where was Dora at that time?"

"She go next door to deliver a lunch."

"Did you see who hollered?"

"No, only hear holler."

"Was it a man or woman?"

"Not know for sure, sorry."

I thanked the old gentleman, left the shop, and moved on down the street. I then had two pieces of information for the chief ranger.

It was past lunchtime, but I wasn't especially hungry, so I bought a corn dog from a sidewalk vender and a beer in a small bar. The bartender allowed me to eat my corn dog as I drank my beer.

While I ate, I wondered if Melody stopped for lunch or just continued to work to get everything in order.

In the back of my mind were eight questions. Really only one question with eight answers. What were the Rainses, Chums, Parkses, Chance, and Rhonda Bulkowski doing when Pinn died?" Rhonda said she was with a biker who called himself Devil. But anyone can say anything, true or not.

Finally, the heat of the desert southwest made itself known to me, and I decided to go back to the room for a short nap. Perhaps Melody would finish her work early, and we could sneak off to a cool spot, then later have a delicious meal, and neck as a late dessert.

Melody finally rang my cell at about 5:30. "Am I too late for a fantastic dinner and some fun later? All of the people on tour have been questioned about Pinn's death, and their alibis, or lack thereof, submitted to the ranger group.

"The Chums said they were at a karaoke contest here in the lodge and won a prize. That was easy to check, and they were definitely there. They were absolutely innocent.

"The Rainses said they were at a nature presentation in the amphitheater and met some people from another tour. The rangers are checking that out and should know for sure by tomorrow. That just leaves the Parkses, the Chance boy, and Rhonda. Maybe tomorrow we will get something from them."

After her short story about her day, I told her mine. She was as flabbergasted about Pinn's activities as I was.

She observed, "A real criminal, looking and acting as meek as a lamb. No wonder someone maybe whacked him. I'm surprised he made it this far."

Then she breathed deeply and said, "What about it, big boy, time for some fun?"

I gave my approval, and we made plans for the evening.

First, we both needed to freshen up from the hot day's activities. She said she would return to her room and meet me in my room about 6:15 or 6:30.

As I hung up the phone, I was already starting to undress and head for the shower. About halfway through my bathroom activities, I heard the shower in Melody's room start to run. I knew she was back and getting ready for the evening.

In a while there was a knock on the sliding glass as she appeared outside. I unlocked the glass, and she fairly floated into the room. Her choice of dress was extremely provocative, and her perfume was almost overpowering. Both caused me complete distraction as I attempted to maintain my equilibrium. She reached back, closed the curtains on the door, and then applied every female wile she possessed to drive me totally up the wall. I could have been angered by her actions, but instead I enjoyed, beyond explanation, her every move. When she finally kissed me, there in the subdued light, the male in me began to scream in my mind. Had she allowed me more time than what was necessary to return her kiss, I would have committed an act that would have put me on the same level as Old Slender. But just in time, she said, "Where and what are we eating for dinner?"

I stood there for a moment, drawing in as much oxygen as my body could handle, trying to regain my senses and, at the same time, not wanting to let her out of my arms. *Damn her, either I've got to bed her or get away from her. She and I can't have it both ways.*

But, without letting her know how far she had driven me, I answered, "Today while I was on my research detail, I passed a small hole-in-the-wall restaurant. It had a sign in the window stating, 'We serve the finest western grilled steak in Canyon Country. Try us, and if you do not agree, your steak is on us, no questions asked.'"

I continued, "No one makes a statement like that unless they really believe it's the truth. Why don't we try them?"

With that damned smile, so beautiful it drove me almost out of my mind, she answered, "You're paying, big boy, so wherever you say, let's go."

"Surprise, surprise," as Gomer Pyle would say, the steak was as good or better than the others I'd had at Big Leroy's and Reggie's back down the road.

As we walked back to the lodge, Melody became very serious. "Perhaps tonight it would be better if we simply kissed good night and went our separate ways. Being together may not be our smartest move."

For a second time, I was confused. What had I done this time for her to seem so cold after our earlier activities? So bluntly, I asked, "What's the problem this time? Haven't I done or been what you expected? Has this mess with Pinn caused you to have second thoughts? Have you maybe decided I'm not what you're really looking for?"

As I looked directly into her face, huge tears began to appear in her eyes, and I thought, *Here it comes.* I could imagine her saying, "I don't think I want to be around you anymore!"

But instead, she caught her breath and whispered, "No...don't think that. It's entirely the opposite—I'm beginning to feel a little like a whore, because I have been setting traps for you and you have been gentleman enough not to take advantage of me."

Then she continued, "Damn me, I want you to take advantage of me so much I hurt, but I don't want you to think I'm that kind of woman."

So once more, I had to tell her what I was thinking: "My Sweet Melody, my Teen Angel, I don't care what kind of woman you are, as long as you are my woman. But if you don't stop being so damned sweet and beautiful, you will finally catch me in one of your traps. I'm only a human male and can only handle so much of the woman you are before I can't stop myself. I was close to that moment in the room, before dinner."

"I know," she said, "and that's why I thought it best we cool it. Just for tonight, you understand; tomorrow I'll want you twice as bad, but maybe by then I'll control myself better."

When we reached the rooms, I stepped inside her door, kissed her, and ran my hand up her back under her blouse, and her breathing increased. I said good night and slipped back out her door, then into mine, and retired for the night.

CHAPTER 30

There was a knock at my door before the alarm went off. I slipped into a pair of shorts I had for just such a situation. Then I opened the door.

Melody was standing there fully dressed and ready for the day. She slid into my room and put her arms around me and kissed me in a way that scared me just a little. Then she pulled away to arm's length and said, "The bank has decided to end the tour right now. They feel that if we go on, there is a possibility that one of the ones on the bus might be a killer. Since no one has been charged and the ranger has decided not to hold anyone here, we are to turn back. We'll remain here today, and I'll get all the necessary arrangements for the return done before I hit the mattress tonight.

"It's also my duty to escort Bonnie Pinn to the airport in Flagstaff today. The bank decided it would be better for her and the tour if she flies back to Missouri. And, Chief Ranger Gray Fox said Jeb's body would be shipped home as soon as the total investigation is completed. The rest of us will leave early in the morning and make the trip home in two days."

She pressed against me and whispered in my ear, "Please don't plan anything after 10:30 tonight. I want us to have the last evening of the tour for ourselves."

Then she quickly kissed me again and said, "I've got a ton of work to do, so I may not see you until after 10:30 tonight."

Before I could say much else, she ran down the hall toward the main desk.

I took care of my necessary morning chores and then went to the dining area for breakfast. Melody wasn't there.

As I left the dining area after eating, I contemplated just finding a spot on the canyon rim in the shade and wasting the whole day there. But it wasn't to be.

As I cleared the main front door of the lodge I was met by the Sly One, Ranger Gray Fox.

"I hear the tour is over and you are all starting the return home tomorrow."

"Yeah, Melody told me the plans earlier this morning."

With a little bit of hesitation in his voice, he asked, "Gray, is there any way I could persuade you to stay behind and assist me in more investigation? My staff is small, and I don't have any money to pay you. But, you seem to have an inner sense about you that enables you to hear and see things others don't, so maybe together we could solve this mess."

Without hesitation, I answered, "I would not have a problem staying out here awhile; the only problems are a place to stay and transportation."

Before I could blink, that Sly Fox answered, "My aunt has a small cabin with a spare room in one of the side canyons, and I have an old pickup that still runs pretty good. Would that convince you to stay?"

"Only if you will answer one question I've had since we met."

"Shoot," he said.

"I do a little reading, and somewhere I read that the Navajo and Hopi cultures still survive around the Grand Canyon. Are you Navajo or Hopi?"

With a dry laugh, he said, "No!"

I said, "You misunderstood what I said. Which are you: Navajo or Hopi?"

"Neither. I'm full-blood Havasupai, and my people have been in this canyon for innumerable years."

Then it was my turn. "You sly son of a gun, now I have to go back and do a lot more homework."

He snorted and giggled, and we shook hands on the deal we had made.

Then I said, "Before you go, I have a couple of pieces of new information you may not have."

I told him of Pinn's little escapade at the laundromat and about the person in the lunchroom bathroom at the same time Pinn was setting up his scheme with Miss Strawflower.

He immediately said, "I don't think the husband is the killer. Pinn would have been too much of a chicken shit to try to take on a man. Women were easier prey."

Then I corrected him a little as I explained Henry Chum's situation. "He probably felt that because of Chum's race, he would also be easy prey."

The Fox made another observation: "I still believe if it's murder, it's one of your group. And I also believe the person at the lunch shop would be the prime suspect. Too bad the old man didn't see who it was."

I agreed but stated, "If it was murder, we still need to find out who did it and, even if we feel it might have been justified, remove him or her from society."

We shook hands again, and he headed back to his office as I headed out to look for more information.

CHAPTER 31

I was a little at a loss as to where to look for new information, so I decided to go to the canyon rim and work my way back to The Village. Perhaps there was something that we all missed in that area that would be of importance.

As I crossed one of the parking lots, I saw a group of bikers. I wondered if it was the same group that the Red Flag claimed as her alibi.

Then I noticed the back of the leather jacket on the front biker. In large gold letters, I read, "I'm the Devil Incarnate!"

It had to be Devil, "the Leader of the Pack."

I motioned for him to stop, and amazingly he did. I chose my words carefully as I said, "I realize what I'm about to ask is extremely personal, so perhaps if you choose to answer, you might want to do it in private."

He answered, "Ask away. I'm the Devil, and I have nothing to hide."

So, I shot directly from the hip but spoke softly. "A lady has given your name as her alibi in a possible murder case. She said a few nights ago she was with you all evening and night. I'm sorry this is so personal, but can or will you answer?"

With a broad grin of snowy-white teeth, he asked, "Rhonda, the big good-looking redhead?"

I nodded.

"You damned right she was with me! We spent the evening and night together. She told a lot about herself and her husband. She was hurting bad, and I hope I made her feel better!" He continued, "If you talk to her again, tell her Devil said she is one fine lady, and he wishes her only the best of luck." Almost as an afterthought, he also said, "If she is charged with anything, contact me, and I will damned well stand up in court for her. Oh yeah, my real name is Dr. Jonathon DuVal, and I'm a philosophy instructor at the University of Berkeley."

Then a darkness appeared on his face as he took time to think deeply, and then in totally seriousness, he spoke, "If you have the chance to talk to her husband, tell him the Devil said he's one damned fool for screwing around on a woman like her!" Then he suddenly revved the engine of his bike, causing dense smoke to roll from twin tailpipes as he shot out across the lot.

About fifteen bikers fell in behind him as they all roared out of view down the pike.

As I walked back toward the lodge, a broad grin spread across my face as I said to myself, *DuVal...Devil—that guy is almost as good with names as I am.*

CHAPTER 32

I was lying on the bed watching some silly show on the TV, not really paying too much attention to what was happening. It was past 10:30, and my thoughts were about Melody and Lily. Melody was beginning to become more important than Lily, and I hoped Lily understood. And I believed she did. I knew she always tried to make me happy, and I believed she always wanted me to be happy. Happily (and sadly), I was almost as happy as I had ever been.

Then there was a light knock at my door. I got up and opened it, expecting Melody coming directly from the computer in the lobby. Instead, she stood there in the hallway wearing a lightweight raincoat, with soft sandals on her feet. She quickly stepped into my room and pushed the door closed.

Before I could move, she was pushing my T-shirt up to my neck and attempting to get it over my head. I didn't understand, but I assisted her as the T-shirt fell to the floor. Then she slid her hands down each side of my elastic-topped shorts and pushed them off my hips, and they also dropped to the floor. There I stood in only my briefs. Next she checked the door to be sure it was locked, and at the same time she turned off the main light switch, leaving only one small light over the headboard on. Picking up the remote, she switched off the TV.

All her activities took place in about two minutes, and I wasn't quite sure what to think. Then she held up one finger, as she liked to do, a signal to stop.

I stopped!

Slowly, oh so slowly, she stepped out of the sandals and, with her foot, pushed them under the TV stand. Then slower still...she turned her back to me and began to do something to the front of the raincoat. I supposed she was unbuttoning it, but I wasn't sure!

Then she turned slowly around to face me once more and let the raincoat slide off her shoulders. She was as nude as the day she was born except for a lace thong that barely covered anything.

She slowly walked over to where I was standing, placed her body almost against me, leaned her head closer, and whispered just loud enough, "My love, this is an invitation. The ranger told me today that you are staying out here awhile to assist him. I am going to have you tonight before I go home tomorrow. I want you to know what will be waiting for you when you get back to Missouri. Now I'm going to take your undies off, and you will need to remove mine."

In a few moments, there was no question—I wanted to be with that woman for the rest of my life.

I don't remember exactly what happened next, but later as we lay there in each other's arms, I was absolutely certain, if I had my way, she would be the next Mrs. Casper Gray. And I believed I heard Lily cheering me on.

Melody aroused a little and said, "Please set the alarm for about 3:00 a.m. so I can get back to my room before anyone suspects anything."

I did as she asked.

Then she nestled back into my arms and placed her face in the hollow of my neck under my chin. Shortly I heard the soft breath of sleep.

When I heard the alarm, I rolled over and shut it off and then noticed Melody was already gone from my bed. I noticed that the meager clothes she wore into my room were also gone. I concluded she awoke earlier and left then. I settled back, and in a few moments, I was once more sound asleep.

I awoke to the sound of a soft knock at my door. I asked, "Who?"

A very familiar voice whispered, "Get up. It's time for breakfast, and I will meet you in the dining area."

Then in a much softer whisper, I heard, "Or should I not wake you, just make you?" Then I heard a sweet giggle as it faded down the hall.

In a short time I was dressed and hurrying to breakfast. I was hungry, but at the same time a little distressed. After breakfast,

Melody and the rest of the tour would turn back east for home. When I started the tour, I never thought I could miss anyone as much as I missed Lily. But I missed Melody terribly, and she hadn't even left yet.

Then I saw her helping the same little old lady with her breakfast and coffee. An ache in my being hit me as I thought of how she looked to me last night and how she also helped me so much. I had to force myself to remain what would appear to be just one of the tour members as she continued doing her tour work.

In a short time she joined me at the coffee area and filled a cup for herself and then led the way to a table for breakfast.

As we ate, she reached under the table and squeezed my hand for just a moment. Then she dropped her napkin, and as we both leaned over and reached down to pick it up, she quickly said, "I left you early last night because if I had stayed I would have kept you awake the rest of the night. And now I know I really do love you, and I want you to get home as soon as you can, so I can show you how much."

I handed her the napkin and tried to return to eating my breakfast. But I was completely full, at least for a time, anyway.

After we had finished the ham, eggs, and coffee, she asked me if I would carry her suitcase from her room to the bus, as she had not been able to get it outside her door in time for it to be picked up by the hotel staff. I followed her back to the room, and she fairly shoved me into the room ahead of her.

As soon as we were inside, she slammed the door behind us. She flew into my arms and was kissing me before I could make a move. All I could do was throw my arms around her and return every move she made. Finally she released me just a little and said, "I only had you for a short time last night, and it's been so long since I felt that way, and now I have to leave again. Please don't stay out here too long; I want you so bad."

I held her as tight as I could and said, "That old saw cuts both ways, so I'll move as fast as I can, and then I'll catch the next plane home."

I kissed her for a long moment, and then it was time to get her suitcase under the bus.

As the bus pulled out of the parking lot and slowly lumbered down the street, I felt like a part of my very being was torn from me. I knew I had not felt this low since the moment I realized that Lily had passed.

I murmured, "God, let the Old Sly One and me get this thing solved quickly. I have another mystery to solve in mid-Missouri: How much longer can I live as a single man?"

CHAPTER 33

A s I stood there in the parking lot waiting for my heart to settle back to its place in my chest, I tried to formulate a plan of action for the coming days. I knew Melody would only be there with me in voice, as I knew I would phone her frequently as loneliness set in.

I had forgotten to tell her about the Devil supporting Rhonda's alibi, so I would tell her the first time one of us phoned.

I also needed to phone the Gray Fox and tell him about Devil. And, I needed to know if the Rainses' alibi was supported by the people in the other tour group. The Rainses had the people's names, so if that tour had already left, they could still be contacted using hotel records. The Fox probably already had that information, if it was true.

Bonnie Pinn and Bulkowski were each other's alibi. But, what if they got rid of Old Slender Ass so they could be together? I needed to question the chief about that too.

I looked at my watch, and she'd been gone ten minutes, and it felt like a lifetime. I had to believe she loved me and would be waiting for me at home. If I couldn't believe that, I was lost.

Hard as I tried, she just kept floating through my mind. I knew I had to hurry and get my mind working on something else, or I'd end up a basket case. With her gone, all I had to keep me sane was concentrating on Pinn's death and trying to make heads or tails out of the bits and pieces of information.

Everyone had a story or alibi. But were the stories true?

I was leisurely wandering around the area when, out of nowhere, the tall lanky photographer appeared in front of me, headed my way.

Next he blocked my way as he stopped directly in my path about two feet from me.

"Hey, I saw you on the rim the other night, and later I heard you were involved in somebody's death. Are you the one?"

I wasn't in the mood to be bothered, but I didn't see any way to sidetrack, so I mumbled, "Yes."

"You was with a fine-looking little bird, if my memory serves me right. Ain't I right?"

"Right."

"Is they a chance I might get some pictures of you looking for something havin' to do with that death? They say you're working with the Old Redskin Ranger on a possible murder case. Is that so?"

"I can't talk about it, because it's police business."

"Never know, I might know something you need. Might trade what I know for some pictures."

Suddenly my mind kicked in, and I thought, *Perhaps he did see or hear something*, so I decided to go on the offensive a little.

"When we met you the other night, had you been working that area the night before?"

"Yeah, I was, been there for a couple days before. That is, in the general area in general terms."

I didn't know what he meant by that, but at least he was talking.

"Did you see anyone walking fast or running away from that general area the night before you met us?"

"No, didn't see anything except what's in my pictures. Man, I want the big frame! All I want is one big frame. If I ever get that frame and you're involved, can I have the photo credit?"

I told him it would not be up to me, because I was working for the US government at the present time.

"Can you tell me the time that the man died? I might have seen something and didn't realize it."

I thought for a moment and realized that this was already public knowledge. It was on the news, so me telling him would not divulge any secrets. So I told him the time.

Suddenly, for some reason, another thought flooded my brain. "Do you have a cell phone?"

"No, mine's a satellite phone, so I can call from anywhere at any time."

I asked, "Can I have your number in case there's a chance for a big frame?"

"Sure, I'd be a fool not to have you in my loop. With you working for the rangers and the feds, I might get a chance at the big one."

I thanked him, excused myself, and got back on my prepared detail.

I resumed my walk around The Village trying to find anyone who might have heard or seen something that would shed new light on the old evidence. I walked into a little bar connected to the back of the bike rental building to have a short beer and try to get away from my thoughts and feelings of desire for Melody.

I had barely tasted my mug when the bartender came down the bar to where I was seated and asked, "Weren't you on that tour from Missouri, the one the man who was killed was on?"

I really wasn't supposed to discuss any part of Pinn's death with anyone, because of the ongoing investigation. So, I just nodded my head in the affirmative and took another drink.

But he continued, "I recognized you from the big group picture they showed on television after that man died. And I saw his wife and another couple on the parking lot, I guess, a day or so later. His wife didn't seem too broken up over his death. Fact is, the other man's wife seemed to be the only one really torn up about it."

Though he was simply rambling on, I suddenly began to listen closer to what he was saying. Then I decided to maybe lead the conversation a little.

"You're talking about the tall slender guy as the one who was killed?" I asked.

"Yeah, and his wife was the big gorgeous redhead."

I almost blew it as I started to correct him that it was the blond who was his wife. But I caught myself just in time and said, "Who was the other couple she was with?"

"You know, the well-built guy and the slender blond."

"You're talking about the guy who looked like a pro football player?"

"Yeah, and that blond, even at her age, was still hotter than hell!"

He stopped and thought for a moment, and then he grinned in an evil manner and even laughed. "I guess they were in here the night the other guy died. But, man, let me tell you, he had his hands down her blouse and up her skirt all night. She kept slapping at his hands and saying, 'Bob, wait until we're back in the room.' Finally, about 9:00 or 9:30 they left. I'll bet he enjoyed himself when he got her into bed."

Shortly, I lied and told him I just remembered I had to meet someone at the lodge in a few minutes. I paid my tab and left.

So Bob Bulkowski and Bonnie Pinn's story checked out. Their alibis appeared to be ironclad.

CHAPTER 34

As I cleared the door of the little bar, I looked at my watch once again. It was almost lunchtime, and I had held out as long as I could. I started looking for a shady spot where I could sit down and make a phone call. Ahead of me I saw a low rock wall running under a small brushy growth—not a tree but a little shade. As I started to position my butt to sit on the wall, my phone rang.

As I put the phone to my ear, I heard heartbreaking sobs.

"I don't have much time, but I miss you so much. The others are eating lunch, and I'm hiding in the bathroom. I love you and want you."

Now it was my turn to get thick-throated and almost unable to speak as I croaked, "Damn, I love and miss you so much too."

Then I heard a cross between a sob and a giggle. "Just like a couple of lovesick teenagers, but I don't care. Cass, I miss you so much, and we've only been apart a few hours."

As we talked, our minds and voices became steady, allowing us to carry on an adult conversation.

She said they would make Oklahoma City later that night and go on to Jefferson City the next day.

I told her about meeting Devil and how he supported Rhonda's alibi. And also about Bonnie and Bob's night at the bar, and the bartender's story.

She asked about the Rainses, and I told her I hadn't heard anything from the Sly One about that yet.

She observed, "The Parkses and the Chance kid are the only ones from the neighborhood group without a solid alibi."

I agreed and said they were the ones I was going to try to find something out about next.

Then with a light sob, she finished, "I can see through the bathroom window; the bus is loading, so I have to run further away from you again."

Then I said, "I love you, I want you, and in a few days I plan to have you. Don't go out with any of the other team members before I get home from this game."

She giggled and said, "My momma told me not to let that slick-tongued hellion get me pregnant. So don't you have any plans for anything like that!"

Then she whispered lightly, "Even if you did, I would love you and it forever."

My only answer was, "I know I'll love you forever."

The spot I chose to sit was comfortable and almost cool, so I decided to try to contact Ranger Gray Fox before I moved on.

He must have been momentarily distracted, and I listened to it ring for several cycles. Finally I heard the familiar deep voice of Old Sly. "Gray, what would cause you to disturb my beauty nap? You know us old Indians need all the rest we can get to stay ahead of you white men."

Then he chuckled as I butted in. "I have what I believe are ironclad alibis for Rhonda Bulkowski, Bob Bulkowski, and Bonnie Pinn." I told him about running into Devil DuVal and repeated the story he told me.

Ranger Fox said, "One less suspect."

I also repeated the bartender's story about Bonnie and Bob, and Bob's sex nutty tah-tee-dah in the little bar.

"Maybe the son of a bitch became ashamed of himself and just jumped," Fox appeared to muse to himself.

Then it was my turn to disagree. "Just before he went over the edge, he saw something. Then he put his hands up in front of his face in a defensive gesture. No, I believe if he jumped, something or someone caused him to do it."

The Native ranger did not speak for a few moments and then finally broke the silence. Like Melody, he had calculated the numbers, and then he quoted the answer to those calculations. "It appears everyone but young Chance and the Parks couple have pretty convincing alibis for the time of Pinn's death."

I corrected him one more time. "No, the Rainses have not been accounted for."

Then he apologized, "Sorry, I forgot to tell you the Rainses' story was substantiated by two couples from another tour. They were at a nature presentation." Gray Fox paused for a few moments and then said, "Well, then I guess my job is to bear down on Chance and the Parkses and their story and see what I find."

Then I asked, "What is their story? Melody didn't say, and you never told me either."

"They claimed to have been in the lodge bar all evening after dinner. But I haven't had time to check it out, as I have been running in circles trying to put out the tourism fires that Pinn's death has ignited. The state of Arizona and the tribal council here are afraid this might hurt the Grand Canyon's bottom line. I knew that would happen, so that is why I asked you to stay and help. So far you've done yeoman's work."

With a grin I said, "I suppose if I continue, you won't be unhappy."

"Far from it. Solve the damned thing if you can." Then he cackled like an old hen laying an egg. "Of course if you do, I'll just claim all the credit."

I laughed out loud as I said to him, "A typical red-faced politician putting the hurt on a white man."

He giggled and returned, "Every chance I get."

I bid him a good afternoon and hung up the phone as I pondered my next point of advance.

CHAPTER 35

Now it appeared my investigation was going to be concentrated on Shane Chance and the Parkses. Of all the possible suspects, they appeared to have the strongest motivation to want Jeb Pinn dead.

The Old Ranger Fox said their alibi was drinking in the lodge bar at the time Pinn died. So it appeared that my job would start at the lodge bar.

First I went to see the lodge manager to find out who was working in the bar the night Pinn died.

He was more than willing to give me all the information he could supply. He told me the council wanted the case closed as quickly as possible because it might have heavy ramifications on the canyon's financial situation. It sounded like he and the Fox had been talking to the same individuals.

I took the names of the bartenders and servers who were working that night and went to the bar to talk to any of them who might be on duty.

A little luck was with me, as one of the bartenders and two servers from that night were on duty when I got to the bar.

They had already been prompted as to who Chance and the Parkses were. As soon as I asked about them, the bartender pulled out a copy of a credit card receipt with Mr. Parks's name on it. It listed the drinks ordered and the time they were ordered. The early orders were for three drinks at a time, and then later only two at a time were purchased.

I asked, "Did one of the customers leave when only two drinks started being ordered?"

The bartender said he didn't know but maybe one of the servers might remember. He called the servers over, and I asked if they remembered the three drinking that night. One server said he didn't recall who they were, but he served the table where they were.

The second server thought for a moment, then his face turned red, and he almost screamed, "Oh yes, I remember them. The young guy got sick and vomited all over the place. Joe and I had to clean it up. Hey Joe, you remember the little shit that vomited all over everything, that we had to clean up after?"

Then Joe asked, "Wasn't he the one who also screwed up the men's bathroom, that we also had to clean up?"

The second server said, "One and the same, the little bastard."

Then I asked, "Were they all three here the entire evening?"

Both servers said that the older couple never left their seats the whole evening. But they both said the kid ran back and forth to the bathroom when he wasn't lying under their table.

Then I asked, "If you were asked by a judge about what I just asked you, what would be your story about the kid and the older couple?"

Both agreed that the couple drank all evening at the table they were serving and the kid got sick and messed up the area around the table and the men's room in the hall.

I decided I would pass the information along to Foxy and let him decide if it was worth the effort to pursue Chance and the Parkses' story any further.

I looked at my watch and saw it was pretty late in the afternoon, and I was missing Melody again.

I also thought about Pinn's demise and decided I had pretty well wrapped up the case as far as the neighborhood group was concerned. Unless Chief Ranger Christjohn Gray Fox saw things differently, all the members of that group had pretty tight alibis. I would even say ironclad alibis.

Suddenly I felt hot; some of it was the temperature and some of it was the old male hormones attacking my sanity. I decided it was time to find a super cool environment, something tasty to eat, maybe a libation or two, and a loving conversation with the woman I intended to make the ghost's wife. Then I thought, *I'm sorry Lily!*

But then I believed I actually heard a sweet voice from the past say, "Go get her, Casper. I love her too!"

As I almost ran back to my room, I suddenly remembered I didn't have a room any longer. I should have moved out of the room before noon.

CHAPTER 36

When I reached the front desk, I was totally mortified. I explained to the desk clerk that I had forgotten to check out at noon, and I didn't know what to do about it now, at 4:10 p.m.

The desk clerk grinned and said, "The big man said you were good for another night, just put it on your credit card."

I was a little perplexed and said, "What big man? The lodge manager?"

"Na...the big, big man—Ranger Gray Fox."

Then I really grinned. The Old Red Sucker, he socked it to me again. One more victory for the Red Man!

I thanked the desk clerk and headed for my room. I was a little blue as I opened the door, because Melody was no longer in the room next door. As I headed for the bathroom I saw a gift-wrapped package sticking out of the top of my overnight bag. I stopped and picked it up. It was not very heavy and was soft to the touch in my hand. Carefully I opened it and found a pair of Melody's black panties. Pinned to the band was a small card with four words written on it: "Kisses...I love you!"

My bathroom visit had to wait. I dialed my phone and waited for an answer. After a couple of rings, I heard a sweet voice whisper, "I love you!"

"I love you too!" Then I continued, "Are you anywhere close to Oklahoma City yet?"

She quietly replied, "It will be close to midnight, one side or the other, when we get there. Maybe even later, as we haven't stopped to eat dinner yet. Did you learn anything new today about the case?"

I told her about the Parkses and Chance at the lodge bar, and that Gray Fox's group had cleared the Rainses.

She slowly replied, "Everyone has an alibi. What does Gray Fox think?"

I told her I would tell Chief Gray Fox about young Chance and the Parkses in the morning.

"Does that mean you'll be coming home in the next couple of days?"

I told her that would depend on Gray Fox and Arizona state law. But I would leave the minute they okayed it.

Then I suddenly remembered: "Did you leave me a gift in my overnight bag?"

"No, not a gift. That package contained a promise, kisses, and other goodies for you as soon as you get back."

Then Angel's persona broke to the surface for a few moments. "Get home so you can give me your ring to wear round my neck."

"Little girl, it will be around your neck before you know it. That's a gold-clad promise."

We continued our conversation for a few more minutes, and I asked how the Bulkowskis were handling each other.

She giggled and said, "They haven't had their hands off each other since we left this morning." And she said she also asked them if they desired separate rooms in Oklahoma City, and they both said, "Hell no!"

I heard Melody say, under her breath, "Maybe they'll make it after all." Then she continued, "Coming up to the dinner halt—have to go. Will I hear from you tomorrow?"

I told her I would call as often as I could and then said, "Goodbye."

As I put the phone away, I remembered that sometime soon I should hear from Volkens about the ring. I also remembered I needed to have them include a gold chain for Melody to wear it on.

I finally made it to the bathroom and freshened up a little.

I decided to return to the little steak house for dinner. I wanted to go for two reasons. First, it's the last place Melody and I went together, and second, the food was excellent.

When I got to the steak house, the counter man remembered me and asked if the lovely lady would be joining me. It hurt a little as I told him no.

The steak was better then than it had been the night before. When I mentioned it to the waiter, he grinned and said, "Our steaks grow on you...or they grow in you and make you fatter."

I told him I was very satisfied, either way.

I knew I shouldn't, but I stopped in the lodge bar and had a couple of very small Turkey and Honeys on the rocks. Then it was off to bed. I knew if I was to stay any longer, I would either move out to Fox's aunt's cabin or be paying top dollar for the room I continued to occupy. Oh well, I would talk to Fox in the morning and decide then.

I turned out the light to try to quickly fall asleep.

CHAPTER 37

B ut as I lay there in the darkness, my mind continued to play and replay all the information I had accumulated.

"Damn it," I said to myself. "All the probable suspects appear to have ironclad alibis. Young Chance and the Parkses have the bartender and the table servers. Bulkowski and Bonnie Pinn have the other bartender. The Chums won a singing prize. The Rainses have people from another tour. Rhonda Bulkowski can depend on the Devil. Dub Waller was or is in the hospital. And Melody and I have each other, plus Miss Strawflower.

As I slowly blasted away at my own thoughts, I berated myself. *There's something I'm missing, but what is it?*

Then my mind awakened with a start. *He is so obvious, I simply looked right past him. What about Krash? He's so damned crazy and weird, perhaps he could have killed Slim!*

I wanted to immediately jump out of bed and try to check it out. But, I decided I would do better rested and wide awake. So I rolled over, closed my eyes in sleep, and pleasantly dreamed of Lily and Melody, in that order. One was with me, and hopefully the other might, in the future, agree to be. Not a bad mental state to be in. Either way I considered myself to be a winner. And besides, no matter what happened, Lily would always be with me.

When I awoke the next morning I already had a plan formed in my mind. If I approached Krazy correctly, he was just loony enough to admit he was the one responsible, if he was guilty.

But first I had to get moved out of my room, locate the chief ranger's aunt's cabin, and get his old truck for transportation.

As I ate breakfast, I placed a call to the head ranger. In a short time, he answered. I told him about the work I did at the lodge's bar, and that it appeared the Parkses and Chance had pretty tight alibis also.

Then I asked about the room at his aunt's and the old pickup for transportation. And I asked, "If this is the final word, do you want me to stay or go home?"

"Do you have any other ideas?" he asked.

"Funny you asked that. Yes, I do have one more angle to check."

"Then leave your bags in your room, and before checkout, I'll move them to my aunt's place and leave the truck there in the parking lot. The keys will be at the front desk."

I thanked him and hung up the phone.

After a very satisfying breakfast of the usual eggs, bacon, sausage, coffee, etc. in the Canyon Lodge dining room, I walked out to the parking lot to look for Krash. I wandered out to the spot where he usually parked his old photography van. The van was there, but Ole Krazy wasn't. I assumed he had his satellite phone with him, so I dialed his number on my cell.

After a dozen or so rings he answered with a vengeful timbre in his voice. "Who in hell's name is this, and what in Sam Hill do you want? I just had a blue jay trying to attack a California condor, and your dumb ass ruined my chance at sure fame. Who in the hell is this?"

"It's me Jack, Casper, and I need your help right now."

In a surprisingly friendly voice, he replied, "Okay, Boss. Give me a few minutes to collect my junk, and I'll meet you at my van."

"I'm at your van now," I answered.

"Okay, I should be there in about ten minutes."

I had decided to just straight out ask him if he had pushed Old Slim off the rim. I hadn't planned to use a rhyme, but there it was.

After more like thirty minutes, Krash came out of the brush growing along the edge of the rim carrying several cameras and other pieces of photographic equipment. He unlocked the back doors of his van, stowed away the tools of his trade, and closed and relocked the doors.

Turning to me, he asked, "What can I help you with, Boss?"

Without giving him time to think, I blurted out, "Why did you kill that lanky son of a bitch?"

Then in return, without giving it a moment's thought, he replied, "If you didn't lie to me about the time and date of Pinn's death, my state-of-the-art camera will show I was pho-tog-ra-fatin about a half mile down the canyon at the time he fell. All my pictures have the time and day they were taken automatically added to the photo. I already checked earlier when you told me about his death, and I was taking pictures of the sunset over the canyon at that time." He continued, "Fact is, he went over the rim at about the time I was shooting toward the same area."

My mind kicked into gear at almost warp speed. "How far away can you get a recognizable image with that fantastic camera of yours?" I asked.

"Oh, if the atmosphere is clear, I can get a clean picture of someone skinny-dipping at about a half mile. Only thing is, in a landscape frame as large as I was shooting, you'd have to enlarge the frame quite a bit more for a bare butt to appear as something other than just a dot in the picture."

Suddenly a new approach occurred to me. "Could Pinn and his murderer be on one of your sunset frames, and you might not know it?"

"Could be, Boss. All I can do is check the frames with the correct time and date on my computer and see what develops." And with that little play on words, he released a, "Ha, ha, ha."

"Why didn't you tell me that this might be possible earlier?" I asked.

He grinned a big silly grin and said, "You never asked me earlier, Boss."

CHAPTER 38

Krash bragged as he explained his extraordinary interest in photography. "One day you'll see my pictures in magazines and hung in museums. One of these days my name will be up there right next to Joe Rosenthal! You know, the picture of the marines raising the flag over Iwo Jima in the Second World War."

As he talked his eyes became animated, drool appeared on his lower lip, and his voice increased in volume and took on a dreamy quality. "All it will take is one big frame, one big frame...and my fortune will be made. Krash the Fantastic!"

Quickly I made a verbal observation. "I suppose your equipment is of the quality that what you are telling me is really possible?"

In a mouthy mood, he said, "My major camera is a Japanese prototype that I have been given the honor of testing for the Fuji Corporation. I'm not at liberty to tell you any of the trade secrets, but I can tell you it has two to three times the photography capabilities of the latest pro Nikon, the Nikon D5."

He explained that the year before he was in Japan and saved a child from being hit by a car, and the father was one of the top Fuji officials. During an exchange of information, he explained he was a photographer, and the father explained he was a Fuji official and offered to allow him to test one of their latest cameras.

Then Krash continued his prior train of thought as he said, "With that beauty I can photograph a gnat's ass, and after enlarging the frame, you would be able to see if he had a hard on! If Pinn's sorry ass is somewhere on one of my photos, I will sure as hell find it."

With that, Krash went to work on his photos, and I excused myself to get a cup of coffee. I hadn't gotten far from Krazy's van when my phone rang. I answered, and it was Volkens of Chicago, and Mr. Singer was speaking. "Mr. Gray, I'm proud to inform you your special ring order is ready for shipment. Can I be of any other service to you?"

I answered, "Yes, could you include in that order a nice 10-karat-gold chain heavy enough to hang the ring around a girl's neck?"

"Yes sir, and we will do that complimentary."

I thanked him, and he connected me to his secretary for me to make final payment and supply a shipping address.

I guess I stirred up a real pain in Krash's rear, because before I hardly had time for a cup of coffee, he was on my phone and on my behind telling me he needed me front and center. With bravado in his voice, he told me he had Pinn's final seconds of life on a flash drive, and I needed to see them.

I wasn't sure what he really had, but I was wild to see it, whatever it was. Being sure I had my notebook, I took off for his van.

When I got to Krazy's van, he was standing outside with a grin a mile wide, leisurely drinking a warm can of soda. He had told me he never drank anything colder than room temperature. He said cold drinks shrank his brain.

The moment I got close enough, he chided me for being so slow. He yawned and said, "It took you long enough. I've been waiting for hours!"

He turned toward the back of his van and said, "Come on in; you will really want to see this. I believe it will solve your so-called murder."

When I stepped up into the van, Krash already had things set up for me to look at. He had a computer screen that looked about four by six feet in size, and a beautiful picture of a canyon sunset was already displayed.

He sat down in front of the keyboard and invited me to be seated on the chair next to him. As I seated myself, he was already enlarging the picture on the screen, moving toward the moment when it would change from a recognizable picture to pixel dots.

Suddenly he stopped enlarging and moved the lower left part of the picture to mid-screen. And there he was. Mr. Slim was standing in the picture clean and clear. Krazy quickly moved to the next frame, and Pinn was hanging in space off the rim of the canyon. I didn't see anyone else in the picture, so I blurted out, "The SOB either fell or jumped."

Krash the Fantastic slowly spoke, "I believe from how he looks in the picture, he jumped."

Immediately a new puzzle rushed into my mind as I said, "If he jumped, it's suicide! But why?"

Then I thought to myself that probably all he could have been charged with was assault on the young lady.

"I don't know, Boss, but now it's your problem to find out." With that, he handed me a thumb drive and said, "There are five photos on this stick, and all of them are of Pinn's last seconds alive. Good luck in your hunt, and remember, if there's any fame attached, it belongs to me."

Then with a grin on his face, he said, "Now get the hell out of my way so I can get back to watching the animals screw or whatever else I might shoot that could make me famous."

I looked at my watch and realized it was close to lunchtime, so being proper, I offered to take Krash for lunch as a thank-you gift for his work.

At first he declined, but as I insisted, he replied, "Okay, Boss. It looks like you can afford it, so I'll just take you up on the offer."

He knew of a place I had not been to in my search for information. Old Krazy said they served food his body could tolerate. I wasn't impressed with weeds and grass as a substitute for meat and potatoes. But a deal is a deal. I knew I could always find an ice cream shop later if I needed something else.

We discussed our lives and living habits as we partook of the bounty that was placed before us. I'm joking about the bounty, of course. However, the falafel burger was at least passable, and you have to work very hard to harm the taste of a potato.

Finally, the Old Photographer said he was full and had to get back to work.

"That one big frame!"

We thanked each other one last time as he headed for his van.

I headed the other direction with thoughts of love and beauty dancing in my mind. Maybe I would see Melody in the next couple of days.

CHAPTER 39

As I headed for the lodge, a sudden remembrance shot through my mind. I no longer was living at the lodge—I had a room at the aunt's, even though I had never been there.

Because I was almost to the lodge before I remembered, I decided to see if the old truck was there.

Yep! She was there, all two thousand pounds of rusty scrap iron. I walked into the lobby and asked at the desk for the keys. As the clerk handed me the keys, I also asked if I could sit in the cool and make some phone calls.

He replied, "Mr. Gray, you are no longer a guest of this lodge, you are a friend of the canyon. Help yourself."

I thanked him and located a seat out of the way of the paying guests.

My first call was to Fox. When he came on the line, I explained to him about Krash's photos.

His only question was, "Do they show anything we don't already know?"

I had to admit they did not.

"Well it doesn't look like murder, but he's just as dead, whatever it was," Fox mused.

Then I asked the chief, "Does this finish my work here? I don't mind helping, but I have things I would like to be doing back home."

There was a pause. I assumed he was giving something some thought.

"Gray? Would it be asking too much for you to stay a couple more days? I have to report to the state and the council before the case can be closed, and I'd appreciate you being around if I can't answer some of the questions. You understand. Maybe you could."

Then I had to think a minute. "How long are we talking, Chief?"

"Three days tops."

"Okay, I'll force myself to look at you for three more days."

"I appreciate it, Gray. Goodbye."

My next, and most important, requirement was to call my love on the bus and tell her how soon I would be home.

With nothing on my mind but love and sex, I placed my second call. I figured at this time of day the bus would be burning up the road either in Oklahoma or southwestern Missouri.

I heard a click and then, "Hello, my love."

Before she could say more, I blurted, "A couple more days and I'll probably be flying home. Fox says my job is finished out here."

There was a long silence on the line.

"Hello, Melody, are you there?"

In a dreary voice, I heard her say, "Yes."

"What's wrong? Are you ill?"

"No, just mad as hell at myself."

"What's wrong?" I repeated.

"I thought you would be tied up out there for a couple more weeks, so I volunteered to guide another trip for the next couple of weeks. One of the other girls became ill, and I said I would take her rotation. Damn it, damn it, damn it!"

I thought I heard another sob and then, "Will you forgive me for being such a fool?"

Picking my words carefully, I replied, "Nothing to forgive; it's your job. If we were married I might not think that way. But you have to do what the job calls for."

"I'll make it up to you when we are both in the same place at the same time. I promise, I'll do whatever you want, all day or all night."

"I will love you wherever you are, whenever. And now it's my turn to say I'll be waiting when you get home." We talked a few more minutes, and then her job called again. We said goodbye.

I went back to the desk and asked the clerk if my luggage had been picked up. He said Gray Fox had collected it earlier and taken it with him. Oh yes, he had left the truck with written directions on the seat as to how to get to his aunt's.

I went out to the old truck and proceeded to try to find my way to the cabin. Would you believe it, the old truck didn't have air-conditioning. I knew I would be a mess by the time I found the cabin. Old Red Man got me again.

About forty-five minutes later, I pulled into a beautiful little oasis in a side canyon. There was a babbling spring, big trees, and a coolness I couldn't explain. And the lady who came out of the cabin—I assumed she was Fox's cousin, as she was younger than Melody.

As I introduced myself, I decided I'd better be certain I was at the right cabin.

I stuck out my hand and said, "I'm Casper Gray, and I'm looking for Ranger Gray Fox's aunt's cabin."

She took my hand, and as we shook hands, she replied, "I'm Tama Claybasket, and yes, I'm Gray Fox's aunt. His mother was the oldest child, and I'm the youngest by a little more than twenty-two years. So I'm younger than my nephew."

Then I laughed and said, "Gray Fox didn't tell me that you were younger, and he assumed I would embarrass myself by saying or doing something stupid when we met. But, I got by our introduction without fulfilling his assumption, so that puts me one up on the high-and-mighty chief ranger."

She said, "I understand. No, he doesn't like it much that I'm younger but still his aunt."

As we continued to talk, she led me into the cabin and showed me my room.

It was cool in temperature, though there was no AC; it had a homey feeling to me, and it was decorated with Native American curios and artifacts. It made me feel comfortable, like being in my own historic home with Lily.

I thanked Miss Claybasket and felt the old male itch work its way up my spine. Though I loved Melody dearly and completely, this young lady was difficult not to notice.

Then I thought of Old Slim and said to myself, *Keep your mind on business, look but don't touch, and you'll probably live to see another day.*

Then in the background of my conscious mind, I heard something and realized the young lady was addressing me. "Would you like to take your meals here with me? I sometimes work for the ranger group, so Chief Gray Fox has assigned me to assist you if I'm needed. I'll have time to cook for you if you so desire."

I thought for a moment and then asked, "Does Gray Fox take his meals with you?"

"Most of the time he does. He lives in the next house down the lane, behind my cabin. He thought if you ate here, the two of you could go completely over the Pinn case and make sure neither of you missed any vital information."

"Let's try it with me eating here, and if the chief and I can iron this thing out quickly, I'll be able to get home sooner."

"Oh, and my husband and I do lots of volunteer work in the evenings, so we will not disturb your work."

With her last statement I felt a weight lifted from my shoulders. I thought perhaps Old Sly was attempting to line me up with his aunt. But, I guess all he had on his mind was ranger business.

I had a glass of tea made from some local native plant and then told Tama I was going to get a little exercise by walking to Fox's house to see more of their beautiful spot in the canyon.

She said she would be leaving for work, but the door would not be locked if I needed to get to my things. She explained that the area was a holy spot protected by the spirits of the old ones from ancient times. She also said, "If you see one of the old ones working in the canyon, don't be afraid. Just wave and go on about your business, as they will do the same."

I assumed she was mouthing mythology from her culture, so I decided to play along.

"But, Tama, I'm a white man, won't they take offense about me being here?"

"In the past they may have tried to kill you, but if you are not consumed by evil, they will not approach you today."

CHAPTER 40

We both left the cabin at the same time, her by bicycle, me on foot—her to town, and me walking down the lane.

Shortly I saw Fox's house. It was a historic ranch-style with a raised veranda completely encircling the building. I suddenly felt tired, and there were lounge chairs on the veranda, so I decided to rest for a spell.

I had no more than made myself comfortable when I became aware of a man of small stature appearing from out of the bushes a few yards farther down the lane. He had a heavy walking stick in his right hand and was trailing a rope behind him in his left hand. Suddenly a second figure appeared out of the bushes behind the first. The rope was tied around his neck, and his hands were tied behind him. A rock was tied to the rope that bound his wrists—a weight used to add pain to the poor fellow's misery. I also saw he had bleeding welts and bruises covering his almost-nude body. The first figure stopped, turned, and brutally hit the bound figure with his heavy walking stick. The man opened his mouth in what should have been a loud scream, but I heard no sound.

I jumped up from the lounge chair and looked for something to use as a weapon to help the bound man. Then they both faded into nothing, and I felt a cool breeze touch my face.

I shook my head and found myself still sitting in the lounge chair. I half giggled as I thought, *You fool, you fell asleep.* Then my giggle became a shortness of breath, and perspiration popped out all over my body as I realized the bound figure was Jeb Pinn.

I jumped up from the lounge and ran at full speed back to Tama's cabin. As I ran, I heard beautiful bird calls, saw blooming flowers, and once more felt the coolness given off by the babbling spring. But all I could think about was Pinn and his damnation.

As I began to feel the weariness from my run up the lane, I stopped and reconsidered—it had to be a dream, perhaps brought on by my work on the case, by fatigue, by unconscious thoughts of Miss Strawflower and ZuZu. Ah ha...or the damned tea. I'll bet that damned tea was made from cactus leaves. But...what if it was real? Could I have really seen one of the old ones and...Pinn?

Gray, you're an educated man. You know there are no such things as ghosts. I decided I had better forget it, or they could come to take me to the loony bin.

I forced myself to think of Melody and her love and, oh yes, her fantastic body. I knew she was real because I'd already sampled the goodies.

I decided to leave a note that I would not join the Fox family for the evening meal. Then I went back to town for one more run at the little steak house.

When I returned to the cabin later, it was not quite dark. My note had not been moved, so I assumed everyone was out for the evening. I found soap and towels in my room, so I showered and proceeded to an early commission to sleep. Tomorrow Fox and I would probably also put the Pinn case to bed.

CHAPTER 41

After a restless night in a new bed, I awoke to the smell of all the dishes of a regular breakfast. I scented eggs, bacon, perhaps sausage, something with a corn base, and a lot of sweetness in my nose. The scent was very clear and close by. I raised up, looked out the window, and saw smoke coming from the chimney of a small building about thirty feet away. The door of the building was open, and I could hear the soft sound of a woman singing.

I got up, closed the curtains over the open window, and commenced to get dressed.

As soon as I was prepared for the day, I walked out into what I'd thought, yesterday, was the kitchen, but no cooking was taking place. Fact was, there was no stove or cooking apparatus in the room. However, Chief Gray Fox was sitting at the table with a mug of coffee in front of him.

"How was your night's sleep?" he asked.

"I was a little restless for some reason."

"It was Tama's damned stories that caused you not to sleep. She told you about the old ones, didn't she?"

I hedged as I answered, "She may have mentioned it, but I don't follow spirit stories very well."

As I said *spirit*, I wondered why I didn't say *ghost*. Maybe I would have laughed about my nickname.

"Did she tell you she thought one of them killed Pinn?" Fox said.

"No, she only said they would not hurt me unless I was totally evil."

We heard footsteps outside, so he said, "Don't let her get you stirred up with her tales."

Tama came through the door with a platter of food. Most of it I had guessed correctly. The corn smell was corn cakes, and the sweet smell was some type of syrup, piping hot.

She prepared four plates and placed two of them in front of the Sly One and me. The other two she placed at two other spaces and seated herself at one. Then she hollered, "Tom, come on to breakfast before it gets cold."

Through the door I had entered earlier, a tall Anglo strolled into the eating room. He said, "Hello."

And then he seated himself beside the young lady, and she volunteered, "This is my husband, Tom Dodd."

I must have put on a puzzled face, as she said, "I'm a landowner, so I go by my Indian name, Claybasket." She then asked me, "How did you sleep?"

"A little restless."

Then her face took on a strange expression, but it quickly passed. "I hope you like country cooking."

I assured her I loved country cooking.

The meal was fantastic, the conversation was not confrontational, and Tom revealed he was doing research on the old culture in the canyon in hopes of writing a book.

Immediately after finishing his breakfast, the chief excused himself and said he was headed for the office. Tom picked up his knapsack and archeology tools and headed farther into the canyon.

When Gray Fox reached the door, I thought of Krash's flash drive and the pictures of Pinn's death.

I said, "Just a moment, Chief. I have something for you." I handed him a copy I had made of Krazy's flash drive. "Perhaps you might need these as evidence some time down the road."

He took the copy, thanked me, and headed out the door.

I looked at Tama, and she made a statement that scared the hell out of me. She abruptly stated, "When you look at me, you like what you see, don't you?"

I began to stutter and fume and try to make words, but nothing I tried to say made sense.

"Don't be embarrassed or bothered. I was not accusing you of anything, I was only stating facts. I was only trying to get your attention so you will listen to me."

"Well, damn it, you've certainly got my attention now."

"You didn't sleep well last night because he was watching you.

He wasn't sure you were not going to try to hurt me."

"Who? Gray Fox? Your husband?"

"No. The Old One. As I told you yesterday, he protects this canyon and its true people from harm. He killed Pinn, you know? Not because he raped a girl in Missouri, but because he tried to rape a Havasupai girl here."

"How do you know all this?" I asked.

"Though my nephew does not believe, I too am a protector. And, though you are not a Havasupai, you have some of the traits of a protector. I believe now, after you came to the aid of Miss Strawflower, he will be your protector too. That means that no human can take your life; only the God you worship will take you when your duties on earth are complete.

"Now, Casper Gray Ghost. Yes, I know who you are; it was revealed to me. You call yourself ghost because you can hear and see without being heard or seen."

"I'm hearing this, but I don't know what to believe," I stammered.

"You saw him, didn't you? I can feel his presence on you and around you. What did you see?"

I knew my secret was out, so I calmly told her of my introduction to the Old One. And, I told her of seeing Pinn with him.

"Pinn should have never brought his evil ways to the canyon. Or if he was coming, he should have left his evil in Missouri. The Old One can see and smell evil for hundreds of miles. Old Slim, as you call him, will suffer endless misery for eternity."

"You're saying none of the tour group is guilty of murdering Jeb Pinn?"

"Jeb Pinn was not murdered, he was executed for spreading evil."

"Then yesterday I was not dreaming—I really saw the spirit of the Old One and the ghost of Jeb Pinn?"

"Was the Old One wearing a loincloth with the sign of the owl when you saw him?"

"What is the sign of the owl?" I asked.

"It looks like two upside-down, attached letter V's with a black circle on the inside slope of the outside leg of the left V, and a black circle on the inside slope of the outside leg of the right V. Two pointed ears to hear and two round eyes to see."

I felt a shudder go through my body as I thought, *To hear and see, without being heard or seen.* Casper Gray, the ghost. No...Casper the owl.

CHAPTER 42

I still was not definitely sure about all of that, but I know I was nearly scared shitless.

"So you believe I am chasing the wind trying to find a murderer in our tour group?" I asked.

"There is no murderer in the group of people who were on your tour."

"Have you ever seen the Old One?" I asked.

"Many times. The one most vivid time in my memory was him saving my life when I was a child."

"What happened, that he had to save your life?"

"Once, I too fell from the canyon rim, and he caught me on the handgrip of his walking stick and raised me back to safety. He even whispered to me, 'Now you belong to me!'

"Had you attempted to touch me yesterday when you evaluated my looks, he would have hurt or killed you. Afterward, any evidence found would have made it appear that it was simply an accident."

She then became much more serious. "Our culture is very old. I know that right now you still cannot totally accept what I have told you and what you have seen. But in our culture, it is the truth. Owl Gray, for whatever reason, you possess a little of the power of the Old Ones. Do not use it for self-gain or to be foolish, or the power that can protect you, may destroy you."

"Then you're telling me to go home to my love and not try to prove one of the tour people killed Pinn, because none of them did? But what if evidence comes to light that proves, beyond a doubt, that one of them did kill him—what do I do then?"

"The Old One will make sure no evidence will ever be found strong enough to even get an indictment. And he will speak into the ears of any lawyer or judge, warning them that if they get involved, their careers will be destroyed."

I told her I believed I would start preparing to go home, and as soon as I could get the chief's okay, I would be on a plane.

As I stood up from where I had been seated, I looked out the window, and there on a low limb, in the tree closest to where we were, was a large almost-black owl. With a mighty pump of his wings, he arose from the limb and sailed off into the underbrush.

As she stood up, she announced, "Christjohn has asked me to prepare a Bar-B-Que tonight in your honor. Are there any locals you would like me to ask to be in attendance?"

I thought of Old Krazy. But then I thought, *No.* Then I thought, *Hell, why not?* So I told her I had met a strange bird at The Village and he was fun to talk to and might be fun at a party.

She gave me a strange look and said, "Do you mean Jack Krash?"

"Yes. Do you know him? Is that okay?"

"Oh yes. You do know he is brilliant and very wealthy?"

"No. I thought he was some kind of a kook. All he seems to be interested in is photography."

"And, the big frame!" she said.

I laughed, and she giggled. "He'll be a great addition to our gathering."

I decided to call Gray Fox and tell him I believed I would leave. He had as much information as I did. And if he needed me, I'd only be a call, an email, or a three- or four-hour flight away.

I caught him in his office.

"Chief, I think I'm going home tomorrow. You know as much about this mess as I do. If you really need me later, I can come back."

I heard him growl a little, and then he cleared his throat. "You're probably right. I'm waiting on the state and the council to make a decision, and that might take a week, a month, God, who knows. In this case, Casper, it doesn't matter if a politician is red or white, they're still damned politicians. And hell, I'm one too."

Then after a moment or two he continued, "Hey man, if I forget to tell you tonight, just know I've really enjoyed working with you. If you ever want to have a job again, I could use a man like you."

I thanked him for the compliment and said, "Goodbye." Then I began to pack what few items I had with me.

A while later I dialed Melody's number and hoped she was available. In just a short while, she was on the line. I could hear hurt in her voice as she said, "Hello."

"Angel, are you okay?" I asked.

"I want to die. You are going to tell me you are coming home, and I have to leave tomorrow."

"That's why I called—I wanted to tell you goodbye and I love you before you left."

"I know you love me, but I want to feel you love me, and that won't happen for two more weeks."

Then an idea hit me. "Babe, tell me one of the big cities you will be in on this trip, and I'll fly to meet you for a couple of days."

"Cass, that will cost so much, and I'll be busy."

"It was working on our tour, so it will work out on your tour. How about it, will you help me make it work?"

"Hell yes. You know I will."

"Then I won't say goodbye, because I'll see you pretty quick after I get home."

"When are you coming home?" she asked.

"Tomorrow, I believe. I've done all I can out here, so it's time for me to come back to Old Missouri."

I heard another sob and the words, "And I leave early in the morning."

I then said, "I love you, and I'll see you as soon as you can tell me where to meet you. Goodbye."

The last call on my list was to the air service in Tusayan, a small airport at the edge of the canyon, to make arrangements for a flight home, if one would be available the next day.

I was in luck—a flight to Kansas City had a seat available at 11:00 a.m.

As I started to enter the cabin to get a drink of water, I saw the Old One down the road toward Gray Fox's house; he smiled and waved. Damn, he looked like a man living his life today. But I knew he was only an entity of the spirit world. I raised my hand and waved back.

I looked into the cabin, and Tama was seasoning a large slab of meat for the Bar-B-Que.

CHAPTER 43

Everyone began to arrive at the ranger's home after 6:00 p.m. The festivities were scheduled to commence at 7:00. Tama had outdone herself. The meat was on a large rectangular steel-bar grill. The coals no longer had a red glow, but there was enough heat remaining to keep the side of mutton hot enough to be edible. On the side were potatoes, homemade bread, a green salad of some exotic Arizona plant leaves, and nopales. To drink there was tea of the unknown plant, beer, and spring water.

The feast was festive and tasty, and everyone ate their fill.

Tama was dressed in a traditional costume of a puffy-sleeved, red cotton blouse paired with a heavy purple bulky skirt. She also wore pieces of vintage southwestern native stone and silver jewelry. She could have been straight out of a painting done in the 1800s.

Christjohn was in full Arizona ranger garb, with the additional US government hardware.

Old Krash, believe it or not, was attired in a well-fitting business suit, including a tie. However, an impressive camera hung from a strap over his shoulder.

I was a little embarrassed, as I had not packed anything formal for the tour. Therefore, I appeared in Dockers and a nice short-sleeved sport shirt.

Later, as I circulated among all the guests, I noticed the majority of the rest of those in attendance were dressed similarly to me.

After the meal, the party began to gravitate into forming small groups and engaging in small talk.

Krash eventually asked an explosive question: "Who was the skinny old man in a loincloth who stepped out in front of my van as I came along the lane to the house?"

I saw a somewhat frightened look appear on Tama's face, and Gray Fox turned quickly and said something to one of the other guests as if he had not heard Krash's question.

Thinking quickly, I deflected the question as I replied, "There are several old people living quietly a little ways further back in the canyon. They hunt for small game to supplement their cook pot. Probably one of them."

"But why wear only a loincloth?" Krash persisted.

I blurted what I thought might head him off. "It's so damned hot around here, I've thought seriously about wearing just a towel myself."

A small ripple of laughter arose from the group, and Krash did not respond.

I thought to myself that if Krash ever got a picture of a man long dead and remaining only as a spirit, he would have his "big frame."

The conversation groups ebbed and flowed until some of the guests began to trickle to their vehicles to return home.

A sudden question popped into my head. I looked around until I found Old Krazy, and I asked him, "Hey, Jack, has anyone ever taken a picture of a ghost?"

Without thinking, he started a verbal display of his photography knowledge. "I don't know if it's possible or not. Sometimes it's been tried, using infrared film, but I've never seen any pictures that I absolutely believed to be authentic. In today's photography and computer world, however, anything is possible, even if it's fake. Getting a picture of a spirit? I don't think it can be done." Then his mind clicked in, and he said, "Why did you ask?"

"After the fantastic work you did with Pinn's death, I was wondering what else might be possible with the fancy cameras you have."

"I can do great things, but sorry, Boss, no ghosts today!"

But in my mind, I was still thinking, *If you thought you might get the big frame by getting a picture of a real ghost, I bet you would near kill yourself to try.*

I looked around and realized that Tama, Christjohn, Krash, and I were the only ones left in the house. The party was over.

Krash, realizing the same thing, excused himself and headed for his van to drive back to one of the parking lots at The Village.

Tama and I started for the door to walk back to her cabin. As we stepped out Gray Fox's door, the old sly son of a gun held out his hand and said, "In case I miss you in the morning, once more,

I thank you for all you've done. I'll keep in touch and give you the final decision from the state and the council, when they finally reach a decision."

I took his hand, and then Tama and I walked back to her cabin, and I said, "Good night."

My bed did not have Melody in it, but it felt so good as I closed my eyes.

CHAPTER 44

I awoke to the pleasant smells of familiar food being prepared. I raised up and looked out the window, and the cooking was again being done in the little building. Then I was really curious and swore I would ask why Tama cooked in the little building.

My eyes next wandered to the tree limb where the black owl was yesterday. This time there was no owl, and I realized I had slept peacefully all night.

I closed the curtain, dressed, and prepared everything for the flight home. As my mouth began to water, I hurried as fast as what I thought was politely acceptable to the dining area.

Tom and Christjohn had already finished their coffee and had begun to put away their food. Just then Tama came into the room carrying two heaping plates of a fantastic breakfast. She placed one in front of me and placed hers in front of where she planned to seat herself.

Without waiting for anyone else to speak, I declared, "I'm just plain nosy, but why do you cook in the little building outside? This kitchen area is beautiful!"

Tama grinned and replied, "This room is cool too. If I cooked in here it would be hot. I'd rather cook where it's hot and eat where it's cool!"

With a thumbs-up signal, I replied in return, "Me too!"

The chief immediately verbally took the floor. "Gray, you will either have to take a tram to the air service, or you can take the old truck and leave it in the parking lot. I can have it picked up in a day or two. Just leave the keys with the agent at the air service."

I thought for a moment and decided that would be easier than carrying everything to the tram and then having to ride, maybe for a long time.

I thanked him for his favor and said, "If it is not too much trouble, I would appreciate that."

133

He nodded his head as he got up, excused himself, and headed for his SUV.

Tom said he was going to stay in and write up the research he had done yesterday.

I then excused myself and started carrying my luggage out to the old truck.

Tama and I talked for a while about our lives and how we had evolved to the places in our lives where we were at that moment.

When it was time to leave, she wished Melody and me the best, and I thanked her for her and Tom's hospitality. Her last words as I waved to her from the old truck window were, "He was called El Buho Viejo, and he was killed by one of the early Spanish land barons for attempting to defend his family and neighbors from the cruelty of the evil dons."

I didn't know how she could know that. Perhaps...he told her? I remembered from my college Spanish class that *Buho* was owl. I deciphered: The Old Owl.

I looked in the rearview mirror, and through the dust, I thought perhaps I saw him one last time.

CHAPTER 45

I was on the plane and headed for Kansas City. I had called earlier and asked my neighbor to come to the airport to pick me up. He said he had nothing else to do, but I intended to pay him, just the same.

The flight attendant had to wake me when we arrived in Kansas City. Everyone else was off the plane, and I was still napping.

I collected my luggage, and my neighbor was waiting as I exited the gate. We loaded my belongings, and he headed us toward Jefferson City. I checked my watch, and it was about 4:00 p.m. I called Melody, and they were about four hours out from their overnight stop.

I asked her, "Have you decided where I can meet you for a couple of days?"

When she replied, she had it all worked out: "I think if you can fly to Philadelphia on Friday, we can have Friday night, Saturday, and Sunday together. Most of that time is just seeing the city by bus, and I won't have to be with the tour every minute. Basically we would just meet them for meals. I have to be sure everyone has a bed and food."

"Early Friday or later in the evening—which would be best for me to meet you?"

"Dinner is always at 7:00, so meet me in time to eat with me."

"I'm en route from KCI to Jefferson City, so I will start making arrangements when I get home tonight."

"Are you completely finished with Pinn's case? Or will you have to go back for anything?"

I told her I believed I was totally finished, and it had to be an accident or suicide. I decided I would not tell her about the Old One now. Maybe I never would...what did I really know?

The neighbor and I reached Columbia, Missouri, a little after 6:00. The food on the plane wasn't much, and I was starting to feel the sensation of hunger in my gut. I offered to buy dinner someplace in Columbia, and my friend agreed. Since it was right on the way to Jefferson City, we pulled into the local Cracker Barrel and tried the special of the day. Fried chicken is one of my favorites, so I was totally satisfied.

By 8:30 I was home in the old familiar surroundings. It was not quite dark, so I touched Lily's urn, said hello, then stepped out the door and walked up to the edge of the river bluff. Right at dusk the view almost took my breath away. The setting sun was brilliant on the river, and I could almost visualize the Old Ones of this area as they carried water in their earthen pots from the river back up the cliffs to their village here on top.

After regaining the feeling of belonging in this place, I returned to the house and prepared my room for sleeping and peace for the night. I questioned whether to call Melody or wait until morning. Oh well, I missed her so much, I would just disturb her both times. I dialed her number, and I don't think it even rang before I heard her voice.

"Hello, love. I was hoping you would call. If you hadn't, I was getting ready to call you. Are you home yet?"

"Just fed the garbage and threw out the cat."

She giggled and said, "You're never serious about anything. I hope you're serious about us. Are you still coming way out here to see me?"

"Philadelphia. I'll try to make reservations tomorrow."

"Already done—see my friend Suzy at the bank tomorrow. I called her, and she already has it all worked out. I told her I would die if you didn't come out, and she said she would make the arrangements so you couldn't back out."

"Damn, now I've got the whole company trying to trap me. One beautiful little witch is not enough; the whole coven has to stir the brew."

"Please say you're joking. I didn't mean to do something behind your back."

"YES, I'm joking. The only thing I would not joke about is: Don't invite any of the other beautiful little witches to one of our night parties. I don't think I'm man enough to handle more than one hot little witch at a time."

Then she joined in the fun. "You'd better not try to bed one of the other witches while I'm around. One of you would be carried out, and the other would be TOAD."

"Okay, enough of the crap," I said. "All I want to do is get to Philadelphia, being toad or not."

We talked love and other things for a while, and I finally said, "Been a long day, I love you, good night." Then I hung up.

I was right, my bed was peaceful and quiet.

CHAPTER 46

When I went to the bank to pick up my flight information about Philly, I didn't talk to Melody's friend, as she was out of the building at the time. I received my tickets and instructions from the branch manager or whatever his title was. However, I was pleasantly surprised that the bank had picked up the tab for my airfare. It seemed that Old Sly Gray Fox had contacted the bank and explained how I had worked to help close the Pinn affair, so they decided to reward me in some way, and that was it.

Finally the Philadelphia Friday rolled around, and I had decided this time I would simply leave my truck in a paid parking lot at Lambert Airport in St. Louis.

My flight was leaving at 9:30 a.m., and I would arrive in Philadelphia at about 5:00 p.m. Yes, that appears to be a long time between takeoff and arrival. However, the bank had scheduled a plane change with a four-hour layover in Chicago to save on airfare.

I found a place to park the truck, took out a cheap insurance policy the lot offered against damage to my vehicle, and headed for the departure gates.

I was in the air by 9:35, next stop, Chicago in about an hour. I wondered how much the bank saved by scheduling me this way. *Oh well, don't look a gift horse in the mouth.*

Finally, at 4:41 p.m.—Philadelphia. I gathered my carry-on property and headed for the baggage carousel.

When I reached the doors to the area where people are picked up by special transportation, I was surprised again. A taxi driver was standing there holding a card with "Casper Gray" written on it.

He grabbed my suitcase, and away we went to his taxi. The suitcase went into the trunk, and I climbed into the back seat. Then the taxi driver said something that seemed to embarrass him. "This complimentary taxi ride is provided by a little witch who is warming the brew without the assistance of the whole coven."

With that he quickly swung out into traffic and never said another word until we arrived at the Hampton Inn.

I tried to tip him, but he mumbled, "The little witch took care of all the bill and tip."

I thanked him anyway as he placed my suitcase on the curb, then he jumped back into his cab and sped away.

Then out of the main door of the hotel came six or eight ladies muttering over and over, "Double, double, toil and trouble, fire burns and cauldron bubbles."

As a grin conquered my face, I thought, *Macbeth, in Philly?*

Then they surrounded me and forced me through the doors of the hotel and into the lobby. Melody was standing there with plastic champagne glasses and champagne for all of her tour. Then everyone in the tour crowded around us. Without any embarrassment or attempt to hide the fact that we were involved, she kissed me. There was an immediate outburst of whistles and applause.

Then she announced, "This is Casper Gray, the ghost, who says he loves me and wants me to go steady. What do you all think, do I accept his proposal?"

There were more whistles, applause, and a loud, "Yes, if you want him!"

Then she grabbed me and kissed me again. It was my turn to be embarrassed. But before it went too far, she announced it was time to get our things and board the bus to go to dinner. Seeing my suitcase, she quickly suggested we take it to my room before we left. Surprise, surprise, my room was next to hers. As I unlocked the door, she shoved me inside with my suitcase banging against the wall. Before I could move, she was in my arms and saying, "Hold me, hold me, hold me, and don't be gentle."

I grabbed and kissed her roughly as I ran my hands over her body.

She breathed heavily and said, "Do we have to go for dinner?"

I loosened my grip and laughed lightly. "It's your group—do they get to eat or not?"

Sounding like a little girl who was not getting her way with something, she slightly stomped her foot and said, "Yeeess, but I want to stay here, just you and me."

I said, "Maybe later, Angel," as I ran my hand over her delightful rear.

I stood back as she straightened her clothing and smoothed her hair. She then turned to me and stuck out her tongue.

I leaned toward her and ran my teeth down the side of her neck. I felt her shiver as she pleaded, "Please don't do that, or you'll get me started again."

We left the room and made our way to the bus, where she began supervising the loading.

She sat next to me as we rode to Omar's Southside Steak House, but she did not touch me, and I felt she did not want me to touch her.

As we ate, I touched her hand several times, but she did not react to that either. I wasn't sure what was going on, but I believed she would explain sometime, so I decided to enjoy my steak and looking at her, even if I could not touch.

We returned to the hotel, and when we reached our rooms, she said nothing to me, opened her door, entered, and shut the door. Now I was more than confused. I was just a little irritated. After making the trip out for us to be together and then having this kind of treatment, I was almost ready to call the airport and try to fly home immediately. But, I knew I would have to wait until morning to get anything done with my ticket, so I prepared for bed. As soon as I finished showering and putting on my pajamas, I crawled into bed.

Suddenly, I realized my door was opening. I knew I had closed and locked it, but I did not engage the chain. As fast as I could move, I grabbed the telephone to use as a weapon to defend myself. As the light from the hallway shined into the room, I recognized Melody standing in the doorway. I could see a key card in her hand. Then I realized there must have been two key cards for my room, and she had kept one. I reached up and turned on my reading lamp as she closed the door. With the look of someone gone mad, she violently pulled, twisted, and yanked the clothing from her body.

Throwing herself into the bed with me, she placed her face close to my ear and rapidly whispered, "Love me, hold me, love me, love me, love me!"

As I put my arms around her, she began to try to smother me with her kisses. Before I could resist, she was loving me in ways I never thought of. After a few minutes she relaxed and lay beside me with her fingers twirling my hair. And then she whispered once more, "I couldn't wait any longer; it's been so long."

She rolled on to her back, and I raised up on my elbows beside her and looked down into her face.

I decided not to wait any longer. "If everything works out, would you be Mrs. Casper Gray?"

Then the little witch turned the tables on me as she replied, in the voice of Angel, "I believe I would, but we haven't even officially gone steady yet."

I leaned down and kissed her, and then the love was slow, gentle, and exciting.

Around midnight or a little after, she returned to her room, and...she took the extra key card with her.

CHAPTER 47

As I closed my eyes, I thought, as crazy as the action had been, I was certainly glad I had come out for the weekend.

Then sleep overtook me. But as I drifted away, I sensed something or someone else in my room. I should have felt fear, but I didn't.

Morning seemed like a continuation of the southwest tour. I called Melody's room, and she was almost dressed and prepared for the day. I told her I loved her and was glad I came out to see her.

She said after last night she finally felt as if we were really meant to be together.

I thought to myself, *I really hope this means we will always stay together.* But I didn't say it.

We met outside the rooms and headed for the breakfast room.

She whispered, "I was afraid to come in your room this morning because I was afraid I wouldn't let you leave, or do my job for today."

I squeezed her hand as the answer. I understood.

Breakfast may not have been that great, but with Melody across the table from me, it was spectacular.

I supposed she had left Jefferson City before the ring was delivered. I said to myself, *Oh well, maybe when going steady is made official, back home, the rewards will be more exciting than they have already been here. Jackpot!*

Then I realized Melody was speaking to me. "Are you going with us on tour today? I need to get everyone moving, and then I could return here, if you want me to."

I replied, "Don't take me wrong. I'd love to spend the next month, or forever, alone with you. But, same old song—it probably would look bad for your position. Why don't we tour with the group and party alone later?"

This time she squeezed my hand and mouthed, "Thank you."

I had been to the Liberty Bell, Franklin's grave, and Independence Hall with Lily many years before. But forgive me, Lily, it seemed more exciting this time with Melody.

Strangely, I felt the presence of a part of Lily with me and also the presence of something else, just out of range of my ability to completely sense. El Viejo?

Tama said I would always have him with me after the Pinn affair. I knew I needed to get that mess off my mind. But, for some reason I couldn't quite do it yet.

After a long day of seeing the historical aspects of Philadelphia, I was glad when the dinner hour was upon us.

Strangely, I can't remember the name of the restaurant we visited that night. However, I'll never forget the food. Big Leroy's and Reggie's couldn't hold a candle to What's its face in Philly. Probably Melody's sexual allure was blocking my ability to think correctly or remember much of anything.

Yes Melody, Teen Angel, that little witch, or whatever. She's really all that mattered in the mind and heart of Casper Gray.

Ten o'clock, and lights out, brought it quickly home one more time. The card flashed, the door slammed, and Casper was once more under the influence of either the spirits or the witches. Either way, he was more than ready to take the consequences.

I didn't hear or see her leave, but I definitely missed her when I awoke.

She must have sensed I had just awakened, as my phone began to ring.

"Up, up, sleepy head. If my attention affects you that bad, I may cease to spend time with you after 7:00 or 8:00. Are you going on the bus tour around the city?"

"Only if I can breakfast first, and then if some teenager named Angel will sit next to me on the bus."

"I believe both requirements can be fulfilled. We go to breakfast in ten minutes."

"Make it fifteen, and I'll escort you," I said as I closed the shower curtain.

Breakfast was once more, Melody.

The bus tour was fun because also, once more, Melody. Dinner, then the hotel room made the day complete. Once more because of Melody. The only down side was, the next day I had to fly back to St. Louis. But the up side was, by the same time the next week, she would be headed home to be with me.

CHAPTER 48

In an unhappy state, I arose from the bed and prepared for my day. I didn't have much to pack, but I knew I was dragging my heels as I put things into the suitcase.

Melody's call was also quiet and subdued as she asked if I was prepared for breakfast. I assured her I was ready for breakfast but not for the rest of the day. In a few moments she slipped into my room, and I had to really work to control my emotions so I wouldn't do anything wrong.

A few kisses, and then we left the room and walked hand in hand to breakfast. It was probably good, but I didn't enjoy it.

After we'd eaten, she accompanied me back to the room to get my belongings to check out. The hotel had a shuttle that would take me to the airport.

As soon as all my bags were in the van, I kissed Melody and climbed into the back. Then I noticed as we kissed, the tour had been whistling and cheering in the background. I didn't get much out of it, but Melody thanked them.

I waved as the shuttle pulled out of the hotel drive and headed to the airport.

Thankfully it was not long after my arrival at the departure gate that we boarded and the plane took off.

I was able to sleep a little, so it did not seem long before the announcement was made that we were preparing to land in St. Louis. The flight was direct, flying west.

After collecting my gear, I picked up my truck and burned I-70 and US 54 home.

The rest of the day was a total washout, as I missed that woman terribly. I don't even remember eating anything after I got off the plane.

Thankfully, I was so worn-out, I slept well when I hit the bedroom. I guess I thought of Melody some, but not much.

When I awoke, all I could think about was finding something to do to raise my spirits.

Ah ha—fishing. Perhaps catching a fish or two to eat would help. Damn, I love a good crappie fry. And I thought maybe I had the things at the house to make hush puppies, and hey, maybe homemade ice cream. One hell of a party for one. Then the blues hit again, and I decided I would just fry fish and have some canned beans alongside.

I gathered my fishing gear and slipped away to a little creek nearby that my neighbor said usually produced a pan-sized crappie or two when a quick lunch was needed. I was in luck—a few minutes and two eight- or nine-inch fat, black crappies were on my stringer.

Back at the house, it was a quick cleaning job and then on to the stove.

I decided to slice and fry some small canned potatoes for alongside, as beans did not sound appetizing at the time.

After lunch, I began to try to think of something to do to take my mind off Melody.

Then I remembered Old Slim's death, and my curiosity once more kicked in.

CHAPTER 49

As I settled into my comfortable work chair in front of my computer, I turned on the tower and the screen but had no idea what I was looking for.

As the screen brightened, so did my mental attitude. Krazy Krash had shown me the picture of Mr. Slim's suicidal leap from the canyon rim, but I wanted to take a closer look at the digital photos to see if there was more in them than our eyes had detected earlier. I knew that in old chemical prints sometimes part of the picture may not have printed. But with digital, most of the time there are no foul-ups, and if there are, when you enlarge to the point that the picture changes to pixels, you may be able to see if part of the picture is missing or there has been an electronic foul-up.

After waiting through the computer's start-up routine, I was finally able to insert the flash drive that Krash had given me into the USB port and began to visually scan the pertinent frames concerning Slim's demise.

As I viewed each image, I was once more enthralled by the rugged primeval beauty of the canyon.

Then I uploaded photo number 3183. The scene was exactly as I remembered it from the moment Krazy and I saw it the first time.

As I enlarged the frame, Mr. Slim slowly appeared in the extreme lower left-hand corner. The image of the canyon sunset was almost centered in the photo, and the visual impression was spectacular. But, my interest in the photo was totally focused on the image of Jeb Pinn hanging suspended in mid-air off the canyon rim, just a split second before he plunged two hundred feet to the ledge below, and his death.

In the image there was about fifteen feet of solid ground back from the edge of the rim where Slim fell, and his image was out beyond the rim about two or three feet. No one else was in the picture.

The image caused me to suppose it was either a suicide or perhaps a horrible accident.

But, my curiosity just wasn't completely satisfied.

I once more began to enlarge the frame. I knew that eventually the image would break up into colored pixels, and that would be as big as the photo could be enlarged.

At almost the final click of enlargement before the image changed to pixels, I saw something strange. Below Jeb's arm, hanging in space, was a small gray something. It was a circular shape that blotted out the colors of the canyon. The next click caused the image to go to pixels. In the pixels I saw a small group of gray dots precisely in a circle. Then my nostrils expanded, and at once I became extremely nosy! I doubted that the gray spot was a photo flaw. What was that gray spot?

I quickly moved to image 3184 on the flash drive. Krash told me that when he was taking the canyon sunset pictures, he was taking a shot about every five or ten seconds. That meant that if a spot of dust or other matter got onto the camera lens and caused the spot to happen, it should still be there in frame 3184. Bingo—it wasn't!

I immediately grabbed my cell and punched in Krash's number on my call list. I impatiently waited and listened to ten or fifteen rings before he came on in a nasty manner. "What in hell's name is so damned important that you have to interrupt my photo shoot just when I have the chance for a once-in-a-million shot. It's not just anytime that you have the chance to photograph canyon ground squirrels breeding! Who in the hell is this anyway?"

"It's Casper, Krash. I need your expertise about one of the shots on the flash drive."

"Oh well, hell, you've already screwed me up, so what do you need?"

"Krash, I would like you to review photo 3183 and enlarge it on your equipment until you see something gray under Ole Slim's left arm. Then call me back and give me your opinion as to what it is."

While hearing a soft chuckle in my ear, Krash, in his crazy way, said, "Will do, Boss. And if it's important, will you give me the credit?"

"If it's the big one, I'll even have them show your picture too!"

It couldn't have been more than half an hour later when my phone rang. I quickly answered, and it was Krash.

"Krash here, Boss. I looked at the frame you asked about, 3183, and there is something gray under his arm."

"Is it a flaw in the digitization?" I asked.

"No, the pixels are perfect, so there's something physical under his arm in the photo."

"What do you think it might be?" I questioned.

"In this part of the country, probably a small bird."

"Would a small bird make a perfectly round image in the picture?"

"Not likely, but what else could it be?" Krash returned. He added, "Could it be a rock he kicked loose as he fell, or how about a golf ball falling out of his pocket, or even his glasses case?"

Then in a thoughtful study, he said, "The pixels are shaped exactly like a ball, and that would be odd, but who knows?"

In my mind I said to myself, *Only the person who killed him—if this is not an accident or suicide and really is a murder.*

After I let Krazy get back to his nature study, I went back to the pictures and uploaded photo 3180 and saw just a part of a human leg on the extreme lower left corner of the frame. Then I closed that picture and opened photo 3181 on the monitor and began to enlarge the frame. That one showed Slim standing off the edge of the concrete sidewalk looking almost straight down into the canyon. I noticed he was standing extremely close to the edge in an area marked off limits to tourists.

Next, I uploaded number 3182 and once more commenced the enlargement process. As Pinn came into view, I saw that he had turned his back toward the rim edge and was seriously looking at something out of the picture in front of him. His heels were only inches from the rim drop-off. His body was in an odd stance with his shoulders hunched; his mouth was slightly open and his head was tilted a little to his left with his eyebrows wrinkled in a questioning manner.

What was he looking at? What was it that was probably the last thing he would ever see?

CHAPTER 50

It was not too late in the afternoon in Missouri, and I knew it was one or two hours earlier in Arizona, so I decided to call the chief for more information.

I was able to reach Gray Fox, so I asked him if anything odd had been found at Pinn's death site—anything that would appear to be just junk. He told me he didn't know what all was picked up by the crew at the scene, but the state boys were good, and they probably picked up spit if they could get it in an evidence container. Then I straight-out requested of him: "Find out if there was by any chance a round object found, actually ball-shaped."

He answered, "As I told you, I wouldn't know what junk was found if nothing indicated it had any connection to the case. But if you think a ball-shaped object might have been there, I'll sure find out." He continued, "I'm curious as hell where this is leading, but I'll wait until I check, to enjoy the fun, if there is something that leads to something else. Then I can hoot and holler with joy if we solve this thing."

Then my mind clicked in, and I thought of something else. "Hey, Big Red," and I giggled a little, "were there any strange wounds on the body not absolutely consistent with Pinn's fall?"

"There you go again, bad-mouthing me and my red brothers. But what the hell is this about a wound? I would like to know what's going on, but I'll wait to find out what you think you know. Then I can laugh at your white ass."

After we both laughed about our racial jokes, I thanked him and said I would be waiting for his call.

Suddenly another thought flashed through my mind. "Hey, Chief, do you have Tama's number handy?"

"What is it, white boy? Now I guess you've caught an eye for my old aunt. She's married, you know." Then he giggled.

"Could be," I said. "But really I wanted to thank her again for the wonderful party. And, oh yes, thank you too."

"You're welcome, and here's her number."

I was thinking as I wrote down her phone number that I had a question or two about the Old One. But I didn't want to cause a stir between Tama and her nephew, so I kept the questions to myself.

CHAPTER 51

The wily Old Fox called me early the next morning before I had even considered what to have for breakfast.

"Gray, what do you know that I don't?" he asked.

Then I answered his question with a question. "Old Red Man, what are you trying to say? What are you asking?"

"Who told you there was a ball at the damned death scene?"

Then I let out a sharp little whistle. "You're telling me there was a ball where Pinn died?"

"Yes, a dirty, scruffy, torn old baseball, lodged in the rocks on the ledge where his body landed. It was not more than ten feet from him. In the picture it looks like something an animal has chewed on for a long, long time. The boys just thought it had landed there sometime before Pinn's death."

I asked, "What color is it?"

"A dirty gray, like you." He laughed. Then he asked, "How did you know there would be a ball close by?"

"It's in one of Krash's pictures, or at least the color and shape is there."

"What do you think it means?"

"I feel it could be a murder weapon, if Pinn was murdered."

"Why did you ask about an odd wound?"

"Did he have one?"

"Most of the wounds were either punctures or tears, and they were all ragged. However, one on his upper left chest was a round contusion, not consistent with a wound caused by contact with stones.

Then I further explained, "I don't absolutely know anything, but could that ball be analyzed, for whatever, or could there be fingerprints? Again, I don't know. I just watch crazy TV shows, and in them the law can do so many things. Does it really work that way in real life?"

The Sly One said, "Probably not as much or as easy as it looks in fiction, but we can sure have it checked out. I'll call and see if the lab can tell us anything about that old possible murder weapon. But you haven't explained why you asked about an odd wound."

"I'll explain that if there are fingerprints on the ball."

Then he told me he would call me back again as soon as he heard from the lab. And he added, "The next time I call, if we have anything or if we don't, I want the whole story, all the facts or suspicions."

CHAPTER 52

A few days later, at a moment when I least expected it, the call came from Gray Fox. He started with the usual pleasantries of the day. How was I doing and what was I doing.

After a few minutes of casual chitchat, I finally broke off our visiting and demanded, "What did you get from the lab? Was there anything that would point to the guilt of any of the tour group?"

Sly cleared his throat and simply stated, "All that the lab could find on that old ball was a half ton of dog saliva and another half ton of United States dirt. If it was used to kill Pinn, there ain't no way on this green earth to prove it."

Then he shifted gears in our conversation and said, "Something else strange has been discovered. The autopsy indicated that Pinn may have been dead before his body struck the ledge."

That statement caught me completely by surprise. But, before I could think or reply, Gray Fox continued, "What was in Krash's picture that caused you to ask about a ball? We didn't see one in the pictures you gave me."

"There really wasn't a view of a ball in any of the pictures, only a blur of a colored shape in the picture showing Pinn over the edge. I just assumed by the gray round shape under Pinn's arm that it might be a ball."

"But why didn't my team and I see it when we reviewed the pictures?"

"You had to enlarge the frame until it was ready to change to colored dots before you could see the round blur under Pinn's arm."

"I still don't understand it, but my deputy that does our computer work will show it to me when I tell him what I'm looking for. Now what about the inconsistent wound?"

"If there had been fingerprints or human tissue on the ball, the tissue may have been Pinn's, and the prints may have been the killer's."

After a slight pause to think, he again continued, "Enjoy yourself for a while, and I will go over all the information we have and discuss it all with the tribal council and the state attorney to see if there's a case or any viable suspect. I'll get back to you in a while with our final findings. Thanks for your time and expertise."

I hung up the phone and for a moment considered Old Red's statement about Pinn possibly being dead before he hit the ledge. Other things seemed more important at the time as I went back to thinking about Melody. Every day I was missing that woman more and more. We called each other several times a day, but it wasn't like being face-to-face or...body-to-body.

After cleaning the house seven or eight times, I decided that was not helping at all. Counting down the hours didn't help either.

Then like a plane coming out of a cloud, it hit me—*She'll be home tomorrow.* I had become so involved with Pinn's death again, that time got away from me.

Oh well, I said to myself. *It'll take that bunch out there a month to come to any decisions on the case.*

Then I remembered I wanted to speak to Tama some more about the Old One. I looked on my desk, found the number Gray Fox gave me, and dialed the number.

After a few rings, I heard first the birds singing in the background, and then Tama said, "Hello. Who's calling, please?"

"Hello, Tama. Casper Gray."

"Oh, hi, Casper. Did you forget something when you left?"

"No, I have a couple of questions about the Old One, if you don't mind."

"No, I don't mind, and Christjohn isn't here. What do you need?"

"You said the Old One saved your life by catching you with his walking stick. How was that possible?"

"I was surprised, as fast as you seem to think, that that question did not hit you when I told my story."

"Tell me now. It may have a bearing on Pinn's death."

"The Old One killed him! It's as simple as that."

"Then tell me about your rescue."

"I was a child and got too close to the edge of the canyon rim and slid off. Before I even had time to scream, something grabbed me out of mid-air. When I looked over my shoulder, a tiny man on the end of a stick had hold of my dress. At the other end of the stick was a full-sized man pulling the stick back, with me on it, onto solid ground. As soon as my feet touched the earth, everything but me disappeared, and I heard the words, 'Now you belong to me!'"

"The little man who grabbed you, what did he look like?"

"Exactly like the full-sized man, except for his head."

"What?"

"His head had no features. It was simply a round ball, and smooth as glass."

"How big around was the head?"

"Oh, I would judge about the size of a baseball."

Suddenly I got a funny feeling in my gut; I wasn't sure I wasn't going to be ill. "You're sure the little figure on the end of the stick had hands and arms that grabbed you?"

"Oh yes! Because if it had not grabbed me, I would have died."

"And he looked exactly like the full-sized man, except for his head, which was a glass-smooth ball?"

"Yes."

Then I told Tama, "I'm going to have to think about that for a while." I thanked her for telling her story. Then we visited for a short time before we ended the conversation.

As I let the story steep in my mind, I began to also plan on what excitement I could create to welcome Melody home. First, though, I decided I ought to call her and see what the schedule of activities was for the tour's arrival home. I dialed her number and caught her on the bus, headed this way. "Hello, love," I said. "Have you been thinking of me?"

No louder than a whisper, she replied, "Every minute of every day, and reaching for you in my bed all night every night."

"When do you think you will arrive in town tomorrow night?"

"Not tomorrow night, the next morning. We've had a stomach virus in the group the last couple of days, and we've lost some time on unscheduled stops. It will probably be almost daylight before we arrive."

"Should I plan to meet the bus? I want to see you so bad."

"I want to see you too, love, but I don't know what shape I'll be in when this thing hits town. Why don't I call you when I know I can be, me with you."

"I don't like it, but I can handle a few more hours."

"I love you, and I'll call as soon as I can."

As we hung up the phones, I made my thoughts go back to Pinn and the Old One.

So, the head end of El Buho's walking stick can come alive and assist the Old One when it's needed. But, why does it not have a recognizable head? Then it came to me: *The stick is an extension of El Buho, and his brain controls both entities.*

Then a creepy feeling ran through my body, and chills ran up and down my spine. The head of El Buho's walking stick was the size of a baseball, and glass-smooth. The shadow in Krash's picture was the size and shape of a baseball. Krash said he did not think you could photograph a ghost, but if the head of the stick was not part of the ghost, it would show up in a photo. Then a shiver of sheer terror invaded my being. Perhaps Pinn *was* dead when his body reached the ledge.

Could he have seen the Old One on the rim and been literally scared to death? Or, did the ghost hit the SOB hard enough with his walking stick to cause a heart attack. A hit with his stick would have definitely knocked him off the canyon rim.

Then a queer thought crossed my mind. Krash had his one big frame, but no one would ever accept it as being true. I still have doubts, and I have seen El Buho Viejo.

I said to myself, *What do I tell Chief Ranger Gray Fox? I need to think about this awhile and come up with the best route to take through this minefield.*

This is so weird, I'm a little afraid to try to tell the story myself.

CHAPTER 53

The rest of the day I spent planning places Melody and I could go and things we could do to build the relationship we wanted to be in. I knew sex was going to be a big part of our lives together, but I did not want it to become the driving force in our lives. I wanted to know all about her. I wanted to learn her likes and dislikes, to determine what our lifestyle would be if she did agree to marry me.

By bedtime I was more confused trying to figure us out than I was when we first met. I decided I'd just wait, and we would have to plan together. And, that is as it should be. As I climbed into bed, I only knew one thing for sure: I would marry her in a minute, whenever she said it was the right time and place.

I awoke with a start. The phone was ringing, and it was still dark. Then my mind caught up, and I realized it was probably Melody calling to tell me they had gotten into town.

"Hello, my love," I said the moment I picked up the phone. "How are you this beautiful morning?"

The sorriest voice I've ever heard said, "Sick as hell. I've caught the damned virus, and I'm going at both ends."

As I jumped out of bed, I said, "I'll be there in fifteen minutes."

"No, you won't. Don't you dare get close to me until someone tells me I'm well."

Suddenly I heard the most horrible sound of upchucking, and then a weak little voice say, "I love you, but I have to get off this parking lot and into the emergency room. The bus brought the whole load of us directly to the hospital. I'll call you as soon as I feel like it; right now I have to get to the bathroom." And she hung up!

My first inclination was to go to the hospital. But damn, I didn't know which one. And, she had given orders for me to stay away until she was well.

It was early, but I decided I could not go back to sleep, so I put the coffee on and dug a frozen strudel out of the top of the refrigerator and put it in the oven. A breakfast fit for a fool—sugar and a drying agent. Oh well, I've always been a fool for sweets, both living and baked, my entire life. Why should I change anything now?

And that brought my thoughts back to Melody. Was there anything I could do to let her know I was worried about her? I looked at my watch, and it was barely 7:00. I decided as soon as 9:00 rolled around I would call the florist and have a big bouquet of something taken to the hospital with my love and concerns. Damn, I still didn't know what hospital. Yes! I could call the bank at 9:00, because they would know where their tour ended up.

I started on my sugary breakfast and ended up eating the whole damned strudel. I decided when I called the bank, I would talk to Melody's friend. *What was her name...Susan? I think that was it. I'll try it anyway, and if I'm wrong, I'll just ask whoever answers the phone to connect me to Melody's friend.*

I wanted to find out if the gold class ring had been delivered, because I wanted it there when she returned to work. I got up from the table and refilled my mug. That's the problem with a coffee pot, you drink till it's dry, and I usually make a pot of eight or ten cups. A man has to be crazy to drink that much coffee at one time. Oh well, you're looking at him.

What I need, I thought, *is a wife.* Oh God, Melody again. Then I was embarrassed as I thought of Lily. I walked over to the window shelf, and I couldn't believe what I saw. A spider had woven a web across the top of Lily's urn, and it was a perfect valentine heart shape.

And then I saw it—what appeared to be the shadow of a small man in the corner of the window. It was there a moment, and then it was gone.

In foolishness I whispered, "You think we should be a couple?"

Then a bird outside the window whistled, and it sounded like it said, "Yes."

Instead of feeling fear, I had almost a feeling of euphoria.

As soon as it turned 9:00, I phoned the bank and was connected to Melody's friend. I asked her if she knew what hospital the tour had been taken to. She said the new St. Marie's because the bank president was on the hospital board. I also asked her if a small package addressed to Melody had been delivered to the bank. She said yes, it was on her desk. I asked if she could put it in a more secure spot.

Then she became curious and asked, "Do you know what it is?"

"Yes, a very important personal gift from her soon-to-be steady boyfriend."

She giggled and said, "She has informed me about a possible future man in her life, but I didn't know about her going steady." Then she snickered. "Do you know him?" she asked.

"I think I've met him, and he's a dork. But you know Melody, she takes in hurt birds and puppies, so she would take up with a dork."

Then her friend became a little defensive as she answered, "She is just a woman who is good to everyone, and if she's dating this guy, he must be pretty special. Oh, who are you anyway?"

"I'm her cousin, and I'm looking out for her. Could you put that package somewhere safe until she's out of the hospital?"

"I'll put it in my desk and lock it for safekeeping. And, if she asks, which cousin are you?"

"Tell her it was Casper Hotboddom."

"Could you spell that last name for me? It's not one I'm familiar with."

"H,o,t,b,o,d,d,o,m."

"I was afraid I would foul it up—I thought you said Hotbottom. I spelled it H,o,t,b,o,t,t,o,m."

"Most people do, but it's an old Havasupai name."

"Oh, okay."

"If you would put the package in safekeeping, I would appreciate it. Thank you. Goodbye."

"Goodbye."

Then I immediately called the local florist and placed an order for flowers to be delivered to Melody.

CHAPTER 54

About noon I was moping around the house, trying to find something to occupy my mind so I would not worry about Melody.

The phone rang as I checked my soup for the fourth time to see if it was warm enough to eat. As I placed the phone to my ear, I recognized the voice on the other end, even though it was very weak.

She spoke slowly, but I did not hear the forlorn sound I had listened to at daylight. "Cass, I have finally slowed down on the vomiting and bathroom calls, but I still feel like crap. They've put me on an IV to keep me hydrated and given me some type of meds to stop the virus. I asked them when it would be safe for a visitor. The doctor said you should wait a couple of days before you come to see me. You don't know how much I miss you."

I butted in and said, "Yes I do, because I miss you just as much. And I will take the chance of catching whatever you have if I can visit you."

"Don't you dare come here. I will refuse to see you if you do. Understand?"

"Yes, but it's really lonely without you."

"We've played this damned game for a couple of weeks; we can last a couple more days."

Then her voice got a little stronger as she asked, "Are you totally through with the Pinn matter? Is there more investigation to do, or do you have any reports to fill out? If you do, get them done while I'm in here, and when I get out, you'll have everything out of the way."

I immediately realized she was thinking more intelligently than I was, because it was a great plan.

"Angel, you're absolutely correct. I can get that mess taken care of, and then we can have all the time for ourselves."

Then she volunteered, "Don't worry about calling me. If I have news, I'll call you. Get the case solved if you can."

I answered, "I love you, and I'll be waiting for your calls. Goodbye, Angel."

She spoke low and slowly, "I love you too. Goodbye."

For two more days, Melody and I talked by phone more and more often. She got stronger as the stomach distress began to become a thing of the past.

During one of her calls, on about the fourth day, she gave me holy hell for the joke I told Suzy at the bank. She said when Suzy told her that a cousin had called to check on her, she was completely at a loss as to who the cousin was. She said when she was told it was Casper Hotboddom, she wanted to kick my hotbottom into next week. And she also told me Suzy said a package was waiting for her at the bank, that Hotboddom knew about. Then she asked, "Okay, hotbottom, what's in the package, another one of your little jokes? Some jackrabbit crap, or did you find a buffalo chip to send me?"

Before she could really get rolling, I butted in, "No, it is something I hope that you will really enjoy. A lot of thought went into it and also a lot of love."

Then it was her turn to butt in. "It had better be something pure gold, or your hotbottom will pay the price. You'll get no special goodies for a while if it's not something that will take my breath away."

Inwardly I smiled. I could bet it would take more than her breath away. It might even produce goodies I hadn't even thought about. "If you don't like it, I might try to find some other little angel/witch who would enjoy it."

"Well, we'll know for sure very shortly, as Suzy is going to bring it to the hospital as soon as they will let her in my room. She's so curious as to what it is, she's starting to itch."

"What about you?" I asked. "Don't you feel a little curious also?"

"No, because I'm sure it's one of your silly little jokes."

Our conversation moved off in another direction, and I allowed the little surprise to slip to the back of her mind. That evening, I finally decided it was my time to call her.

The phone rang only once before she was on the line. And

before I could get more than a couple of words out of my mouth, she spoke, "Cass, can you pick me up tomorrow? They say I can go home. They took a blood test, and it did not show any signs I was still carrying the illness." Then before I could speak, she continued, "And if I feel strong enough, I can go back to work when I want to."

"You don't plan to take another tour out for a while, do you?" I asked.

"Not for a month or so, or until I'm totally okay."

"Yes, I can pick you up tomorrow. What time should I be there? Are you going home or coming here to stay with me for a while?"

"Cass, I can't come to your house to stay. Don't you realize I have never been to your house, and you have never been to mine?"

Suddenly a hot flash sizzled in my brain. *No! We don't even know about each other's living arrangements, and we, or maybe just I, have been thinking seriously about marriage.*

"No, Love, you will need to take me to my house, then we will start dating in the normal way. You will visit me, and I will visit you." Then a very serious sound came into her voice. "Does this change anything between us?"

"No. I love you, no matter if it's in your house or in my house, but I do understand we need to do some serious planning as to how we can make our love work. I didn't realize that the Pinn mess had stopped me from considering all the angles."

"I don't want to ever lose you. If coming to your house is what I need to do, I'll do it in a minute. I love you!" she hoarsely whispered. And I could hear the tightness in her throat as the tears began.

"Angel, I will be in your room in fifteen minutes. I won't let you hang up and wait all night before I show you that nothing else matters but you and me together."

I put the phone down and headed for the truck. I don't know if I broke any speed laws, but I was at the hospital in less than twenty minutes. And I was in Melody's room in less than five.

I didn't look to see if anyone was in the room when I rushed in, I simply grabbed her to me and held on tight. And immediately she made the same move.

After a few minutes we were able to continue our serious conversation. And before I left to go back home, there was no question about our love.

As I started to leave I noticed the package from Volkens was on her roller serving table, opened. As I was going out the door, I saw her pick it up and hold it in her lap with both hands. I wondered if that little package was what brought on our earlier deep phone discussion.

I didn't have a very peaceful night's sleep, and I was at the hospital as soon as I thought Melody had eaten her breakfast.

She evidently was very anxious to go home, as she was dressed and had all of her personal effects packed in a plastic drawstring bag. I did not see the Volkens package, but she had her purse in her hand and did not lay it down. But, at the same time, she did not mention it. And I did not let her know I had seen it. At about 10:00, she signed the necessary forms, and she was wheeled to the exit, where I assisted her into the truck.

She had to direct me to where she lived. It was so odd—we were into a deep relationship and had never been to each other's homes.

Her house was situated on a cul-de-sac in a small neighborhood on the south side of the city. It was a small house, but the perfect size for a woman living alone.

Melody produced a key and unlocked the front door. We entered, and I placed her bag of belongings on the couch. Then she invited me to have a seat on the same couch. I asked her if there was anything that needed to be done after an absence of ten or fifteen days. She said she had a cleaning lady that came in every week, and so the house was clean and taken care of.

Then out of the blue, she made a statement: "I want you so bad I hurt, but I'm still too weak to be able to love you right now. Do you understand?"

I hoped my answer did not hurt her feelings, but I needed to clearly explain where I stood. "I want you also, but sex is not what keeps me around you. I love you, the person, and I want you, the person. Sex is exciting, and yes, I enjoy it, but I would not enjoy the sex with someone else the way I enjoy it with you. You're the one who makes our relationship what it has become. When you are ready, I will be also, but I would never demand attention when you were not ready."

She grabbed me and kissed me, and then I went to the market for something to eat for lunch. After a sandwich and some loose salad, I cleaned up the eating area as Melody went into her bedroom to lie down and rest.

She was sleeping, so I locked the door and went back to my house to prepare for the next few days as I made plans to take care of Sweet Melody.

CHAPTER 55

For some days Melody and I simply coexisted. She was free of the virus but still weak. However, every day she exhibited signs of more strength. I would go to her house and fix breakfast at mid-morning. We would hold hands or each other, but no serious or exciting love was ventured. I was a little curious about the cooler atmosphere, but I chalked it up to the aftermath of the illness and loved her as much as she would allow.

Later, I would prepare a late lunch or an early dinner. Sometimes we would drive to my house and spend some time sitting on an old wooden bench in the shade of a huge, ancient burr oak tree at the edge of the bluff overlooking the river. That old bench had become one of my favorite spots, and Melody seemed to enjoy it too.

The first time she walked through my house, she said, "Any woman in her right mind would trade her soul to live her life here!"

I would never demand her soul, but damn, I would trade mine for her love. And yes, I was determined to continue to remain cool. I couldn't fathom the answer to her present attitude, and I also realized that, curiously, she had not mentioned the ring. I had no idea what it all meant; she still kissed me deeply and held me close, so I decided to wait for her to supply an answer, whatever it was.

One morning after breakfast, which I had eaten alone as Melody had returned to work, I took my usual walk up to the edge of the river bluff to survey my little kingdom and try to determine where our relationship was headed. By now I was developing a little fear. Perhaps our little fling was no more than a summer tour romance and she was working up the nerve to tell me so.

Gray Fox finally called just as I returned from my walk; I was still savoring the beauty of the river and the vast river bottoms teeming with wild growth and the structured fields of hay and grain.

As I answered the phone, I heard his deep strong bass voice inquire about my health and welfare. Then he changed the direction of his greetings and began to discuss the realities of the possible murder case.

"Gray, I've spent the past several days going over all the information and the little pieces of evidence we were able to gather after Jeb Pinn's death. I streamlined everything and presented my findings to the tribal council and to the state's DA.

"Now, no matter what you think, it's very necessary for the people out here to make decisions based on looking at things from all directions.

"First, everyone on that tour, including you, by your own words had almost ironclad alibis. Second, there is no evidence tying anyone on the tour to Pinn's death. Yes, there is the baseball and the picture, but no evidence of anyone touching the ball. Third, an accidental death might cause a decline in tourist trade, because an accident means the canyon might be too dangerous to visit. An unsolved murder might mean there is a killer nearby, and that also could hurt tourism. However, if it were a suicide, no one but the victim can be blamed. So, as it stands, the tribal council, the state's DA, and I feel that Mr. Pinn must have jumped to his death."

I slowly and deliberately cleared my throat and replied, "And, the state of Arizona and the Grand Canyon would not be financially responsible for what would probably be a long and costly murder trial, without much possibility for any type of conviction. And, secondly, without an accident, no lawsuits will be brought against the canyon for liability."

I thought about mentioning seeing the Old One and Pinn. But with the Fox, it might cause a family rift, and he would not listen to a ghost tale anyway. So, I decided to keep what I saw to myself.

The Sly One answered, "Gray, you understand the total situation clearly and precisely. Thanks again for all your help. And treat that little girlfriend guide of yours with love and affection. Come back and see us sometime. Goodbye."

As I hung up the phone, in my mind I had to give that Sly Old Fox credit. I guess Melody and I were not as smooth as we thought we were as we snuck around the hotels, lodges, and motels. Gray

Fox knew what we were doing. I wondered how many more, on the tour, also knew. And now I was also wondering about other things, in a different vein.

CHAPTER 56

I had hardly enough time to digest what Chief Gray Fox had said before I received a call from crazy Jack Krash. And the moment I answered the call, I knew he was full of excitement.

"Hey Boss," he said. "I finally got a big one, and you are the one I have to thank! After you left the canyon, I cornered Old Red Face and asked him what the final word was on the murder. He told me it was not murder, but a simple case of suicide. Then I asked him if it would be okay for me to sell the pictures of Jeb Pinn going over the wall to a crime magazine. He answered that he saw no problem, as it would show the public that the Grand Canyon was not a danger to tourists, since he did not accidentally fall and was not pushed, so it was not a murder. Meaning, neither the state of Arizona nor the canyon had any responsibility for what happened. Pinn did himself in.

"The magazine is going to run a story, and I'm going to be recognized as Jack Krash, up-and-coming freelance nature photographer.

"Hey, Old Buddy, ain't that a real hoot? It ain't the big frame, but it's one hell of a start. If you get involved in anything else that might call for pictures, let me know. Who knows, next time you may have a real murder, and I might get to shoot the pictures of a real corpse. Man, would that be a big frame or what?

"It's great to know you, and be good to the little tour guide. Goodbye."

I would have loved to have said, "You're welcome." But I didn't even get one word in. Oh well, that's the way the Krazy Krashes.

And Gray Fox, the canyon, and the state were proven to be free and clear of the whole affair.

CHAPTER 57

Melody called early one morning and asked if I had seen the sports-page headlines from the morning *Jefferson City Post*. I confessed that I had not yet gone down to the main road to retrieve my copy. I explained I had slept a little late and was just finishing my first cup of coffee.

She said, "I believe you will be very surprised about what is written there. And, it will probably enlighten you about some important facts."

I asked, jokingly, "What's so important, or who died?"

Her simple reply was, "Jeb Pinn!"

Then I was really curious. "Tell me what the big secret is," I begged.

"Just get off your backside and go get your paper and read what is happening in the world."

I agreed to do exactly that, but first things first. "If I drive to town, will you have time to go to lunch?"

"Yes, but only if you have time to also find a backcountry road to take care of some other details that I need assistance with."

I thought for a moment and then replied, "I'm fairly certain I can supply the assistance, but a dark, nighttime country road would be more appropriate, I think."

"If you apply yourself correctly, the job shouldn't take long, and the task can be accomplished fairly rapidly."

To that I could not think of anything to say, except, "And if the job is done quickly, we might have time to discuss this big secret of yours afterward." At the same time I was thinking, *What brought this on?*

She giggled and said, "If, afterward, you're in any shape to accomplish anything else."

I stopped the conversation right there and said, "Goodbye until later."

She answered, with another giggle, "Goodbye and good luck—you'll need it."

Curiosity was burning me up as I drove down the hill to the mailbox to pick up the paper. That was a drastic change from my usual slow, enjoyable walk.

First, what's on the sports page, and second, why does it seem that my lover, Melody, has returned? Something to do with Old Slim's death?

I could hardly keep from tearing the paper as I roughly removed it from its protective wrapper. With bated breath I quickly unrolled and opened the bulk to the sports section of the *Post*. Across the entire page was a screaming headline! "CARDINALS MAKE SURPRISE DEAL!"

The local sports writer, Jock Hanks, started his column by writing, "Shusssssh, Cardinals put one over on the baseball world. Shane Chance, an unknown local lad, signed a multi-million-dollar deal to pitch for the Red Birds."

Then Hanks continued by explaining that Chance did not start pitching until he entered Quad-States Junior College, of north Missouri, two years ago. He only pitched a few games the past season when all the other pitchers were injured. He had been a third-string, walk-on catcher until late this spring. In late April he walked onto the mound, and it seemed that after that he never left. His record ended at 7 and 0, with five shut-outs. The college was so small that nobody paid any attention to his heroics.

"Except the Cardinals did!"

An old, long-ago bench player for the Birds, Seth Herrly, saw young Chance pitch and notified St. Louis.

"Now it looks like they may have purchased a full-blown musical hit, for a song. It is quietly reported that the young pitcher has a consistent, blazing, ninety-seven-mile-per-hour fastball with the accuracy of a military sniper. His bread-and-butter pitch is a blazer, high and tight in the strike zone, to both right- and left-handed batters.

"It is also reported that one of his pitches, this spring, hit a bat scant inches above the batter's hands and sheared it in half, with little or no splintering of the hitter's wood.

"In my view, that is a killer fastball. And if Chance proves to be only half as good as reported, the Cardinals have pulled off a true major-league coup. Jefferson City has done it again. Go Jays!"

After reading that far, my mind completely failed to comprehend the rest of the article.

I said to myself, *I would call it "a real killer" fastball. And perhaps Jeb Pinn would also.*

From that moment on I ran Pinn's death and all the facts over and over in my mind. Could a sharp blow from the head of the Old One's walking stick cause a killer heart attack? If it could, then a blow from a one-hundred-mile-an-hour fastball could also cause the same attack. But I guessed that after my conversation with Gray Fox, it really didn't matter either way, as the case was officially closed, and I couldn't come up with anything that might change the council's final verdict. *Even if Chance is a killer pitcher or a killer, without any concrete evidence, he would be only a suspect.* And besides, he had an ironclad alibi. Several servers saw him asleep under the Parkses' table, and the Parkses swore he was there.

CHAPTER 58

About 10:30, as I was finishing the little bit of cleaning and dusting I try to do every day, I received a call from Melody. She asked if I could pick her up a little early for lunch. I assured her it would be no problem. She told me that she had informed her boss that some new information had come to light on the death of Jeb Pinn, and she needed an hour or so to check it out. She said he told her to take whatever time was necessary to clear up that mess, as the board wanted the bank to be able to put that problem to rest. She added, "We'll have time to put more than one problem to rest."

I pulled up in front of the bank at about 11:15, and Melody came out of the bank door and joined me in the truck.

Her first question was, "Do you think he did it?"

As I drove out of the parking lot, I replied, "If he didn't, it's one hell of a coincidence that he can throw a baseball high and tight at one hundred miles an hour. But there were no fingerprints on the ball, so where does that leave the investigation? I don't think Old Foxy would even consider bringing charges."

I repeated his explanation about what the canyon needed to stay out of trouble with publicity. The only way he would charge the boy was if old Krazy had super-clear photos showing him throwing the ball...and Pinn would also have to be in the picture.

Melody put her hand up under her skirt and wiggled a little on the seat. Then she pulled her legs up onto the seat. Suddenly I saw in her hand a pair of black bikini underpants. She held them up on one finger, twirled them in the air a couple of times, and then placed them in her purse and set it on the floorboard.

She grinned and said, "On to McDonald's or Wendy's for a quickie lunch and then a road trip to somewhere. Oh, and make that drive-through."

She raised up and looked behind the seat, then reached down and extracted the old blanket I kept to cover things in the truck bed, to lie on when I had to look under the truck, or to sit on to change a tire.

Then she asked, "Do you know of a cool, secluded spot we could take our sandwiches and have a picnic, big boy?"

I detected Melody's persona leaving and the Angel returning to the old rattletrap truck and trying to confuse me with her beauty and charm.

"A good quarterback always has a route to run in the backfield, so I'll find a place for a picnic and maybe more."

We did a teenage buzz through McDonald's and then out the route to a small secluded fishing hole I had discovered earlier. The farmer and I were the only ones with keys to his little back pasture, where a small stream ran through. With the farmer out of town for the week, I didn't think we would be disturbed.

When we parked the truck in the shade of a big sycamore tree on the bank of the stream, Melody fairly leaped from the cab. She quickly found a hidden level spot behind some bushes in the deepest shade and spread the old blanket. She took the sandwiches and fries out of the bag and set the soft drinks down for us to enjoy. Then she removed her blouse and bra.

In my mind I could see her the last night of the tour. "Now, big guy, do you want to eat burgers, or do you want to sample other goodies?"

I decided I would stretch the joke a little as I replied, "Little girl, the goodies are so tempting, but it's been a long time since I et. I think I'll try the burgers first."

Melody's persona returned as she dropped her skirt to the ground and stepped out of it. Standing there totally nude, she laughed at the top of her lungs and stated, "Cass, let's just see if you can eat the burgers before sampling the goodies."

With that she slipped into my arms and began to fumble with my clothing. Quickly, I assisted her with my duds, and I must admit I was more than willing to wait to eat the burgers.

But during the rustling of the blanket, the soft drinks turned over, and we had to eat the burgers dry.

When we finished the beef, Melody made a small confession as she began to get dressed. "Today was the Teen Angel's way of proving she wants to go steady and to thank her Cassy for allowing her to wear his ring around her neck. But she has one question. What do the letters on the ring mean?"

Holding her partially clad body against me, I explained, "The CSB stands for Centrail Savings Bank, and the SWT stands for Southwest Tour. So, it is telling Angel that she is my Teen Angel forever, after the Centrail Bank's Southwest Tour of 2017.

Then from somewhere, I don't know where, she produced the ring and chain and said, "Please make it official—clasp it around my neck."

I did, and then I kissed her one more time.

CHAPTER 59

While I was holding her, she began to volunteer a confession: "While I was sick, I had time to seriously think about out little tour romance, and I was afraid that was all it was. Then the ring came, and I thought it was one of your great jokes. I thought it was gold-plated lead or brass. Later, one of the bank officers, who is also a property appraiser, saw it and whistled. 'Where did you get that?'

"I told him it was a joke gift from a friend. He coughed and replied, 'If you have a friend who can afford to throw away five big ones on a gag gift, I would love to have a friend like that.'"

As she laid her head against my neck, she whispered, "Cass, I'm so sorry I doubted your love and thought you were joking about loving me so much. I know better now, and I will wear the ring forever."

Then she placed her finger vertically against my lips, her signal for me to remain quiet. "Please hear me out before you speak. I must say some more things to you."

Fear rushed through my mind as tears welled up in my eyes.

"Please, Cass, don't cry. I love you more than you will ever know, and I will never let you go, but I must tell you something."

Then I was completely confused as she continued, "While I was ill, I had time to rationally think about you and me, and I became very scared. I knew I loved you more than life, but I realized we really did not know each other that well. And when I visited your house, I also realized we hadn't even become friends before we became lovers. Then you started playing the Teen Angel game, and I couldn't resist it or you.

"What I want to do, if it's okay with you, is to go steady for a while before we talk further of marriage. No, there is no other man in my life. And I would die if I lost you. I just want to marry you when we know each other as well as we know ourselves. Now, if you can't do that, I will marry you tonight, because you have become everything to me."

Then Angel appeared and said, "Mr. Quarterback, will you accept me as your steady until I graduate? My momma would be very disappointed if I quit school my freshman year to get married."

Then she removed her finger from my lips, and I kissed her and said, "Angel, you know that I could never say no to anything you want. So when you graduate, I'll be waiting at your door in my old man's pickup to haul you away to be my wife."

Then Melody and I tried to kiss and hug as she continued to finish getting dressed.

As she completed dressing, she giggled as she looked at her watch.

I said, "Since when is looking at the time funny?"

"I wasn't giggling at my watch; I just remembered my panties are in my purse in the truck."

I lightly giggled also as we picked up the blanket and headed for the truck.

As I started the truck, Angel's persona returned as she lovingly slid over as close as she could to me, almost under the steering wheel with me. Then she reached up and kissed me on the neck. All too soon, we arrived back at the bank.

Melody quickly kissed me one more time and then disappeared inside the bank doors.

I grinned again as I thought, *I hope she remembers to put her panties back on.*

CHAPTER 60

As I drove home, many thoughts flooded my mind. It appeared that I would have someone to share the rest of my life with. Many years ago I believed that someone would be Lily, but fate did not see it that way. And, I believed Lily would approve and be happy for me.

I thought of all the players in the sad summer tragedy and how any one of them could have done the dastardly deed. Was it the Owl Man as Tama believed?

As *Tama* believed? Maybe me too!

Mostly, I thought of Melody, Sweet Melody, the song in my heart.

I parked the truck in the barn and walked up the slight grade to the house.

There appeared to be a special glow on Lily's urn. Perhaps it was the afternoon sun playing through the window. Or perhaps she was glowing for me.

As I snuggled back into my easy chair with just a touch of Wild Turkey and Honey on the rocks, I said to myself, *There was no criminal justice reached in this affair.*

Then, as I looked at Lily's urn once more and raised my eyes toward heaven, I continued, *But perhaps this might be a little of God's justice.*

The Bible says, "Vengeance is mine; I will repay, saith the Lord."

As I paused and took a small sip from my glass, a sobering question crossed my mind. *Was the God El Buho Viejo worshiped the same God I worship?*

I believed it had to be the same God, the One who teaches, do good, not evil. The Old Owl stood against evil, even unto death. And now he haunts the world continuing to fight for what's good and right.

Then my thoughts moved on to Sweet Melody and Teen Angel. I expected more days of enjoyment and happiness, and perhaps a loving wife like and unlike Lily.

Last, I thought of The Krash and Ole Red—a man would never find closer friends than they.

Then I drank the last swallow from my glass, set it on my lampstand, closed my eyes, and smiled with complete satisfaction.

GIFTS FROM

EL BUHO

The Sequel to *Alibis: Murder on Tour*

Prologue

About two years ago, I told you a tale of murder at the Grand Canyon.

After the conclusion of trying to determine how Jeb Pinn met his death on a tour to the US desert southwest in 2017, my love, Melody Muldune, her alter ego, Teen Angel, and I have managed to move forward with our deep loving relationship.

Melody continued to work as the tour director for Centrail Savings Bank in Jefferson City. As Teen Angel, she pretended to complete her freshman and sophomore years of high school and is now close to the end of her junior year of study. As soon as she graduates in another year or so, she and I will perhaps approach marriage in a really serious manner.

Teen Angel has been wearing my ring around her neck on a gold chain for over two years, and sometime in the near future I plan to replace it with a golden wedding band on her finger.

What I have just told you may sound dorky, but it's a game Mrs. Muldune and I have been playing since just after we started our relationship on the southwest tour.

I'm Casper Gray, and my personal story is just as strange as the beginning of the tale I have just started to tell you. Bear with me for a while longer, and I will clarify more about myself as this story unfolds.

Though Melody and I are deeply involved in an intimate relationship, I live in my historic house located on a high plateau overlooking the mighty ol' muddy Missouri River, while she resides in a small house on the southern edge of Jefferson City. However, she spends more and more time—both days and nights—with me in my home, as we have both grown to love it so very much. When and if she says, "I do," it will become home to both of us, legally.

But enough of the boring details in the latest chapters of Owl Gray's life. I'm sure you are more interested in the adventures that continue to make a middle-aged male's life exciting.

Chapter 1

For a week or so, a large, almost black-hued owl has taken up residence on a limb of the old tree on the edge of the bluff. I have a bench under this tree where I can sit in the evenings and watch the sun go down over the river below. An owl in a tree is not that unusual. But, in my past tale of Jeb Pinn's death, it was whispered that a black owl was a spirit messenger from a long-dead wise man, a keeper of the peace. Though that legend may sound strange, many of the Native Americans of the desert southwest region believe it to be completely true. I'd been told the spirit of an old Havasupai man still lives in the canyon lands of Arizona and protects his people, their land, and their way of life. Stranger yet, perhaps I have personally met him face-to-face, and perhaps he's visited my own domain from time to time. And sometimes, when he makes his presence known, he appears in the form of a great, black owl.

I was told by a very pretty Havasupai woman, one who perhaps is also recognized as a Native wise woman, that the long-dead wise man is called El Buho Viejo, the Old Owl.

But if the black owl that has taken up residence in my old tree is El Buho Viejo, what message of happiness or gloom and doom has he found important enough to deliver to me at my home in Missouri?

I did not have to wonder for long. Almost before I started to think about the black owl, I received a call from Chief Ranger Christjohn Gray Fox at the Grand Canyon.

I had barely tried to start speaking when a strong booming voice greeted me with, "Gray, you low-down white-eyed detective, I need your help...bad! I have a strange death out here, and I have neither the time nor the manpower to get anything done. Could you help out some, if you can get away from the little tour guide for a while?"

"You big red devil, are you getting too old or too lazy to take care of business?" I asked.

"All fun aside, Gray, I have, I think, a murder, but I have no body, just a pool of blood and a missing man. And the whole mess is out of California.

"The reason I really need you is, you may have to work here in the canyon and perhaps into California. The missing man is from California, and he's been playing games here in the wilds around the canyon. There are two things I know for sure: He's a lawless loser, and he's probably kin to some of the families who have been in this area forever."

Then there was a pause, as I supposed he was waiting for an answer. But before I could speak, he started to speak again.

"Gray, this time we will put you up in a motel, not at my aunt's house. And furnish a rental car for your transportation."

I quickly answered, before he offered to locate a date for me also. I felt he really needed my help. "Chief, I will need to do some checking here before I can answer a request like that. Can I call you tomorrow or the next day with my answer?"

"Don't take too long—the trail is already almost a week old, and we need to get started before everything goes cold and falls apart."

"Chief, I'll try to get back to you later today or early in the morning. Catch you later."

"Oh, wait a minute, Gray. I guess it is only fair to tell you that Krash is already involved out here, so you may have to put up with his craziness as well as trying to make heads or tails out of the death mystery. Hope I can still depend on you, if you can get away from Missouri."

"No problem," I answered as a thought went through my mind. "Krash might be a big help in some way. His photography certainly was when Pinn died."

I heard a grunt on the other end, and Gray Fox was gone.

Chapter 2

I had barely hung up the phone when it started to ring again. As I said hello, I recognized the voice on the other end.

"Casper, it's me, Tama Claybasket. Do you have a couple of minutes to talk?"

As I answered in the affirmative, she continued, "Casper, we have a real mess out here, and I believe El Buho is involved once again. It appears there has been a murder, but no dead body can be found. However, the real problem is, the supposed victim has been digging into affairs that concern the Old Ones, and the Old Owl is in flight."

I broke in on her story and explained I had just gotten off the phone with her nephew, Gray Fox, and he had asked for my help.

"Can you come quickly?" she asked. "You may be the only one that can head off El Buho."

I told her I would try my best and then explained I thought I was being approached by the Old Owl also.

"Hurry, we need your help now! No, make that, I need your help now!"

"Tama, I'll give it all I've got, if I can get away."

As I hung up the phone, I knew that if I did not go, Melody would be the only reason. The first thing I needed to do was find out what she had planned for the next couple of weeks. I knew she had a longer tour coming up, but I wasn't sure when. We just always enjoyed each other until she had to leave on a tour, and then we enjoyed each other when she returned.

I pressed her number on my phone, and she said hello very quickly.

"Melody, how soon is your next tour? I know we have talked about it, but I've ceased to be bothered about your travels, because it is such great fun when you get back home."

"Cassy, I'll be leaving Monday morning for two weeks in New York City. But why are you asking right now?"

I explained that I had received a call from Gray Fox asking if I could help on a murder case. And then I fully explained what had happened. However, I did not mention El Buho, as I had never divulged anything to her about him or how he fit into Pinn's death. Neither did I mention that Tama had also asked for my help.

No, there was no male/female interest, it's just that both of us had a real connection to the Old Spirit, and I really wanted to help.

"When would you want to leave?" Melody asked.

I explained that Gray Fox said he needed me as soon as I could get there.

Melody giggled and said, "If you could quarterback the team tonight after such a winning season, you could probably leave tomorrow, if you are still able to walk and can get a flight."

I said, "I'll have the trainer wrap both my ankles after I finish my whirlpool treatment, and I should be ready for one of our big games."

Then I heard her quietly mock-yell, "Go Jays!" as I hung up the phone.

I immediately called the airlines in St. Louis and was able to book a flight the next morning. Then I called my neighbor, and he was also available to drive me to the airport.

Last, I called the Old Gray Fox back and told him I would arrive the next day. He said he would set up my living and transportation needs and have someone at the airport to pick me up.

Then all I had left to do was prepare for the old ball game that Melody and I would be playing that night. Oh yes, as soon as I packed, but I thought I could do that in an hour or two.

Since I would be gone for a while, I decided to go up to the old bench and sit and look at the river for a few moments, just to enjoy the view.

As I prepared to seat myself, I saw a black owl feather on the bench. As I reached to pick it up, my eyes were drawn to a shiny object lodged between two of the boards of the old bench. As I drew the shiny little disk from the crack in the boards, I realized it was a small silver coin. And then a large winged shadow floated over my head and disappeared. As I looked more closely at the small coin, I realized it was a half *real* from Mexico, dated 1799. For a few moments I sat there in thought and wonderment. Finally I put two and two together, and the only answer was a question crossing my mind: Was the coin a clue or an invitation? Then a third thing crossed my mind—the large black owl. At once, I knew I had to get to Arizona immediately.

Chapter 3

My flight departed St. Louis at 8:20 in the morning and arrived at Tusayan airport, in the canyon, at 11:30 local canyon time.

During the flight, I had time to think about Melody and our time together the night before. She turns my temperature up to boiling every time I touch her, and last night was no exception. We played Teen Angel and the quarterback games for a while, and then it was time for serious lovemaking. I still want to marry her more than anything else I can think of, but going steady is a lot of fun, for now. And, going steady presents no permanent commitment for the near future, so I have time to think things through before I have to make any tough decisions.

I certainly did not want to leave after our evening of love, but she has her job...and life, and I have mine.

When I landed in the canyon, Tama was there to pick me up. She said her nephew, Gray Fox, was almost underwater from the murder case, and she grinned from ear to ear. I immediately understood the grin. When she said *nephew*, she was thinking, *And he is so much older than I am.*

As we rode on toward the motel, I asked her what was going on.

And she answered, "For the time being, I would rather you talked to Christjohn first. He will have the lawful facts and lab results. And, you know I will talk about El Buho and how he is involved. And none of that approach would ever stand up in any court in the land, or in my nephew's mind."

I told her I understood. But then I asked, "If I find anything I can't explain to myself under the law, would you help with what you might think from El Buho's point of view?"

"Yes, but I don't know if I know enough, to know what I know."

"Just be there for me, and I will decide what you know or don't know and if any of it will help me."

I looked up, as we had arrived at the Canyon Sunshine Lodge. The lodge was rustic and appeared to have many years behind it. But, as I discovered a little later, it was nice and comfortable, and it had a place to eat common food and get a good night's sleep.

As I got out of Tama's SUV, she pointed to a late-model Subaru pickup truck parked in front of my room and said, "Casper, there is the rental unit you will be using while you are here. It should get you around the immediate area and to California if it becomes necessary for you to go there. Plus, your meals are paid for here at the lodge. But if you invite a guest to eat, you will be responsible for the cost of their meal."

I assured her I felt that was more than fair, and I thought, *The only guest I would probably invite would be Melody, and she'll be in New York for several days, not out here.*

I gathered my baggage from the back of Tama's vehicle as I thanked her for the pickup at the airport and the one in the parking place. She responded that the keys were at the front desk, and I was to ask for Steve. As I turned to enter the office of the lodge, she waved and drove away.

In a few moments I located Steve, and he assisted me with getting settled in my room as he produced the Subaru's keys. I thanked him and retired to my room to prepare to meet with the Big Red Ranger.

Chapter 4

After a few minutes to catch my breath and take care of bathroom needs, I proceeded to the Subaru and drove toward the canyon ranger station. Hopefully I'd connect with Gray Fox and get the rundown on the presumed murder in the park.

Luck was with me, as the Big Ranger had just returned from lunch and was seated at his desk, allowing his meal to settle a little.

He saw me enter the station door, and I heard his deep voice. "Gray, damn it's great to see you. With you here I have to believe this mess will start to make sense. I sure haven't been able to make heads or tails of any of it. Oh, sorry, how was your flight out, and how is the little tour guide?"

"Good or probably great, in both instances. The flight was short, and the young lady is leading a tour to New York City for a couple of weeks. That means we need to get this thing cleared up in about fourteen to twenty days. Now, tell me what happened."

"Why don't we go for a ride while I tell you about it? Then we'll end up at the rental house where the victim was living when he disappeared."

The chief began by telling me that a few months back a tale started to circulate in the area about an ancient treasure. Mexican gold and/or silver was reported to be hidden somewhere in the surrounding hills, valleys, or canyons.

Almost at the same time, a man by the name of Mickey Lopez appeared in the area and began to question anyone who would talk to him about old Mexican coins. Specifically, he was asking if anyone had found any old coins anywhere nearby.

I broke into his story and asked, "About what time in history were the coins thought to be from?"

"About 1775 to about 1800, or so the people he talked to said. But, Gray, there are always old coins being found where people have lived during the period being talked about. So what does that mean?"

My mind was churning a mile a minute as I thought back to the little coin I had found in the crack in my old bench. And, oh yeah, the black owl wing feather.

Hot sweat began to run down my back. I felt glad that I had packed the little coin and had it with me at the lodge, in case I needed it as proof of odd happenings pertaining to early Arizona and Mexico history. And, I also remembered the mint date—1799. This was during the approximate period of Spanish involvement in the history of the desert southwest, and less than fifty years before the United States acquired this area from Mexico. The Jefferson City area was not even colonized until after Lewis and Clark's expedition shortly after 1800. My coin may have been lost by an early explorer, but how did it end up in a crack in an old bench that was probably constructed after 1900? The sweat down my back flowed faster and heavier.

Suddenly my mind went back to what Gray Fox was saying. "So you see, there seems to be no sense in what is going on."

I broke in once more, "Do you suppose this Lopez found the treasure and was killed for it?"

"Do you really think there might have been a real treasure around here?" the Fox asked.

"You remember the old saying—sometimes truth is stranger than fiction. Maybe there was some Mexican silver or gold hidden around here, and it was found, either by Lopez or someone else."

"How do we go about finding the truth or the treasure, or both?" Gray Fox continued.

"Why don't you give me a day or two to nose around, and perhaps I might find more information. Probably not the treasure, but information leading to the treasure and Lopez's death or disappearance."

"My aunt refers to you as Ghost Gray and says you probably knew more about this mess before you heard about it than we did after it started."

About that time, Ranger Gray Fox pulled up in front of a small house in what appeared to be a depressed residential neighborhood. He said, "Here is the house where we found the blood and clues that indicated that Mickey Lopez was killed here."

"How do you know the blood is Mickey Lopez's blood?"

"The fool injured himself poking around in caves and crevices and had to have medical treatment at our little local hospital, and his blood work was on record there. When we sent samples of the blood found in the house, it matched his blood work that was on record."

When we walked into the house, a very sickening scent caught me by surprise. The chief told me it was decaying human blood. As we moved to the back room of the house, I saw a large brown stain on the floor and what looked like scrape marks through the stain and disappearing at the back door.

Gray Fox once more started an explanation. "We think Lopez was stabbed to death, as we found a bloody knife on the floor next to the stain. The blade of the knife was totally covered with blood. And we also think the scrape marks through the stain were made by his heels as his body was dragged out the back door."

I took time to look over every part of the room, and it appeared that Gray Fox's scenario was more than likely the correct assumption.

I walked through all the rest of the rooms, and then we prepared to leave. As I passed one of the windows that was partially in shadows, I saw a reflection in the glass of a dark owl wing feather, and a chill crept down my spine.

When we reentered the ranger's SUV, he spoke once more. "Well, Gray Ghost, or Ghost Gray, did you see anything I might have missed?"

I was dying to say, "Yes, you missed El Buho," but I knew that would be a mistake, because he did not accept the existence of the Old Spirit, so I just said, "Chief, it remains to be seen if either one of us saw anything or nothing."

Then I remembered Gray Fox's last statement when we talked by phone.

"Hey, Big Red. How is Krash involved in this murder investigation?"

"Oh, White Eyes. He's not really involved with the murder; he's just doing some photography work for the department. We've started having drug problems in the park, and he is taking random pictures of the tourists to determine who is only here for a day or two, as most real tourists are, and who is staying for a longer length of time. I figured drug runners and dealers would be here longer, or maybe permanently. Krash doesn't get close to the people; he takes their pictures at a distance. Then the department checks mug shots from various locations against his pictures, which enables us to arrest people that are a match. Then we can tell them their mug shots were to blame for their arrest, and Old Crazy Krash stays in the clear."

Then the chief giggled as he said, "It's funny, even if Krash is caught taking pictures, he has a great cover story of his own. After I allowed him to publicize his pictures and the story of Pinn's death in that cheap magazine, the station started getting requests from people who wanted to meet Old Crazy, purchase copies of his pictures, and get him to speak to groups.

"You know, Krash doesn't need to make money, but he sure eats up the recognition. He even gives the people who purchase one of his canyon pictures a computer disc or thumb drive with Pinn's death pictures on it. That way they can enlarge the photos on their own computers until they can actually see Old Pinn jump off the rim.

"But if you need him anytime to assist you in the investigation, the department will also pay him for that."

Then he hit the accelerator, and we quickly buzzed back into the region from where we started. A little later we arrived at the ranger station.

In just a short time I returned to my room to prepare for, hopefully, a satisfying dinner. But, before I left my room, I wrote down all that the Gray Fox told me and all I had seen. Yes, and I wrote about being made aware of the presence of El Buho Viejo.

And then I became aware of another presence in my thoughts that had slipped my mind, as I had become totally involved with the mystery of Mickey Lopez. I pulled my cell phone from my pocket, punched in Sweet Melody's number on quick dial, and waited for the voice of an Angel to reach my ear.

Chapter 5

The meal was superb—a meal fit for a hungry snoop. There was beef roast, baked potato, green salad, and hot rolls. And last, a dessert of my choice of fruit pies, topped with handmade vanilla ice cream.

My God, it was so tasty.

But the meal was not nearly as tasty and sweet as the call to my Sweet Melody. Absence does make the heart grow fonder! And when the call was finished, I could hardly get her out of my mind.

However, I had no choice, as I needed to be prepared to meet Tama early on the morrow and discover what secrets she may have gleaned from the Old One.

As my head hit the pillow, I finally was able to let my thoughts return to my love. And as sleep overtook me, I knew I would dream great visions of that woman who owned my heart.

All too soon the alarm screamed me awake. I crawled from the comfort of the linens and hit the floor. After a shower, shave, and other necessary bathroom details, I got dressed and prepared for breakfast and the rest of the day.

Like the dinner the night before, breakfast was tasty and satisfying. It was the usual eggs, meat, and toast with jam, and coffee, milk, hot tea, or water.

About 9:00 a.m. I pulled into the yard of Tama's home in the side canyon. As I drove, I watched for the apparition of El Buho as he involved himself in his daily activities. He would be doing work, that morning, the same as he had been doing for about the last two hundred years. But, I did not see him.

As I slid out from under the steering wheel and stepped out of the pickup, I caught a glimpse of an odd happening: a large black owl winging his way across the bright sunny expanse of broad daylight. Then I knew where the Old One was and what he was doing. He was monitoring Tama's and my actions.

As I got close to Tama's front door, she suddenly appeared and welcomed me back to her home. She played the part of the perfect hostess as she again served me a great iced tea made from some unnamed canyon plant leaf. And again, it was extremely satisfying to my body and my busy mind.

Tama invited me to sit, and we commenced a discussion about the recent murder. Before much was said, she confided that she believed El Buho Viejo was once more involved in this death, the same as he was in the death of Jeb Pinn.

Then I asked, "Does all of this have to do with some ancient treasure? Gray Fox said there were rumors that a hoard of silver or gold might be behind the murder and disappearance."

Tama answered, "I really don't know. All I do know is El Buho is not doing much work in the canyon, and his spirit is in the air almost continuously. Something is happening that we do not know about or that we cannot see."

Then I told her that he had also been visiting me in Missouri and had left a small silver Spanish coin with a mint date of 1799 that I believed was a clue.

Tama dropped her head and said, "That date is about the time El Buho was born. I believe I should give you a little more information about the Old Ones. Especially El Buho."

Since Tama had explained the Old One, El Buho, to me after Jeb Pinn's death, I began to become more and more involved with her story.

Knowing something about American history and being a former action-movie buff, the stories of Zorro, by Johnston McCulley, started to creep into my conscious mind. I wondered if McCulley, back in the early years of the twentieth century, had heard whispered references to a poor man's hero in the southwestern United States and decided to use him as a basis for his action hero, Zorro. El Buho, if he really existed, would have supported the creation of that character. And then another death occurred, just recently, in the region of the canyon, and I was once more getting drawn deeper and deeper into the muck that was stirred up.

Chapter 6

As Tama and I sat and continued to discuss the recent death and how she believed El Buho was involved, she slowly disclosed more and more of the legend of El Buho Viejo.

First she let slip, either intentionally or unintentionally, that he was born around early 1800 in the tiny village of San Angel, near what would become the tourist center of the Grand Canyon. His Christian name was Miguel Lopez, and his mother was a lowly Native American woman of the Havasupai culture. However, his father was a soldier from one of the groups of Spanish explorers going through the region during that period.

In later years one of his sons or grandsons would follow the flow of humanity across the western desert into Southern California. And the family line descended down to the present time.

Slowly, ever so slowly, Tama continued to let her tongue slip as she divulged more information.

It seemed that Miguel, being of half-Spanish blood, was allowed a little more freedom in his thoughts and actions than the other Native young men of the region. Perhaps out of naivete or self-assurance, he began to rise to the surface as a spokesman for the Native population. For several years, even until he reached almost middle age, he was permitted by the Spanish dons to express what he believed, and sometimes they actually acted on his recommendations. And sometimes those changes improved conditions in the poor people's way of life.

But one day, one of the old, more powerful dons died.

As his son assumed control of that family's wealth, he also demanded more submission from the Native population. Miguel approached the young don and must have demanded redress of some grievance.

The young don invited Lopez to his hacienda to further discuss the question over a glass of wine. Miguel was encouraged to enjoy the wine until he was drunk, and then the young don and one or two of the more radical gentlemen drowned him in a cask of wine. As Lopez breathed his last and disappeared below the surface of the bloody red liquid, a large black owl swooped down from the rafters of the wine cellar and sailed out of the door and into the cloudy sky above.

When Miguel's body was extracted from the wine cask, a black owl feather was gripped tightly in his hand.

At least that was the tale of the owl that Tama Claybasket told me. Was it real, or only a legend carried down through the ages by the Native Havasupais?

Almost as if coming out of a trance, as she finished her story, Tama shook her head and took another drink of her tea.

Then the most obvious question came into my mind, and I asked, "Tama, you just said that El Buho's Christian name was Miguel Lopez?"

"Yes, it is from legend and actual historical church records."

"And you do know that the victim of the recent murder was named Mickey Lopez?"

"Yes."

"Could there be kinship between El Buho and Mickey Lopez?"

"I am sure it is more than likely, but Mickey came here from California, so I cannot say for sure. You know, there are probably no records, anywhere, that would confirm kinship."

Then a thought went through my mind. "Gray Fox said Lopez was a petty criminal. Do you suppose there are any pictures on file in California, when or if he was ever really arrested? Or do you suppose if there are pictures, would Gray Fox have asked for copies?"

As she pulled her cell phone out of her apron pocket, she replied, "I'll call the station and check with Christjohn or whoever is on desk."

In a moment she asked someone, and they confirmed that they had a mug shot from Los Angeles. Then she told me, "Give me your cell number, and I'll have them forward the picture to you."

In a few moments I was looking face-to-face at Mickey Lopez.

Immediately I emitted a belly laugh, and then I almost roared. Realizing I was laughing at the dead, I quickly begged Tama to forgive me. But all my warped mind could think of was that Lopez's name should have been Mickey Mouse. The poor man had a nose that stuck out like a mouse's nose, ears like small half-moons, and a small mustache that looked like whiskers. Lopez looked like a mouse from a Disney movie. Well, at least I now knew what he looked like, if during my snooping I should happen to find his body.

After my idiotic thoughts passed, Tama and I visited for a few minutes, and then I headed back to the lodge.

Chapter 7

Once back in my room, I considered what could have been the motive for Lopez's murder. Could there really be enough gold and silver hidden close by to precipitate a cold-blooded killing?

I decided the first thing I needed to do was take a few notes. New ones from this case and a review of Pinn's death. *If El Buho is once more involved, what is his concern? Is Mickey Lopez a descendent, and is El Buho seeking revenge on those who did the dirty deed? Tama believes he whacked Pinn as revenge for the attack on a Native girl. If Mickey is a descendent, the Old Spirit would be running wild. And that is what Tama believes is happening.*

A feeling of depression crept into my mind as the memory of one of mine invaded my brain. Lily, my beautiful love, once more appeared in my mind's eye, and I knew if the circumstance of her death had been foul play instead of a natural death, I would have reacted the same as the Old One.

Then suddenly a new direction swept away my thoughts of Lily as a new approach entered my thoughts. *If the coin I have is from the time of El Buho, the treasure would have to be in the area he was familiar with.* The next time I talked to Tama, I'd try to find out if she knew where El Buho lived during his life. Then I might get closer to Lopez's killer—and the treasure, if it existed. I did remember I had seen him at Gray Fox's house and working in a small field along the road to the ranger's home.

After writing a few notes and questions to be asked, I decided to go to the lodge's café and grab a late lunch and then try to locate Krazy Krash and get reacquainted. After he told me about getting some recognition for helping to solve Pinn's death, I felt he would be more than ready to give assistance if I needed any. I supposed he was still searching for the one big frame that would make him a world-famous photographer. I was a little sad to know he may have gotten the big one a couple of years ago, but I was not at liberty to tell him so.

Not knowing for sure, but making an educated assumption, I believed I would find his rolling photo lab parked on one of the tourist lots near The Village. That was his favorite haunt and within easy walking access of the cafés and stores in the area.

As I drove the pickup along the main drive to The Village, I spotted his vehicle in a shady spot near the back of one of the parking lots. So I signaled and turned into the lot. Pulling up next to Krash's rig, I saw that the screen door was closed but the entry door was open behind it, so I assumed Old Krazy was in.

As I knocked, I could see through the screen, and he was busy at his computer console reviewing some people, canyon, and animal shots.

He looked up from his work and turned his head toward the door. A smile exploded on his face as he almost yodeled, "Hey Boss, come on in and have a pop."

As I opened the screen he was reaching into a bag and pulling out a warm soda. He had once told me cold drinks caused his brain to shrink. So, he never put his drinks on ice.

I slipped into the chair next to him and opened my hot pop as I thought, *Whoop dee do.*

As I slowly sipped my drink, Krash excitedly explained that he was becoming more and more famous every day. He was selling some pictures, and his name was becoming known all around the canyon, and in some other cities.

One more big case with pictures to prove it, and his name would be a household word.

I stood up, slapped him on the back, and said, "Now Krash, don't forget your friends when you get to the top, cause we'll all be down here looking up."

He smiled a big faceful and replied, "Boss, I'll never forget you—you're the one who discovered my big break in my pictures of Pinn's death, even though I didn't know they were there. You know you're one hell of a detective, Casper Gray, and I'm proud that you say I'm your friend."

I thanked him for the compliment and then continued, "Krash, I may need more help. Are you up to being my first-class assistant?"

He answered, "I'm working for the Old Red Chief right now. But when I finish his work, I'll be bright, right, and ready to assist you. You get into all kinds of cracks, and I might get the next big one or the super big one while I'm around you."

He stopped and thought for a minute, then he continued, "You're out here to help the Big Man solve that guy's murder where there's no body, ain't you?"

I nodded and replied, "I'm going to give it all I've got, but I'm sure I will need a good bit of help."

Once more there was a grin from ear to ear as he stuck out his chest and bragged, "Boss, I'm your number one man."

We passed the time of day for a few more minutes, and then I took my leave and got back into my truck.

As I left the parking lot, I gave Old Krash a lot of thought. He was probably crazy, but I felt you could depend on him when the going got tough. And that was what you looked for in a true, honest friend. Then another thought found its way through my muddled brain. With Gray and Krash on the trail, how could any malcontent stay free from the law for very long? Then I laid my head back and roared with laughter. And then I saw a black shadow flash across my windshield and heard a perfectly mimicked echo of my laugh. I had to suppose El Buho was happy with the way I was working the case.

When I got back to the lodge, there was a written message from Tama asking me to meet her at her home the next day to hear more about El Buho. She said she did not call in case Christjohn was with me—because of his dislike of her legends and myths. There was a PS saying that we would meet about 9:00.

Chapter 8

Tama finally saw fit to reveal more of the tale of the life of El Buho. That part of the legend appeared to have a vein of provable truth in it. She even said she would take me to the location and let me see the truth for myself.

She explained that the young dons who drowned Miguel Lopez all met their deaths within a year after his. It was determined that four wealthy young men were involved in El Buho's death. And, the four were buried in chapels located on their families' land holdings. Tama further explained that two of the burial sites still survived near San Angel, and I could see for myself that the young men really existed.

I quietly said, "Tama, just because two young men existed during that period doesn't prove much of anything having to do with El Buho Viejo."

"Would you believe it had a connection to El Buho if he signed his name on their graves?"

"What do you mean he signed his name on their graves?"

"Would you care to see for yourself?" she asked.

We left in my truck immediately and drove to the locale of San Angel. Following Tama's directions, we arrived at a little stone building that appeared to be some sort of chapel. It was at the edge of a large, modern housing development on the floor of one of the side canyons, just a short distance from her home.

The little chapel was about fifteen by thirty feet in floor area, with a height of seven to eight feet, with several holes in its roof. It was built of stone blocks that had at one time been coated with white stucco. However, without consistent care, the coating was in extreme disrepair. And the beautiful bold colors of red, blue, and green that had detailed the building many years ago had faded to dirty brown and black.

We exited my truck and walked into the small building through an open archway. Inside were five or six burial boxes made of carved stone, with carved stone lids.

Tama guided me to one of the boxes and pointed to the carved lid. The name of the person buried inside was partially destroyed, but enough was left to recognize the family name, Hidalgo.

But, next to the name was a chilling black stain. As if it had been painted by an artist, a black owl feather was more than plainly visible.

Tama said it was not painted on; it was a stain formed by water and minerals. And every time the family scrubbed it away, within a few months it reappeared.

Tama continued that the second burial chapel, some distance on down the canyon, had a second burial box lid with a perfectly matched stain. And then as deep feelings of fear ran through my body, I remembered the black feather I found on my old bench back home, realizing it was an exact duplication of the stain I just observed. And I once more wondered what the tiny silver coin from the era of El Buho's life meant.

Tama broke into my thoughts as she asked, "Do you want to see the other burial box at the other chapel? Since the two young dons grew up as neighbors and were such close friends, when they died so soon after each other the families constructed their graves exactly alike. Twin friends as such."

"No, since you told me the truth about this one, I have to believe the second one really does exist. But, do you remember the family name on the other lid?"

"Garcia. Like the name of the fat sergeant in the reruns of the old *Zorro* TV show."

Another chill ran down my spine as I thought back to the idea I'd had about Zorro being a carry-down in history from the legend of El Buho. As we climbed back into my truck, I wondered if we would ever find Mickey Lopez's body and discover why he was murdered and why his body was taken away.

Chapter 9

It had been about a week, and I had very little to show for my efforts except a mug shot of Mickey Mouse Lopez. But, then I remembered the little silver coin. Was it simply an invite from El Buho?

The only highlight of the day was my call to Melody. She said New York was thrilling, but she was sorry I wasn't there to make it a total delight. I told her New York City was old hat for me, and the only thrill I would have, if I were there, would be her. We talked love and a little of what she was doing and a little of what I was doing, then it was time to say I love yous and goodbyes as we ended our call.

Before I could get involved in anything else, there was a knock at the door. I opened the door and found Krash outside.

"Hey Boss, I was wondering if you were terribly busy. You know, I'm supposed to assist you, and I thought maybe you might assist me a little in return? I've taken a few pictures, and Old Red Face wants me to try to compare them to about two dozen mug shots he gave me. Every time I start to do the pictures, I fall asleep. Would you help a little, to keep me awake and compare some of the pictures with me?"

In my mind I thought, *Thrill, thrill, an hour or two with the Krazy Man!*

But a deal is a deal, and I would probably run his legs off sometime in the not-too-distant future, so I agreed to help. And he had been a hell of a help with Old Slender Pinn's case.

I followed Krash in my truck to where he parked his unit, so when we were done, I could return to my room.

Quickly he had his big computer screen on and the computer booted. Across the screen I saw about twenty-four eight-by-ten-inch photographs of a group of people, and on the desk in front of the screen, about a like number of five-by-seven-inch mug shots.

Krash assumed his position at the keyboard as I seated myself in the chair next to him. He then brought up the first photo on the screen and made it appear about two by three feet in size. The people's faces in the shot appeared about one quarter life size.

Krash took four or five of the mug shots and handed four or five to me. Then he said, "Boss, look at the people on the screen and compare each one to one of the mug shots. Then compare the next mug shot. And then again the next mug, until you have checked all I have given you. Then I'll bring up the next eight-by-ten photo from the big lot, and we'll repeat the process until we are finished."

I could immediately see why a person would fall asleep, as this crap was going to become very B...O...R...I...N...G pretty damned quick. But, I made the deal, and I intended to stick to it until the end.

We had covered about half the eight-by-tens, and then Krash's face brightened, and I thought he had hit a live one in the mug shots. But he only wanted to brag a little. "Now Boss, I want you to pay especially close attention to this shot. I was almost, no, I was a full four hundred yards away when I got this frame. I had to take about ten shots of the same group to get one this great. If you will look, you will see there are about ten faces in this photo, and every one of them is looking directly at the camera. Man, I'm not good, I'm Krash the Great! Oh, by the way, this was a marijuana party. Red probably won't get real excited about it, but at least he'll have the picture."

I was just beginning to visually scan the faces and compare them to the mug shots, when a crazy flash went through my mind. *M...i...c, k...e...y, M...o...u...s...e. Mickey Mouse!*

I wondered where that came from. Then a bolt of lightning shot totally through me. "Krash, when did you take this picture?" I asked.

He looked closely at the lower corner of the photo and said, "Boss, the date on the picture says I took this three nights ago. Why?"

I almost stammered as I replied, "Look at the man third from the left; tell me about what you see."

Krash let out a laugh and almost roared, "That SOB looks like a rat!"

"A dead rat," I responded. "That man is Mickey Lopez, the man whose murder I'm investigating."

"Don't shit me, Boss! Are you sure that's him?"

"I have a mug shot in my room and on my phone that is exactly the same face as the one in your photo. You're sure about the date it was taken?"

"Dead sure, Boss." He released a little giggle about his tiny joke.

As I pounded him on the back, I proclaimed, "I agree—you're not good, you're great."

"But Boss, what now? If he's not dead, what does that mean?"

"I don't know, but I do know it means we attack from a different direction."

"Hey Boss, does it also mean I'll be working full time with you and can get away from the rest of these damned mug shots?"

"I can't say for sure, but I would think I will need you full time or almost full time to crack this twisted case."

We chattered about what might be going on for a few more minutes, then I said, "I'll see you later," and headed back to my room.

As I drove, I also thought. I decided the best thing to do would be to immediately inform the head ranger about the new development in the Lopez case.

The phone rang about three times, and the chief's deep voice tickled my ear. "Gray, why would you call this late? You know you're taking me away from my favorite classical music station on my satellite radio."

"Sorry to interrupt, and even sorrier to destroy your whole evening, but Lopez is not dead!"

"Now Gray, I don't mind a joke now and then, and we both play the race game, but I don't need a joke like that when I'm also fighting the druggers."

"Not a joke, Chief—the truth, the whole truth, and nothing but the truth! And I have photo proof to back up what I say. Unless Lopez has a twin or a double living in this world."

Then I went through the full explanation about what Krash and I had found. I verbally highlighted that Lopez was in a group picture of marijuana smokers someplace at the edge of The Village, as I recognized some of the buildings in the background.

He was silent for a longer moment, and then he said, "Take that Big Slender Nut with you in the morning, and have him photograph the whole damned house of horror and fake death. I don't want to lose anything that we might have seen that proves more than what we have. And I am going to call in right now and put out an APB to find and hold that little rat, no joke intended, so maybe we can find out what he is up to. Oh, stop by the station in the morning and pick up the key to the death house. Good night, and thanks a lot for both your and Krazy's work."

And then I heard the phone click as Gray Fox hung up.

Shortly I pulled into my parking place and headed to my room for the night.

But before I totally gave up, I placed a call to Krash's satellite phone. When he answered, I explained the plan for the next morning. He hooted and said, "Away from the damned mug shots. I'll meet you at your room at 8:00 if that's satisfactory."

I agreed as I broke the connection.

My bed was nice and my thoughts and dreams nicer.

Chapter 10

I decided Gray Fox's idea to have Krash take pictures of the fake death house was an excellent plan. It was such a grand scheme, I decided I would go a step or two farther. I would have him take pictures of any visual clues we might find. That way I could review them at any time, if I found I needed to refresh my memory.

At 8:00 the next morning, there was a loud knock at my lodge room door. Krash was there, but he was not in a very good mood. As we stood facing each other on the edge of the parking lot outside my door, I asked him what the problem was. He said he was ready to take pictures, but he would have to use one of his lesser cameras, as there was something wrong with his big jewel. I asked him what was wrong with it. He told me the blasted thing was taking weird pictures. So I asked him how weird. And he began to explain.

"Gray, you remember when you were here working for the chief ranger on Old Slender Pinn's murder? You remember I told you about seeing an old Native in a loincloth as I was driving to Ms. Tama's party? Well, yesterday I saw him working in one of the canyons, and I took his picture, but the damned camera only showed the place where he was working. The damned thing didn't take his picture!"

Immediately fear grabbed my mind! How could I hide the fact that the old man was a ghost when Krash knew a picture would never show a ghost? After a few moments, I decided I would have to tell what I knew, or Jack Krash would never trust me again.

"Hey Krash, I have to tell you something, and I hope it doesn't destroy our working relationship or friendship. The old man is a ghost. And he sometimes takes the form of a large black owl."

"That's crap, Gray—don't be playing games with me. They ain't no damned such a thing as a ghost. I may be crazy, but I ain't no damn fool."

"Krash, I need to tell you a story, and I hope you can keep an open mind. There is a legend in this area that some of the Havasupai people believe to be true. And Krash, I also believe it's true. Ms. Tama told me the story, and she said the Old Spirit saved her life when she was a child. She also believes he is the one who killed Jeb Pinn."

"Oh, come on, Gray, we both know the Chance kid killed him with that damned old baseball that was found on the ledge by his body. Hell, we both know he's pitching for the Red Birds out of St. Louis, and he has a vicious fastball. He knocked Old Jeb's rear right off the wall! And I have the pictures to prove it. And you know there was something round under his arm, because you found it in one of the pictures."

Then I explained all I knew, including the Old One's walking stick and how it had a smooth round grip. Krash then looked at me with the most unbelieving pair of eyes I have ever seen.

"Okay you big liar, convince me. Tell me that this El Buho Vi-ho-ho or whoever can really do things or cause things to happen."

Just then, a dark shadow moved over our heads as a large black owl sailed upward toward the heavens. And a black wing feather slowly, spirally floated to the ground between us.

Krash's eyes grew large and round as I heard him barely breathe the words, "Oh, crap." Then in a louder voice, he addressed me. "Was that him?" He leaned down and picked up the feather.

Then I saw it...on the feather was a white circle forming a perfect seeing eye. When Krash also saw the eye, he threw down the feather and slowly sank to his knees. And once more I heard a lighter voice say, "Oh, shit." Then after a long few minutes Krash slowly got to his feet and then rose to his full height. "Oh yeah, I'll help you by taking all the pictures you want. This case may be my chance for the really, really big frame...lead on, Boss!"

I knew what had just happened was bound to happen sometime, and I was really dreading having to face it. Then it was over, and it really wasn't so bad, with El Buho's help.

Chapter 11

Krash and I got into my rental Subaru and first picked up the death-house key at the ranger station. I turned on the GPS and headed out toward the fake murder scene. Krash asked what he was supposed to photograph there. I told him to take pictures, explaining that ten too many was far better than one not enough. He replied that he understood and that he would do the best job any photographer could. I was sure he would.

We arrived at the house, and Krash went to work. And he was happy he could use his big jewel to do the job. After about an hour, he said he was finished, and he had taken about 150 frames, inside the house and out.

I then told him about the two little chapels and the burial boxes. So I reset the GPS, and we headed for the little side canyon. Krash's memory was very good, as he stated the chapels were located close to Ms. Tama's house and the chief's house. I commended him, telling him he was absolutely correct.

We stopped a short distance from the first chapel, and he took several shots of the outside. Then I drove on and parked just outside the front archway going into the burial area. He took a couple of shots of the arch opening, and then we moved inside the vault. The burial boxes looked the same as they had when Tama and I came out to see them a day or two before. Old Krazy took pictures of all the boxes, from every side and down from the top. He also got the names of all the people buried there, if their box lid had a readable name. He got a very good image of Hidalgo's burial box. After about another hour, we got back in the truck and headed on down the valley to the second chapel.

The building looked exactly like the one we had just left. So, Krash went through exactly the same routine he established in the first chapel. He took photographs of every burial box, from every angle. He took a clear image of Garcia's name and, of course, the black stain in the shape of an owl feather. I mentioned that the Hidalgo box and the Garcia box were exact copies of each other. Krash was impressed that both boxes still existed, and he was in awe of the feather-shaped stains. For a time, he could not stop looking at them and talking about them. El Buho had just about scared the stuff out of him.

After a time, Krash said he was finished with his work and was ready to leave.

As we walked out of the archway, a large black owl appeared above us, again in the bright light of the sun, and spiraled upward into the sky until it disappeared.

I saw Krash staring at the screen of his camera and shaking his head. Then I heard him barely whisper, "No damn image, and I know I had him centered in the lens."

I felt myself grin as I headed back to the truck.

While driving back to my room, Krazy had very little to say. Because I had already told him about the possibility of a hoard of gold and silver, he did ask, "Boss, do you really think there might be a treasure involved in this damned nonsense?"

All I could say was, "Old Buddy, there have been stranger things than treasures found in this old world!"

Chapter 12

I didn't learn until later that the chief's APB bore fruit the very next morning after it was issued.

One of the Grand Canyon's rangers saw Lopez slipping into a small forest of pines directly behind the hotel in the main part of The Village.

Once he was located, Gray Fox instructed his men to keep watch but not apprehend until there was time to determine if he was involved with a group or working alone.

It was a little sad—poor Lopez's facial features were so unusual it made him easy to identify in a crowd. But, with him being a loner, it made the job even easier. He tried to fit in with a group but just could not accomplish the feat.

After it was almost certain that Lopez had no accomplices, the Big Red Ranger gave the command to bring him in.

When Mickey was first located, Gray Fox felt his apprehension was important enough that he took over the investigation personally. And he informed his staff that he was not to be disturbed unless it involved death or dismemberment.

While the head ranger was involved with the capture of Lopez, of which Krash and I were uninformed, we continued carrying on our own massive investigation.

Chapter 13

I hadn't set an alarm the night before, so I slept a little later the next morning. After breakfast, I called Krash and asked if we could go over the pictures he had taken earlier. He laughed and said, "You're awfully late in asking—I've already loaded them to the computer and have them organized for you to look at. Just come on over to my lab."

We quickly ended the call, and I mounted up into my rental horse and galloped over to The Village parking lot.

Krazy had made something he called coffee, but I was glad I'd had the real thing earlier at breakfast. He assumed his spot at the keyboard, I seated myself in the co-pilot's position, and he began the photo review.

I was more than impressed—his pictures were absolutely fantastic. I could see things in the photos that I had not seen in the natural setting. Then I knew why he considered himself "the greatest." If he wasn't, he was awfully close.

Almost the same as the last time we were doing this, I started to become drowsy and lose interest. But suddenly I saw something and hollered for Krash to hold the action. I had suddenly remembered an old axiom from an art class: "Almost nothing in nature is absolutely symmetrical." That is, three trees never grow in a straight line unless they have been hand-planted. The picture showing the bloodstain on the floor, with the drag track through it, jumped out at me. The heel marks in the bloodstain were exactly the same distance apart from end to end. No two dead human feet being dragged would stay the same distance apart. Then I saw a straight-backed chair in the background of the picture, and I knew what had made the drag marks.

The little rat had faked a body being dragged out of the room. We had two facts for clues: Mickey Mouse Lopez was not dead, and no body had been dragged out of his house.

I quickly pointed out what I had noticed to Krash and explained what I had just thought.

Krash wrinkled his nose and squinted one eye and said, "What in hell's game is the little rat...mouse...Lopez playing?"

I said, "Krash, I don't know, but I sure plan to work like the devil to find out." I called the ranger station to tell Big Red what we had learned. He wasn't available, but the officer on the desk said they would contact him by radio, and I would probably hear from him in a short while.

We continued to watch the photo display, but neither of us saw anything else. We finished the house collection just before noon and decided to take a lunch break.

I felt like having a big, thick steak, so I was going to see if the little steak house I found the last time I was here was still in business. Krash said steak was too rich for his blood (not money-wise but food-wise), so he opted to go to a natural-food café. We agreed to meet back at his place in about an hour or so.

I wanted to take a little time and try to phone Teen Angel or Melody, whichever personality came on the phone.

Krash took off on foot to one of the small natural-food cafés he frequented for a quick bite. And I stood in the shade of his rig until I heard Melody say, "Hello."

My first words were to say I was sorry for the gap in our communications. "I'm sorry for not calling for a while; we have been covered up with information and checking out clues."

"Not a problem—we have been on the move continuously since we arrived. I have been a little concerned, but I knew if something happened to you I would hear very quickly. How have things been going?"

Then I explained to her that we had at least learned, from Krash's pictures, our murder victim was alive and well, though we had not located where he was or learned why he faked his own death. I also told her the mystery might be due to a secret treasure hunt for old Spanish wealth. When I mentioned that fact, I heard, "Will it be finders keepers if you find the stash?"

I told her I didn't know yet, but the only treasure I was interested in was the one I was talking to.

She answered that with, "It had better always be that way, because if I go, you don't know all you would be missing."

I assured her I did, and I wouldn't take any chances. We talked for a few moments more, and then she said she had to load the bus to go to the next attraction. So we said our goodbyes.

I stowed my phone and headed to where the little steak house had been a couple of years back. Before I had walked more than a few yards, my phone stopped my progress. The caller was Gray Fox.

"What do you need, Gray?"

"Chief, no dead body was dragged through the blood in the death house. What we thought were heel marks leading to the back door were made by a straight-backed chair." Then I explained the reasoning for my beliefs.

"Sounds legit to me. That will be just one more thing the little punk will have to explain when he's questioned."

"Do you have any leads on his whereabouts?" I asked.

"Better than that, we have him in custody. We've watched him for a couple of days, and no one else has had contact with him."

"Has he said anything yet?" I asked.

"He basically talks gibberish and screams, 'I didn't do nothin'.' I'm going to let him stew awhile longer and then try a pressure interrogation. You want to be there for that?"

I confirmed that I would like to listen in.

"When I'm ready, I'll call."

Chapter 14

After lunch it was back to Krash's lab to continue reviewing the photos he had taken of the house and at the chapels.

I told Krash that Lopez was in custody. He waited a moment and then asked, "Did he say what in hell happened?"

"No, but Gray Fox said he would find out pretty soon when he questions the little mouse."

Krash said, "Well okay," as he turned back to the computer console.

As we got into the chapel pictures, I began to feel as if all we were accomplishing was looking at pretty photographic work. As I looked at pictures of the chapels and burial boxes, my mind continued to wander, and suddenly a new concept took hold in my mind. I once more remembered an old saying: "Anytime you assume something, you may end up making an ASS of U and ME." I had assumed the ranger lab had done a full workup of the blood found at the house. But what if all that was done was just enough to prove that the sample they tested was Lopez's. What if there was someone else's blood there also? Maybe someone else, a person Lopez had hurt or killed, was there too?

Without stopping Krash, I got up and went outside to make a phone call to the ranger station. When I got an answer, I asked to speak to the lab. A technician came on the line, and I asked him if they had done a full workup of the Lopez blood. He said, "As soon as we discovered the sample we tested was Lopez's, we stopped, because it appeared he had been murdered and we assumed that was as far as we needed to go."

I asked if further tests could be done to see if there was more than one donor.

He replied, "Chief Ranger Gray Fox said anything Casper Gray wanted, get it ASAP. I'll personally run more tests and report back to you before quitting time."

I thanked him, hung up the phone, and went back into Krash's lab to rejoin him at the computer. The rest of the photos were just as I thought—they were simply pretty pictures until we had some other evidence that called for photographic support. Krash made some more of his so-called coffee, and we shared a couple of cups as we consumed some passable leftover breakfast pastry.

After a leisurely length of time, my phone rang, and I found myself speaking to the lab technician.

"First, Mr. Gray, all of the blood sample was from Mickey Lopez. He was the only donor. But, that's as far as common sense goes. So, second, the tests indicate that various parts of the sample were harvested at several different times. I found markers containing alcohol of various strengths, and heavy calcium in some but not in others. The real deal was that some of it was in different stages of unstable decomposition."

After I ended the phone conversation, I thought, *I have a piece of the puzzle, a damned odd piece, but I don't have any idea as to what it means.* I just supposed it was one more thing Lopez would have to explain...if he would.

I decided I would give Gray Fox the latest information as soon as I could make contact. But, until then, about all I could do was go back to helping Krash and pass the latest word to him.

As I opened the screen door and reentered the picture lab, I was still wishing the job of looking at pretty pictures would soon be over.

Chapter 15

As I was leisurely enjoying breakfast, I was also thinking it was perhaps time to prepare to return home to Missouri and my Sweet Melody. Lopez was in custody, and as far as I could determine, no murder had taken place. Something strange was going on, but I thought the chief could handle the case from then forward.

I was partaking of my second cup of coffee when my phone disturbed my relaxation. The party on the other end was Gray Fox himself.

"Hey, Gray, I think I'll start my interrogation of the little rat today. Still want to sit in?"

I was thinking of home, but I thought I'd still like to know the whole story of the fake murder. So my answer was yes.

"I plan to start in about an hour, so be at the station."

Then I remembered—I had my mind so involved with home, I almost forgot to tell the Big Ranger about the blood situation.

"Gray Fox, I'm sorry, I almost forgot to tell you there's something odd about the blood found in the death house, or perhaps I should now say Lopez's house."

"What do you mean *odd*?" he asked.

"The blood was old; it was harvested over a long length of time, and it just was not all lost at the same time."

"I still am not sure what you are saying."

"If Lopez lost that much blood, he lost it over a long period of time, perhaps a month or two."

"Now that is strange!" the Old Fox said. "But I will sure work to get the truth about it from that piece of crap."

I told Gray Fox I would be at the station in a little while, and then I went back to the last couple of swallows of my coffee.

I walked into the station just as Lopez was being taken into the interrogation room. Gray Fox was right behind the ranger who was escorting the prisoner, and I was right behind Gray Fox. The prisoner was placed in a chair, and his hands were cuffed to the table.

The first words said were, "I didn't do nothin'. I want to go home to LA."

Gray Fox got right to the point. "Mr. Lopez, what the hell has been going on?"

"I didn't do nothin'."

"If you didn't do nothin', then what was that mess in the house where you were living? There was enough of your blood on the floor for you to have been killed twice. Then you faked your body being dragged out the back door. What the hell is the story?"

"Oh, is that why you have been chasing after me for the past week or so? I thought someone had discovered that I was looking for my ancestral Grandpa's treasure, and the landowners where I was looking had called you."

"No, but what in the hell is the story of the blood?"

"I get hurt a lot, and I was afraid someday I might need a blood transfusion, so I had drawn enough for an emergency."

"You draw your own blood?"

"Yeah, I was an army corpsman, so I learned to draw blood. After I drew mine, I kept it in the refrigerator."

"Go on!"

"The bagful you found on the floor was a batch that was old, and I was throwing it out when I spilled it."

"What about the damn knife?"

"I was going to use it to cut the bag when I got outside in the weeds. But I accidentally punctured the bag before I got through the door. And that's the mess you found."

"Why did you drag the blinkin' chair legs through the puddle of blood?"

"I was so mad at myself for making the mess, I had to have a cigarette to calm my nerves, so I drug the chair out on the back porch to have a smoke."

"And then you just left the mess behind?"

"I was going to clean it up later, but then you guys started chasing me, and I ran because I thought you were going to arrest me for trespassing."

I saw tears form in the poor mouse's eyes, and he began to cry. "Now I'm in trouble, and I never did find my ancestor's treasure. Grandma said it was here, and she gave me a map telling where it was, but I never found it. I found the damn hole it was in, but all that was in the hole was bones. Now I'll be in jail and never get back to visit her grave ever again."

I saw what I thought might have been a tear in the Big Red Chief's eye as he stood up and turned away. Then he spoke. "Man, I have to hold you for other warrants, and for doing what looked like a fake murder."

As the junior ranger unlocked Lopez from the table and began to put handcuffs back on, I saw the Old Gray Fox shake his head. Then Lopez stood up, reached inside his shirt, pulled out a scrap of old leather, and threw it at me.

"Here, take this damned old map and stick it up your ass. There ain't no treasure, and now I'll never get to go home ever again."

As tears formed in his eyes once more, I spoke. "Mickey, what was your ancestor's name?"

"The old treasure map said Alejandro Hidalgo. And his best friend was Diego Garcia. They were buried close to each other out in one of the canyons. But there ain't no treasure." Then he dropped his eyes, and the young ranger escorted him back to his cell.

Though it appeared the guy was a rat, in my mind I thought, *Maybe he's not, but only God would know.* And then I thought again, *Maybe El Buho would know.*

Chapter 16

On a later morning, I awoke covered with perspiration. I wasn't sure if I was catching something or if I was experiencing anxiety and fear. I recalled having a bizarre dream, but I didn't know what it meant. So, I decided to call Tama. If it had anything to do with El Buho, maybe she could fathom its meaning.

When she answered her phone, she sounded a little strange, as if she had been sucking on a booze bottle. Finally I was able to get through that I had a strange dream and needed her help.

With a drunk giggle, she invited me to drive out to her house for a conference. I'd never heard anyone call a conversation a conference, but perhaps that would be what it would evolve into.

I got into the pickup and headed out to the canyon where she lived. I once more paid close attention to see if I would see the Old One working. And once more, no evidence of him or his work appeared along the road. When I pulled up to Tama and her husband Tom's house, Tama was standing outside the door to the eating room.

She invited me inside and seated herself at the table. As I took a seat, I noticed she had a small bowl with what looked like tiny Brussels sprouts in front of her. And I also saw some little leaf parts beside the bowl.

As she spoke, I could detect no slurring of speech, nor could I determine any flaw in her actions. So, I asked her if she was okay. She answered, "I'm okay, I have just been using some of our local plants to clear my thought process."

With concern in my voice, I asked, "Have you been ingesting some type of peyote?"

"Yes, is there a problem?"

"Isn't that a little dangerous? It's a mind-altering drug, isn't it?"

"For anyone who does not use it correctly. But I have been trained by the Old Ones to use it for good, not evil. I was having a little trouble with a dream I've been experiencing, and I thought a little bit of the plant would clear my vision. And I believe it has."

Since I was wanting to talk about my dreams, I decided to ask about hers. "What was your dream, and what did the plant clear up?"

"I have been dreaming about seeing El Buho flying across the sky, and he was being chased by a dirty white owl. El Buho is so powerful, no dumb white owl would even attempt to chase him, for any reason."

"What did the plant do to clear you vision?" I asked.

"As my vision cleared, I saw it was not a dirty white owl, but a gray owl. It was you: Owl Gray! Why would you be chasing El Buho? If anyone is going to run in the presence of El Buho, it should be you, Owl Gray."

I thought for several minutes, and then a clearness came to my vision also. "Tama, could I have been following El Buho to a place he wanted me to go?"

"Casper, I never thought of that. No white man ever followed El Buho Viejo, unless he had evil in his heart. But, yes, El Buho appears to trust you, so perhaps there is a place he wants you to see or learn about."

"So, what do I do?"

"If you see the Old One in a dream or flying in the sky, if he signals, follow him."

"But, what will the signal be?"

"El Buho will make it very clear when he is signaling you. You will not need to question. Now, Owl Gray, what was your dream?"

"El Buho and I are watching a group of children standing on the ground watching us as we are riding a merry-go-round. El Buho is tossing gold and silver coins to the children. He tosses small silver coins to all but one little girl. To her he throws large gold ones. The little girl appears to be ill and moves very slowly. She catches all the coins he throws to her, and they seem to make her illness better.

"And, it's very odd—I actually hear his voice as he points to the little girl. 'Mi hija.' Doesn't that mean *my child* in Spanish? Or am I mistaken in my Spanish understanding?"

"No, your Spanish is correct. But, you are saying he actually spoke to you? You heard him make a sound?"

"Remember, Tama, it was only a dream."

"It makes no difference. You are a very special person, and he has a very special job for you to do, Owl Gray."

For a long time, several minutes, Tama sat with her eyes closed and breathed very slowly and deeply. When she opened her eyes, they looked almost dead white as she began to speak. "Owl Gray, the little girl is deathly ill, and you must save her life. El Buho will help you, but you must do the human things that he is too weak to do. Do not let lust or evil deter you from doing what is good and right. And you all will be richly rewarded."

Tama's eyelids fluttered a few times, and when she opened them, her eyes looked human once more. "Casper, the Old One is depending on you to save his child. All you have to do is be yourself and follow where he leads."

Then it hit me. "Tama, I don't know who the child is, where she is, or how long she has before her life can't be saved. I really want to help, but I don't know how."

"Just follow El Buho's lead, and you will accomplish what he asks."

Chapter 17

I felt we had finished our conversation on our dreams, so I prepared to leave. But then I recalled I had another reason for my visit.

"Tama, do you read or understand any of the old written Spanish script from the earlier years? I need something translated, and I thought you might be the one."

"Not me, but Tom has done a lot of studying of the old dialects so he can accomplish his research. He might be able to help. And you're in luck—he's in the office typing up some of his work."

She called out, "Tom, could you come out here and maybe help Casper with some old writing?"

I heard a mumble, and then Dr. Dodd appeared at the entry arch. "What can I help you with?" he asked.

I handed him the peace of leather and explained I was hoping it could be translated. He walked outside into the sunlight and studied the somewhat faded script. After only a few moments, he said, "Mr. Gray, this is really rather simple. It appears to have been written by a somewhat educated person, and for me, it is easy to understand. However, it is written in a style that could be confusing to someone who only reads street Spanish. The style is classical and, for some, extremely confusing."

I rudely butted in. "Can you read it to me?"

"Better yet, if you have about ten or fifteen minutes, I'll write it for you."

I nodded, and he once more disappeared back through the archway.

As I stood there waiting, Tama handed me a glass of another fabulous iced tea.

In almost no time, the doctor reappeared and handed me a typed page. And before I could speak, he asked if he could keep the leather message as part of his historical work. Something, or someone, whispered in my ear to just give it to him. So I replied,

"Dr. Dodd, you are very welcome to it, as I feel it has no bearing on what I am working on and it may prove to be of great value to you."

He nodded and said, "Thank you."

I then, in return, thanked both of them and proceeded out to my truck. I decided I would wait until I had more time to read and digest the translation before I allowed any more information to muddle my brain.

As I drove back to my room, I was so forlorn—I was afraid I would fail and the little girl would die.

Then I saw him. With a crude tool he was working the earth, and I saw green plants behind him that he had just introduced into the ground.

Suddenly I realized: Life comes, fulfills its time, then withers away and dies. During our life we do the best we can, and the only way we survive, even for a short time, is by not ever giving in to the hardships around us. I was going to find the little girl, and if she could be saved, I was going to find a way. And El Buho had many more years of knowledge than I, so how could we fail?

By the time I got back to the lodge, my bravado had cooled, and I was not so sure of my ability to do what had to be done. But one thing that always caused me to be able to see the brighter side was my Sweet Melody. So I promised myself as soon as I returned from the café down the hall, I would hear her voice and see her in my mind before I surrendered to my bed.

The meal was good. And the phone conversation was fantastic. Melody was there for a while, then Teen Angel put in her two or three cents' worth. But the big discussion was about the end of the New York tour in about another week—would my detective work be finished by then? I had to be honest as I told Melody that we had answered some questions, but I didn't see the end of the whole mystery yet. I kept quiet about the little girl, because I really didn't know anything at all about her. And, my love would only worry as she always did when a child was in danger.

I promised love and kisses as soon as we could both be together back home. We both said, "I love you," as we hung up the phones. A quick shower and shave followed, and then it was into the sack.

Chapter 18

After talking to Tama, I began to pay close attention to everything around me. If El Buho needed me to clear up the new mystery, I intended to be prepared. Then it happened. I walked out of the lodge to get the transcription of the old leather message out of the truck's glove compartment, when I saw El Buho circling in the sky above my head. He would make a large circle and then sail off across the open sky until almost out of sight. Then he would return and repeat the same moves.

Then it struck me. My old movie mind flashed a signal, and I remembered the old *Lassie* TV series from my childhood years. Lassie would make the same maneuver when she wanted someone to follow her.

I close the door to my room, took my keys out of my pocket, and climbed in behind the wheel of the Subaru. The moment my tail hit the seat, El Buho almost flew into the windshield. As I started the truck, the Old Spirit moved out in front of me about fifty yards and floated on ahead. When I cleared the parking lot, he sailed on down the street ahead of me.

The Old Owl was easy to follow. He flew fast on the straightaways and slowed at the turns. In a short time I realized we were headed back to Mickey Lopez's rental. I wondered if there was more information that we had overlooked or that the Mouse hadn't volunteered.

But then the Black Owl turned a new corner and, about halfway down the block, settled on a limb of an old tree in front of another low-finance home. That one was a little nicer than Lopez's rental but was still pretty sad.

I stopped in the street and got out of the pickup with the intention of knocking on the door. Then I saw a young man and woman preparing to get into a pretty ragged vehicle. I walked up the short gravel drive to introduce myself but was nicely rebuked by the young man.

"Sir, if you are not here about our daughter, please excuse our rudeness. We are on our way to the hospital in Flagstaff to see our daughter. She's ill there, and we must go now!"

I stated I understood and that what I wanted was of no importance. And if it proved to be, I would try to contact them later.

They quickly jumped into the front seat of the old jalopy and appeared to blast off as gravel flew in all directions.

I looked up into the old tree, and the limb was empty. El Buho was nowhere to be seen. I stood there for a while and simply let my mind wander. I had to believe the little girl in my dream was the same little girl in Flagstaff, but I still did not know more than that.

As I started to return to the truck, a little old lady exited the house next door and waved for me to wait. As she drew near, she began to speak, "Sir, please don't think badly of the Frankens. They are a fine young couple, but they are under so much stress right now, I don't know how they survive."

I had a thousand questions but decided to let her tell her story.

"Their little daughter is in the hospital in Flagstaff and is so very ill. She has a very rare condition that is probably going to prove to be fatal. There is only one hospital in the world that has ever cured a child with what she has, and it's in Zurich, Switzerland. The poor things wouldn't ever be able to raise the money to pay to get her there or pay for her treatment, if they could sell their very lives. I don't have anything to help them either. And I hurt so much for them, I can hardly control myself."

I didn't know what to say, so I just continued to listen.

"Sir, was there something they needed to know? If there is, you could tell me, and I would pass it along to them when they return."

I assured her it was nothing that important, then I lied. "I thought we might be kin, but my genealogy does not have the Franken name in our family tree."

When I told her that, she spoke again. "Sir, perhaps your family tree is connected to the young lady's family line. I believe she once said she was part Native American from close around here. I'm fairly certain she said she was connected to the old Garcia family."

Then as my eyes were drawn above the lady's head, I saw El Buho dive straight toward the ground behind her, and just as his wing tips touched the earth, he sailed straight up until he disappeared from sight.

I thought to myself, *If that was not a signal from the Old Owl Spirit, I will never see one.*

I thanked the old woman for her time and concern for the little girl, and then I said, "I'm still not certain she or he are part of my bloodline, but if I find they might be, I may get back in contact at a less stressful time." Then I expressed my deepest feelings for their little daughter and said I would keep her in my thoughts and prayers.

As I climbed back into the truck, El Buho was circling above me in the clear, cloudless sky.

Chapter 19

As I backed into the Frankens' driveway, then drove out onto the street headed back the way I had come from, El Buho led me off in a different direction. As I followed his lead once more, I was also thinking about the little Franken girl. She had to be the one El Buho was throwing gold coins to in my dream. But, what did it all mean?

After a few blocks of travel, I realized the Old Owl was leading me back toward the two chapels. "Now what?"

After a while, I arrived at the first chapel. El Buho was perched on the chapel's roof, preening his wings. As I dismounted the truck cab, the Spirit disappeared. However, I proceeded inside the small building, thinking perhaps that was where he had gone. And yes, there he was, perched on Hidalgo's burial box. Beside him on the lid was a nut of some type. It was black with age and partially covered with soil. As I started toward him, he dropped from the lid of the box to the rough stone floor. Then I saw him standing over a small hole in the earth between two of the flat stones that formed the floor of the crypt. I continued to watch as he placed one of his talons into the hole and extracted another of the nuts. Then with a pump or two of his powerful wings, he once more was on the lid of Hidalgo's box. Once more he repeated his previous actions, and three nuts now lay on the burial box lid.

Standing on one leg, he picked up one of the nuts in the talon of the other leg and disappeared. As I visually searched the interior of the small chapel, thinking he had simply moved out of my sight, he suddenly reappeared back on the box lid. This time he repeated his actions two more times, then once more disappeared. I waited for a few moments, and he flew by my nose at warp speed and exited the archway to the outside. I rushed to the door and saw him winging his way down the canyon in the direction of the second chapel.

I fairly ran to the truck and also attempted to fly as I followed his lead down the canyon road.

In a few minutes I saw him circling the second chapel, and then he once more disappeared. This time I was sure where I would find him as I rushed into the chapel. And there he was atop Garcia's box, with the three nuts from the other chapel lying next to his feet. As I observed his actions, he carefully picked up one of the nuts in a talon and then dropped to the floor. Watching me to be sure I was watching him, he forced the nut under Garcia's burial box. As I continued to watch, he repeated his actions two more times, and this time he simply faded into nothingness. I waited for several minutes for him to reappear, and then it dawned on me—when he was finished with his work, he usually just faded away.

With curiosity burning from the top of my head to the seat of my britches, I rushed to the burial box, dropped to my knees, and peered under the edge of Garcia's resting place, but there were no nuts to be seen. Then I was really perplexed. What did the whole damned show mean? I got back to my feet, dusted off the knees of my trousers, and slowly sauntered out to the truck, deep in unexplainable thoughts. As I boarded the truck, I decided I had to allow the latest clue to percolate through my brain for a while. But, I also needed to discuss this with someone, and since I hadn't talked to my soon-to-be wife for a day or two, she would be the one. Besides, I could think better after knowing I was loved by someone, and at the same time my subconscious could work as I relieved some stress.

Chapter 20

Though it was still fairly early in the afternoon, I decided to try to phone my Sweet Melody. But with the state I was in, I decided to get back to the room, safely off the road, before I tried to make contact.

After getting back to the room, taking a quick shower, and putting on some lounging duds, I settled back on the bed and punched in my love's number. I thought perhaps she might have finished with the day's tour in New York, as it was at least two hours later in the afternoon there.

I was in luck, as Melody was in her room, relaxing and preparing for the evening meal.

"Hello, love," I said after she answered. "How are things in the Big Apple?"

"About ready to wind down. A couple more days, and the big wheels will start to roll back to Ole Mizzou."

She really enjoyed using the lingo of a young Missouri citizen. Or perhaps Teen Angel was going to also say hello.

But no, it was Melody who continued on the airway. "How close are you to bringing your little case to a close and heading home?"

"Don't know. I thought the damn thing was over a day or two ago. But as I told you, new clues are popping up like mushrooms." Then I mentioned that a little girl was involved, but her story was too much to talk about on the phone. "But, when you get home, I won't be far behind. I have fulfilled my promise, so I can leave anytime I want to."

"No you can't! You are not one who quits in the middle of a detail." And she giggled as she continued, "And I should know!"

"That's the problem—I really need to prove that to you again."

Then Teen Angel got on the phone and replied, "Only Cassy Gray, not a lineman, not a manager, not the coach, not even the president. I only have eyes and goodies for the quarterback. And

233

you better not be looking at other girls either. I'll kick theirs and yours if you do." And then she gave me the raspberries.

Then Melody returned to the phone and asked, "Are there any strange clues that I might be able to help with? You know sometimes I'm good with puzzles."

I knew I couldn't say anything about the Old One, so I cleaned up the story and said, "Strange, I was in an ancient burial chapel, and some nuts—like peanuts—kept moving from one place to another. Some that animals appeared to have buried, and they had been dug up."

"Was there a period of time between when they moved from one place to another?" she asked.

I didn't want to say only a few minutes, so I just said, "Yes."

"Well, there's your answer. Some animal was moving his hoard from one place to another."

"Yes, moving a hoard could be the answer. I'll have to think about that for a while."

Then a jolt hit me like lightning. But I held the thought until I would be off the phone. I thanked Melody for her help with the clue.

After more pleasurable time and words, we went our separate ways, she to finish preparing to depart for dinner to some fancy restaurant with her tour group, and me to my favorite steakhouse.

Melody had given me a big clue, but I was still hungry, so I decided to put the clue on the back burner until after I got fed.

After another fantastic steak from the greatest steakhouse in the canyon, I returned to my room to try to make sense out of all the things I had seen and heard.

Chapter 21

B ack in my favorite thinking position—in bed, lying back on the pillows with my head against the headboard—I began to rethink what facts and clues I had about the rest of the case.

First, Lopez was looking for a treasure. But the treasure wasn't there. Damn, where was the loot?

Then I remembered I had a copy of the map. And my copy was translated perhaps the best way it could be done—by a professional, not a mouse.

I got up from the bed, slipped on my shoes, and went outdoors to the truck to get the translation out of the glove compartment. After retrieving the written page, I kicked off my shoes and regained my position back on the bed. Then I began to try to decipher the translation.

There was a preliminary note signed by Dr. Thomas Dodd: "This is as close to modern English as I can translate." Then his translation appeared as follows:

> "As I serve Lord and King, I fear not death. My doctor advises me I should fear death, as it is upon me. If that is so, I feel it necessary to take precautions. My brothers and my sisters wait with saliva on their lips, anticipating the enjoyment of my wealth. Thank the Lord who is in Heaven, I have a brother who is honorable unto death, though he carries not my life. (Translator's Note: *Life*, as it is used here, has a different meaning than the act of living. It probably means blood, kinship, religious belief, or something else, but not life as we interpret it.) Putting my trust in him, he will guard and protect my transportable wealth

until my son comes of an age to defend it. If, pray God no, I have no living heirs, I will, in defiance of all that is Holy, take my riches with me into eternity.

------> Alejandro Hidalgo <------

(Translator's Note: This was not signed by Hidalgo. The tiny arrows in some old scripts that I have seen mean that the writer is addressing the person named between the arrows.)"

After reading the words, I turned my thoughts to who may have written it. Then I remembered Tama's statement. "Twin friends."

Then if what she'd said was hard truth, the writer would have been Garcia. Brothers, though they did not carry the same blood. Lopez was chasing after the wrong brother. Then another jolt hit me. He had said something to the effect of, "Nothing in the hole, no treasure."

What hole was he talking about? I saw no hole as we explored the chapels. I wondered if he had dug a hole in the pine forest somewhere.

I knew tomorrow I would be heading for the pine forest where he was taken into custody. I checked my watch, and it was not past 10:00, so I decided to ring up Old Krazy and his great camera.

"Hello, damn it. Can't a man watch a screw movie without some SOB calling right during the good part? Who in hell is this?"

"It's me, Krash. Would you like to go treasure hunting tomorrow?"

"That you, Boss?"

I grunted in the affirmative.

"Is there really a treasure? You think we might really find gold bars and skeletons?"

"Well, possibly skeletons and gold and silver coins."

"Millions and millions, you think?"

"I doubt it, but who knows."

"Could we go now?"

"Morning," I answered.

"I'll be ready at daybreak."

"How about 7:30, after we've both had a bite of breakfast?"

"Could I join you for breakfast, say about 6:45?"

"I thought you couldn't eat real food. It will be meat and eggs."

"I'll force myself, 'cause if we have to dig, I'll need all the energy I can get."

"See you at 6:45. And bring your big jewel to take any necessary pictures."

After that sequence, I was ready for bed. Didn't even have enough strength to call my heartthrob.

Chapter 22

It was quite a blast to watch Krash chow down on a straight man's food. At first he snorted a little, then a frown crossed his face as some pork fat crossed his tongue, and then, as he slowly forgot he didn't like regular food, a huge smile settled on his face, staying until he wiped it away with his napkin. As he laid down his fork, he slightly mumbled, "Quite tolerable."

As we finished up our coffee, he once more spoke. "What's the story, Boss?"

So, I told him all I had discovered up to that time, including about the little girl and her illness. As I spoke of her, I'm sure I saw teardrops appear in his eyes, and I heard him snuff his nose.

"Maybe we could help in some way."

I agreed, but then thoughts of treasure blinded our eyes, and we were off to the hunt.

As I climbed into the cab, Krash deposited a long-handled shovel in the pickup bed. Then over his shoulder I glimpsed an old friend, as great black wings spread and pumped and drove a large bird forward.

Krash settled in the seat and fastened his seatbelt as I turned the wheels into the main stream of traffic and headed out of The Village.

When I got to the location were Lopez was taken into custody, I stopped the truck on the side of the blacktop. As I set foot on the ground, I saw El Buho high above me. He was moving off in the distance and then returning, circling and flying away again.

"Back in the truck," I told Krash.

"Why?" he asked.

I pointed skyward and said, "Our guide wants us to go to a different location."

Krash looked up and replied, "It's him, ain't it?"

I nodded as I swung my legs back under the steering wheel. Then, on down the trail we continued. As before, fast on the straightaways and slower turning corners. And again, we were headed toward the chapels.

As we exited the truck at the first chapel, El Buho perched on a larger cactus and simply faded from view. That little act caused me to assume that the chapel was where he wanted us to be. I told Krash to take pictures of anything I thought might be different from what I had observed before during my other visits.

As soon as we reached Hidalgo's burial box, I noticed something different but couldn't place what it was. I mentioned that fact, and Krash backed up to the archway and snapped a shot. Then in the dirt between two of the floor stones, Krash picked up a small silver plate with a hole in each end. Engraved on the plate was the name Freddie.

"I wonder who dropped that?" he said.

"Probably a child visitor at some time or other," I answered.

He stuck the plate in his camera bag and continued to look over the other burial boxes in the chapel.

After a while, boredom began to set in, and I looked outside. The Old Owl was back perched on the cactus where he had perched before.

I told Krash I believed it was time to go.

Back in the truck, we saw El Buho sailing down the canyon toward the other chapel. We obeyed the rules and followed along. Then it was the same old thing—the Old One perched and faded.

And Krash and I did the same old thing—we went into the chapel.

Garcia's box looked the same as when I had left it last time. The nuts, however, were back on the lid in a straight line. Then I got the same feeling that something was different. No, not the nuts reappearing—something else. Then I remembered El Buho had pushed the nuts under Garcia's burial box. And they had vanished. But at the present time, I still could not see under the box, because it was too dark in the chapel.

I told Krash to help me remember, if we came back, to bring a strong flashlight, so we could look under the box. I looked out the arch, and the Old Owl was perched, so it was time to go.

As we got back into the truck to leave, Krash asked me, "Did we learn anything, because we certainly did not find any treasure."

Then I jokingly said, "You found a piece of silver."

"Yeah, but who is Freddie?"

We both giggled as we headed for home and dinner.

Then I added, "We got whatever information El Buho wanted us to get, because he continued to signal his desires until we arrived at the chapel."

Then we saw him for the last time on this trip as he flew across the truck hood, right in front of the windshield, and faded into nothingness.

Chapter 23

Another night passed, and I was at Krash's lab by 8:00 a.m. the next morning. Overnight I had time to think some more about everything I had seen and heard pertaining to the case. For some reason, the words Melody had said in our last phone conversation were finally heard by my thick brain. I remembered that she had said something about animals moving their hoard. Then it dawned on me: Did Garcia move his hoard...of wealth? Maybe Lopez misread the leather message and thought the treasure was in Hidalgo's burial area, but it was not. Could it really have been moved into Garcia's burial area? I say burial areas because Krash and I had not seen any sign of a hole anywhere. And Lopez had said there was nothing in the hole. What hole? And El Buho signaled for us to go there. Then I saw in my mind, the Old Owl moving the nuts from Hidalgo's bone box to Garcia's, then pushing them into a small space under the box. Could there be some way to pry the burial boxes up and then get into a hole under the box? And if the burial boxes are twins, then both of the boxes would have possible movement.

So, that was why I was waiting outside Krash's lab. I was going to review all the chapel pictures in an attempt to discover what was different the last time Krazy and I were there.

I finally decided that if any of what I believed was true, Old Krazy Krash would not be bothered if he was awakened early.

I started to bang on the door of the lab, and as I suspected, loud bitching came rolling out of the open windows. "Damn it, can't a man get a good night's sleep without some ass banging on the door at daylight?"

"Get up, Lazy. There's treasure to be located, and this time we'll hit."

The door popped open, and there was Krash in prison-striped pajamas. "Treasure you say? Are you sure this time? I'll be dressed in a couple of minutes." Krash disappeared, and in five minutes he was back at the door, fully dressed and ready to work.

I explained that we needed to compare the two groups of chapel photos to see if there were any noticeable differences. And I believed there were, and the differences would solve the mystery.

Krash quickly fired up his computer and downloaded all the pictures from both trips to the burial chapels. I didn't understand how he did it, but he put the photo groups from each chapel side by side on the huge screen. He said that way we would see the differences more easily.

He took the keyboard seat, and I slid in next to him. And away we flew.

As I was watching the stone floor for any evidence of digging, he noticed something very quickly. "Hey Boss, grab a gander at the two pictures of Hidalgo's and Garcia's burial boxes."

I looked, but I didn't see anything except the beautiful carvings of birds, animals, and plants. The handwork reminded me of pictures I had seen of stonework from the ancient Romans and Greeks.

Then he pointed and said, "Boss, I took both of these pictures from the arch entrances, but they're not the same views."

Then, as I concentrated on the carvings on the sides of the boxes and the names on the lids, I saw one box was turned one quarter out of synch with the other. "Damn, Krash, they must turn, slide, or swing above the floor stones. And I'll bet there is a hole or passage under the burial boxes."

"But why are they out of synch?" Krash asked.

"There must be some simple mechanism that allows the boxes to move. And when Lopez found the hole empty and returned the box to its original position, the mechanism fouled up and allowed the box to misplace itself one quarter turn out of synch."

"Hey Boss, let's go now and see if we can find a treasure!" Krash almost screamed.

I agreed, so as soon as we could gather Krash's equipment, plus a big flashlight, we were in the truck and on our way.

Chapter 24

We knew where we were going, and the Big Bird was not guiding. We arrived at the first chapel in a very short time. Krash was like a little kid. He jumped out of the truck, grabbed a shovel and the flashlight, and bounded toward the chapel's archway. I noticed his camera bag was still in the truck seat. So I picked it up and followed him into the burial chapel.

When my eyes became accustomed to the dim light, I saw Krash carefully digging between the floor stones at one side of Hidalgo's box. I picked up the flashlight from the spot where Krash had dropped it and proceeded around to the other corner of the box. Dropping to my knees, I flashed the light under the corner of the box and saw a thin piece of rusty metal in a small gap. After a careful visual examination, assuring myself there were no animals or snakes, I stuck my finger into the gap and tried to move the rusty chunk. For my efforts I heard the grind of metal on metal, and the box began to slide a short distance off center of its original position.

Seeing the box move a little, Krash let out a squall and dove to the floor beside me. "Gee hosses! Boss, you've found it!"

I pushed the rusty piece of metal once more, and we heard the grinding again. But it only lasted a few seconds as the box moved a little more.

"Krash, I'm afraid the mechanism is partially jammed or broken. If I keep working the lever, it may break, and then we would have to destroy the burial box, and I don't want to do that."

"Maybe if I helped it move while you work the lever, we could take the strain off the mechanism."

"Okay, but only once more. If it doesn't work, we give up, because Lopez said this hole was empty."

I pushed the rusty part once more as Krash pushed the heavy stone box in the direction it had started to move. With a constant grind and Krash's shoulder work, the mechanism continued to move the box. When I saw a square hole start to appear as the box moved, I held my breath. When half the hole was visible, I released pressure on the rusty lever, and the box ceased to move.

As I stood up and moved toward the hole, Krash caught his breath and joined me at the cavity. With the light shining, we both peered down into the tiny opening below us.

There we beheld...NOTHING! The hollow area was empty except for dust, dirt, and a few small bones. After a long moment of disappointment, I flashed the light to the side and saw why the mechanism did not work correctly. A small rock was lodged between two rusty iron levers supporting a heavier iron gear. With the shovel, I gently pushed the rock from where it had been wedged.

With a questioning look on his face, Krash continued to stare into the dark recess in the floor. And then he spoke, "Boss? Do you suppose the other old guy's box works just like this one?"

"Old Buddy, I don't know, but the burials were purported to be of twin friends. So if that's the case, there's only one way to find out."

"Let's go, Boss, I'm about to wet my britches."

"Okay, but let's try to get this box back over the hole before anyone sees how it works."

"Okay, I'll push, and you work the mechanism," Krash answered.

I got to the lever before Krash could put his shoulder against the box. I touched the rusty metal, and the grinding began to start, and it did not stop until the box was back into its original position—the position it had been in before Lopez found it. It was once more a perfect twin to Garcia's box in the other chapel.

And speaking of chapels, I'm not sure Krash did not run into the next chapel on foot. No matter, he was so excited that he was at the lever under Garcia's burial box almost before I could get out of the truck. But, no matter how excited Krash was, he remained the perfect professional. He had taken pictures of every phase of our discovery and of how the box operated. Later, he told me he would prepare the pictures in such a way that, if and when they were published, no one would know where the hole was or how the old mechanism operated.

Chapter 25

As I entered the archway of the second chapel, I heard the familiar grind of old rusty levers and gears as the heavy burial box made its slow move from over the opening in the stone floor. Old Krazy had tripped the hidden lever, and the ancient mechanism was doing its work.

Even before the hole was completely exposed, an aura of reflected light escaped from the dark hollow below the stone floor.

I saw that Krash's mouth was hanging open, and he had a look of total astonishment on his face. As I shined the light into the opening, the glow of gold and silver was reflected back into my eyes. I saw piles of coins that had leaked from rotted bags. There were gold and silver service pieces, plates, goblets, knives, and forks. In a partially rotten box, beautiful pieces of jewelry rested. Some of the finer items contained large pieces of fine stones. I was fairly certain I was looking at diamonds, rubies, and emeralds. And to finish the collection, there were a number of jewel-encrusted blades with their sheaths of rotted leather hanging in shreds from them. I looked at Krash once more, and saliva was foaming from his mouth.

As I watched, Old Krazy knelt at the edge of the cavity and reached to touch one of the pieces of the treasure. An odd look of puzzlement replaced the one of amazement that I had just seen displayed on his face. He raised his head and looked up at me. "Boss, something will not allow me to touch any of the stuff in the hole."

"Oh, come on Krash, you're just experiencing buck fever. Let me show you a piece or two."

I dropped to my knees and reached to put my hand on one of the goblets. But my hand could not touch the beautiful golden drinking utensil.

Then I saw a dark shadow block some of the sunlight coming through the archway. As I turned and looked toward the archway, fear replaced every other emotion my mind could experience.

In the archway opening stood a man of medium height. He was old, lean, and muscular. The only clothing he wore was a dingy loincloth with some black marks making a design. Then I remembered the design. It was two inverted V's connected at the ends. Along the insides of the outer slanted lines of the V's were two perfect circles. The design depicted the sign of the owl—two ears and two eyes. The one who hears and watches. And perched on the old man's left shoulder was a large black owl. From long-dead human lips, I heard the Spanish words, "Ayude a mi niña."

From my college Spanish, I thought he was saying, "You'd better take care of my girl."

Then I heard Krash emit a moan and the words, "Precious God!" as he began to shake.

I decided I had to do something, so I spoke directly to the Old Spirit. "Miguel. What do you want of us?"

The large black owl pumped his wings and rose into the brilliant sky as the Old One faded from view. I hurried to the archway and looked up into the heavens. There, circling above, was El Buho signaling to be followed.

As I turned to look for Krash, Garcia's burial box was closing over the hidden chamber, and Krash was scratching his head. "Boss? Did I just experience a bad dream?"

"If you did, I had the same damn nightmare."

I moved to Krash's side and assisted him up from his knees as I spoke in a hurried manner. "Quick man, we need to follow the Old Owl."

"Hey Boss. Why don't we try to open the treasure vault again, right now?"

"No, Old Buddy. El Buho has sealed the vault and perhaps moved the treasure. We must do his bidding right now, or I'm afraid the treasure will disappear forever!"

Chapter 26

As quickly as we could, Krash and I scrambled into the truck. I looked up through the windshield, and El Buho was sailing toward the mouth of the canyon and out along the main blacktop.

In a super short time, the Big Black Owl led us to the Franken residence. The old, beat up excuse for an automobile was parked in the yard. El Buho was perched in the same spot he had occupied the last time he had led me there.

This time I pulled into the gravel drive and parked beside the old clunker. As I stepped down from the truck cab, I looked at El Buho; his face had assumed the features of the Old One. Not knowing what was to happen next, I silently said, *Miguel, guide my words, as I want to do what you wish.*

Immediately I felt words taking form in my throat. I turned toward the side door of the house, and young Franken stepped out into the sunlight.

"Mr. Franken, I heard from your neighbor that you have a very sick child. And I have been sent by a benefactor to tell you that help is coming quickly."

I didn't know where the words I had just spoken came from, but I knew I was meant to continue. But, before I could, Mr. Franken spoke as tears ran down his cheeks. "Yes, our little Freddie is so ill, and there's nothing we can do."

"Mr. Franken, how quickly could you have the hospital in Flagstaff prepare your daughter for a flight to Zurich?"

"Sir, we don't have the money to send her to Switzerland, or any to pay for treatment. And how do you know about Zurich?"

What I said next sounded almost brusque, but I was saying exactly what was coming into my mind. And I still saw El Buho on the tree limb. "Don't waste time with a lot of questions. Can you call the hospital and tell them to prepare your child to make the flight to Switzerland?"

"But who's going to pay for all of that?" Franken begged.

Suddenly Krash rolled out of the truck and said, "Tell them Josiah Jackson Krash. Tell the hospital in Flagstaff to contact my bank—Centennial Trust—in Denver, Colorado, and I will make arrangements for whatever is necessary. And Mr. Franken, did you say your daughter's name is Freddie?"

"Her name is Fredonia. We call her Freddie for short. She was named after an ancestral grandma."

"Well, I believe I know more about that, but we can discuss the subject later. You need to move fast to get the young lady overseas for treatment. And by the way, you and your wife will be going along, so get packed. And I will see that you have an ATM card for $15,000 to be used for all your personal expenses. The card will be delivered to you at the airport."

After I listened to Krash's presentation, I looked past him, and the Old Owl was preening his wings as he continued to rest comfortably on the limb of the tree.

I supposed Mrs. Franken must have heard most of the past exchange, as she stepped out the door, rushed to her husband, and asked, "Who are these people? And why are they doing this for us?"

Once more Krash took the lead. "We are messengers from some of your relatives who wish to see your daughter, their kin, healthy and a blessing to the family."

This time I saw El Buho spread his wings and flap them as if applauding Krash's speech.

Then Krash asked Franken if he had a cell phone. When he answered yes, Krash entered Franken's number into his own phone and told the young man he would keep in constant contact until the family was on the plane. And he also gave the young father his number, so he could be called if they needed more help.

Then Mrs. Franken asked what family members had any concern for her family. Then it was my turn to supply an answer. "It is a branch, I believe, of your side of the family. They claim to be distant relatives of one of your past grandmothers. Her name was connected to the Garcia family."

"Oh, that would be my great-grandmother's family. That is my Garcia connection. But, she was poorer than us. Where does any money come from?"

"As I understand, it was from a far, far distant relative who was very, very wealthy." The Old Owl shot straight up into the open air and actually did a barrel roll, far above our heads. I wasn't even sure the Frankens could see him.

Krash once more admonished them to hurry, as he had called a transportation company to send a car to deliver them to the hospital in Flagstaff.

Then we bid them both goodbye as we got into the truck. As we traveled back to The Village, I asked Krash why he had jumped up and volunteered to cover the cost of the child's care. He said, "It was as if I wasn't talking—a voice in my head told me what to say, and then it said I would be rewarded handsomely for my help. And, did you hear Franken say that they called her Freddie? That little silver trinket I found at the burial chapel was either hers or her ancestor's."

Then I told Krash that we needed to go past the ranger station and talk to Chief Gray Fox. He asked what about. I answered I didn't know, but we would be told when we got there. Then both of us saw the Black Owl flying just ahead of the windshield, and Krash said, "I believe both of us are under the influence of the old man or that majestic bird."

Chapter 27

When we drove into the ranger station parking lot, the chief ranger's SUV was parked in his restricted space. I was sure he would be there because a certain Spirit would have whispered in his ear to remain. I remembered Tama telling me, two years before, that he had the power to assign tasks to people, and they would carry them out. He had reached Krash and me, so I was sure he could affect the chief's actions also.

As we walked in the door, the chief was standing at the front desk. "I've been expecting you," he said.

"Why?" I asked.

"No real reason. I just thought you might stop by."

When he said those words, I felt a chill.

"Oh yes, and the head of the tribal council dropped by also, and is still here. He said he had never met you but really wanted to."

Then I felt words building up in my throat, so I opened my mouth and allowed them to start escaping. "I would like to meet with you and the council head, officially, right now, if that would be possible."

"You're wanting to go home, aren't you? We got the Lopez thing out of our hair, and now you want to get home to that little tour guide."

"That would be great, but I have other things to talk about that would probably be of more interest to you and the council head."

By that time we had gotten into the chief's office, and I was introduced to the council head. After the introduction, the chief asked, "Now, oh Great White Seer," and he grinned as he said it, "what could two old red men help you with?"

"Chief, what I am about to tell you will sound extremely unbelievable. Krash and I have located a vast treasure of gold and silver!"

"Grand, now get on with the rest of the joke."

"Not joking, Chief. Honest Injuns!"

"What the hell are you trying to say, Gray?"

"We found a vast hoard of gold and silver," I repeated.

"You're telling the truth, aren't you? Hell yes, you are!"

"But so what? What does that have to do with me and the council? Can't you just take it and enjoy yourself?"

"No, because it is on canyon and council land."

"And it would never be yours, because it belongs to us."

"Exactly, but there is another problem. It may belong to one of your tribal members. But by the time the courts can decide if that's true, the whole hoard will be lost through court costs. So, I have a proposal. There is a little girl who may be one of the heirs to the treasure. But right now she is being prepared to be sent to a hospital in Switzerland for treatment, because she is very ill. To get her there and have her treated, Krash has put up his own money to pay her and her parents' expenses. If the little girl had the treasure, legally, she could pay her own way. But that's the catch-22. She would also lose so much to the court and take up a great deal of time, which she doesn't have, without treatment. So, here is my proposal: If the Grand Canyon and the council would reimburse Krash and pay for the little girl's medical bills, Krash and I will lead you to the treasure, and it would belong to the canyon and the council, because no one else knows all the hitches and angles. And it is on Grand Canyon land, so it really should belong to the canyon and her museum."

"How much do you think this so-called treasure is worth, Gray?" the council head asked.

"I really don't know, but it is in a container about three-foot square, and the container is level full. The treasure consists of Spanish coins, gold and silver, that are over three hundred years old; a gold table service, probably religious in nature; gold and silver jewelry, some with large precious stones; and a few edged weapons with jewel-encrusted hilts."

"Can we look at the treasure before we say yes or no?"

I started to say we would have to go to the location of the treasure, but Krash said, "Boss, I've got beautiful pictures in my camera." Krash then showed pictures of everything in the hole but did not show them where or how the hoard was stored.

After only a few moments of seeing the beauty of the gold and silver artifacts in the photos Krash displayed, the council head said, "We'll take the deal. Now when can we see and collect the treasure?"

I looked at my watch and said, "It is extremely late, so why not early in the morning?"

"Will the treasure be safe to be left out tonight? What's to keep you two from raiding the site tonight and leaving the canyon and council out in the cold?"

All I could say was that Krash and I were the only ones who knew where the treasure was. And if we had wanted to steal it, we would have never told them about it. But deep in my mind, I knew there was another reason: Only those chosen by El Buho Viejo could ever even touch the treasure. So then I suggested, "Why don't we meet you here at 7:00 in the morning, and the four of us will go and get the treasure. No one else will know what we are about, so that will keep us safe."

After a handshake all around, Krash and I headed back to The Village. Once we were in the truck, Krash asked, "How can we take them to the chapels and let them see how the treasure is hidden? Everyone in the country will lay claim to it if they have any connection to any of the burials in the chapel."

I answered, "El Buho will take care of that. His power is far above anything you and I could conceive of, so he will solve that problem. Remember, he caused us to form a plan to save the little Franken girl."

"I guess you're right. We will just have to wait and see how he handles the whole thing."

With that thought, we parted company—he to his lab and me to an evening meal, a shave and shower, and then an evening call to Sweet Melody. I thought I could tell her that my days out here were finally numbered and I would soon be headed home.

Chapter 28

Because of the realities that the Lopez case was closed, the treasure was found, the Franken child would be receiving treatment, and I might be going home, I was not able to sleep much. So at about 5:30, I rolled out of bed and hit the floor.

But when I opened the door to my lodge room at about 6:10, Krash was sitting right out front, on the curb.

"Where you been, Boss? I've been out here all night!"

Then I knew he was more excited than I.

Without a reply to his remark, I asked, "How about another one of those poison breakfasts that ruin your gut?"

He grinned and said, "As long as you're paying for it."

As we ate, Krazy once more said, "We can't take those two to the chapel; those poor dead will never again be allowed to rest in peace."

And my reply was the same. "The Old One will make everything work out."

When we finished the fiendish food, we gathered the supplies I thought we would need and placed them in the truck. Finally we mounted and drove to the ranger station to meet Big Red and the head councilor.

If Krash and I were excited, then the chief and the head man were ecstatic. Also, they were not only unsteady, they displayed signs of perhaps being inebriated. Then I saw the reason—on the back of each of their shirts was a small black stain in the shape of an owl feather.

Then I noticed Krash had one on his back also. That fact caused me to become very curious. But I believed what I had told Krash, so I decided to allow El Buho to have his way, and not question how.

Though they appeared to be a little drunk, all three carried out their part of the labor without incident. We loaded the equipment into the black GMC carryall that the two Native men had chosen to haul out the treasure. I had brought three large plastic tote boxes and a small blue tarp that would cover all three boxes. We could pack the treasure in the three boxes and cover them all with the tarp. No one would see what we were moving into the Canyon Museum.

It was decided I would drive and Krash would accompany me in the front seat. The ranger and the councilor would occupy the second bench seat and be able to look out the side windows. The rest of the paneled area in the carryall had no windows. Again, no one could see what we were hauling. The only thing that worried me was, if someone saw a big carryall parked at the small chapel, they might remember seeing it on a certain day at a certain time. But then I once more remembered—El Buho.

In a short time, I turned off the main blacktop and proceeded down the canyon to the second little chapel. As the other three were carrying on an animated conversation, I backed the carryall up in front of the archway entrance to the chapel.

As I slid out the door from the driver's seat, I picked up a strange piece of conversation from the other three. I heard Chief Gray Fox say, "I should have guessed. The area of the canyon where we nabbed Lopez. I suppose the treasure is hidden somewhere back in the pines."

Then the plot hit me. El Buho was taking the other three on a virtual treasure hunt. Then I heard Krash chime in with, "Right back there in the brush under a big flat rock. Come on, I'll show you." And then he headed toward Garcia's burial box, just a few feet in front of them.

After a step or two, I heard the head man say, "How far back in this mess of pines is it hidden? My legs are getting tired."

Then Krash answered, "Oh, fifty or sixty more yards. Yeah, there it is just ahead, under that big flat rock."

I stood and watched as the trio went a couple more steps and stopped at Garcia's box.

Krash reached down and tripped the lever, and I heard the grinding of the gears and him saying, "Put your shoulders and legs into it as we push the stone back."

Then I almost laughed as all three bent over and struggled to push the air from in front of themselves. And I even saw sweat pop out on all their foreheads. Then the box ceased to move, and the treasure lay shining in the subdued light.

"Hurry, hurry, hurry—bring a box, Gray!"

I heard all of them yell in unison.

As I turned to get one of the tote boxes, my eyes did a double take. There in front of me was not a GMC carryall but a beat-up old black pickup with one gray fender. So...if anyone saw us there, they would say some poor farmer had just stopped to picnic or rest.

In a few seconds I was at the burial box, and then the gathering of riches began.

After what seemed like a long time, but was probably only a few minutes, the treasure was all in the boxes, the boxes were in the carryall, and the four caballeros were about to ride off with the evil don's riches. But, to be honest, I was beginning to wonder if Garcia had been an evil don.

Then I heard the grinding of the gears as the rusty mechanism began to return the burial box to its original position, and the heavy breathing of the bewitched three as they thought themselves to be pushing the flat stone back over the hole.

As I drove back to The Village and the Canyon Museum, my three companions began to appear more and more sober and alert. But, as they talked of the treasure, they were convinced it had been hidden in the small pine forest under a large flat rock.

As the other three talked and dreamed of the treasure, I contemplated...the eternal peace of the innocent souls in the little chapel would probably never, ever be disturbed again.

Unless...a rodent buries his bounty under one of their burial boxes.

Then we arrived at the Canyon Museum.

Chapter 29

As I backed the carryall up to the loading dock at the rear of the museum, we were met by a welcoming committee. The chief said it was the curator of the museum and the rest of the council.

As I got out of the vehicle, a lady in the group rushed up to me and introduced herself. "Mr. Gray, I'm Dr. Deborah Dill, curator of the Canyon Museum. And I want to personally thank you for the recovery of such a rare treasure."

She extended a gloved hand, and we shook hands as Krash and the others proceeded to move the somewhat heavy boxes out of the vehicle and into the museum's supply area. The curator and the rest of the group closed in around them. Since the tarp had already been removed, they began to ooh and ah about the beautiful metal objects they beheld before their eyes.

I saw the chief move close to the curator and carry on what looked like a serious conversation, while the rest of us removed the items from the boxes and arranged them on three different tables in their various groups. Coins were placed on one table, fine serving pieces on a second table, and the jewelry on a third table. The small number of jewel-encrusted blades were placed with the serving pieces.

When everyone was satiated after visually devouring all the gold and silver items, the curator called Krash and me to the coin table.

"Gentlemen, it has been brought to my attention that the two of you are the ones most responsible for the Canyon Museum receiving these fine artifacts. Being that the museum will never be able to display all these coins, and that some of them will, no doubt, be sold, the council feels it is appropriate to reward each of you with five of the lesser gold 'pieces of eight.'"

As I saw anticipation rise in Krash's eyes, I hurriedly spoke. "Madam Curator and council, it would be in very poor taste for Mr. Krash and me to accept any payment, in any form, for placing these fine artifacts in your museum. When Mr. Krash is reimbursed for the expenses he volunteered to the Franken family enabling them to have their little daughter treated for her illness, we feel that will be payment enough."

And I was a little surprised, but Krash nodded his head in agreement.

And, at that moment, on the far wall of the museum, I saw the shadow of a large bird with its wings spread.

After my declaration, the chief and the members of the council gave Krash and me a round of applause.

With that, the meeting began to come to a close, as some of the dignitaries started walking toward the exit and others quietly conversed among themselves.

I caught the chief just as he reached the door. "Hey, Old Red Man. Have the Frankens gotten on their way across the big water?"

"This morning, if there was no hitch in the airline. They should be almost into Switzerland by now."

"How about this murder case—do you believe it's about solved?"

"Yes, and very satisfyingly, I would say! And yes, you can go back home to that little tour guide of yours. And if I am counting right, you both should get back home to Missouri about the same time."

I shook his hand and said, "I may or may not see you again before I fly out. So take care of things until we meet again."

And then Chief Ranger Christjohn Gray Fox fairly howled as he laughingly said, "I hope not!"

And both of us were laughing as Krash and I exited the Canyon Museum and headed for the truck. I drove Krash back to his lab and told him how much fun it had been working with him once more. After I said that to him, he asked a favor.

"Boss, if you really did enjoy me working with you, should you become involved in any more problems, please let me know, and I'll come to try to help."

As we shook hands, he spoke again. "Boss, if you don't fly out before breakfast in the morning, let me treat you to one of those damn poison breakfasts. Even though it causes me to break out in hives, that stuff is damn good going down my throat."

I agreed to his proposal and told him that if my plane didn't leave until later, I would give him a call.

As I drove out of the parking lot, I saw Krash waving in the rearview mirror. And I thought, *A man could have a hell of a lot worse friend than Krazy Josiah Jackson Krash...Krash the Fantastic!*

Chapter 30

As soon as I got to my room, I called the little Grand Canyon local airport to inquire about making reservations going east to Missouri the next day. I was informed that the first flight going out of Tusayan would be at 10:00 in the morning, and it would go to Denver and then to Kansas City.

I asked, "If I take that flight, how soon will I arrive in Kansas City?"

The young lady answered, "Arrival time in Kansas City would be at 7:00 p.m."

I didn't even give it more thought; I told her I would take the reservation. I gave her my credit card number, and she informed me of the total amount of the fare. As I broke the connection, I thought, *A good time will be had by all.* Then I called Krash and told him I was on for breakfast. He said he would meet me in the breakfast room at seven. I told him I would be there. Goodbyes were said, and I once again broke the connection.

The next thing I did was pack my baggage and check with the desk to see if I had any outstanding charges. They informed me that all the bills, including incidentals, were covered by the chief of the canyon rangers.

With everything else taken care of, there was only one more chore on my list. And that little job would not be a chore, but a real pleasure. I punched in Melody's number as I sat back against the bed's headboard. About three rings later, I heard the voice of an Angel.

"Where are you? I got home last night, and you weren't waiting for me. When are you getting home?"

I started to make a joke, but I thought better of it and replied, "If everything goes correctly, I'll be in Kansas City tomorrow evening at 7:00."

"Do you want me to pick you up?"

"That would be great. Then we can spend the night at the airport hotel and drive home the next morning. And I think the hotel room is complimentary, since I am getting in that late."

"What will I need to pack for my stay in the hotel?" she asked.

"Don't pack anything or wear anything, because I have great plans," I joked.

Then Teen Angel came on the phone and said, "Where would I carry my cell phone, if I followed those instructions?"

Still feeding on the joke, I answered, "Why not just carry a large shoulder bag and wear a string of pearls?"

Then I heard fake crying as she sobbed, "I don't have a string of pearls." And before I could carry on, she continued, "And, don't you dare buy me a string of pearls. No one wears pearls anymore."

Then I broke the line of joking as I said, "Wear whatever you want and pack whatever. You're all I really want to look at and enjoy anyway."

Then Teen Angel carried the joke one more level. "Cassy? Do you want me tomorrow night, or do you want the old broad?"

Then I knew I couldn't pass up the final punch line, as I challenged, "Why don't you both come up to KC, both go to the hotel with me, each of you do a strip show, and I'll decide then."

Then with a joyous sound in her voice, Melody accused, "I always thought you were a pervert, and now you are making a move on a teenager. So I will be there, for sure, to defend against you hurting the poor wittle guoil."

I finally said, "I'll see you at 7:00, because for tonight I've had all the fun I can stand. Kisses!"

Chapter 31

When my little traveler's alarm sounded, I left my bed immediately. Today was the big day, and tonight was a fabulous dream. Two weeks away from Sweet Melody was about my limit. Actually it was sixteen days, and I was ready for love.

I quickly shaved, showered, and dressed, preparing for breakfast with Krash. Before I left the room, I made sure everything was ready for me to catch my flight. I had not made arrangements for a shuttle to the airport, but the last time I just left Gray Fox's old truck at the airport, and the rangers picked it up there. I supposed the rental would work the same way. But to be on the safe side, I called the Fox and asked. He replied that the truck was rented at the airport, and I could just turn it in there. We said farewell, and I moved on down the hall to meet Krash in the breakfast room.

Before I walked into the dining area, I looked at my watch. The time was about five minutes before seven, so I got a cup of coffee, found a seat facing the door, and sat down to wait.

In a few minutes it walked into the room. There was Krash wearing fancy soft-leather shoes, the dressy expensive type. I thought them to be of a British style. He was also wearing a fancy white dress shirt stuffed into a pair of slim-fit trousers, covered by a long dark duster. On his head was a hat with a long bill on both the back and the front. And to complete the costume, he was holding between his teeth a short-stemmed, curved pipe with a large bowl. I almost yelled, "Heigh-ho, Sherlock, where's Watson?"

But then I saw the seriousness in Krash's face, and I decided to hear what game was afoot. I finally caught his eye, and he came over to the table and seated himself.

"Boss, after helping you on two cases, I've just about decided to take up this detective business full time. I think I have a natural instinct for doing the right thing at the right time, being in the right place at the right time, and letting my visual acuity lead me when the situation is shrouded in total darkness. What did Poirot, or Spade, or even Holmes have over yours truly—the Incredible Krash?"

I looked him straight in the eye and replied, "Sit down and eat; this meal is on you." And then I went to the breakfast bar and commenced to fill my plate, because my plane was leaving in a couple of hours and Sweet Melody was waiting.

When we had eaten our fill, I looked Krash in the eye again and said, "You are one hell of a photographer, you do have a lot of natural instinct, and you can get the job done. But, why do you want to be a detective? You appear to be wealthy, so you don't have to work. Why be a detective?" I repeated.

His answer almost made me cry. "Boss, I'm big and awkward, people believe I'm dumb and crazy, but all I want to do is live every moment of my life to the fullest and with the greatest excitement."

Then I saw myself reflected in him, because all I wanted to do was live my life to the fullest also. "Krash, old buddy, all I can say is, if I find myself involved in any more mysteries, I'll call you before I start any investigation, because we make one hell of a team."

As we walked out of the dining area, he turned, shook my hand, and said, "I'm glad my best friend is you."

As I walked away, though I didn't say it, I felt he was my best male friend also.

When I got back to my room, my watch said it was 8:30, so I picked up my bags, left the room, and turned in the key. After I threw my baggage in the bed of the truck, I once more climbed in behind the wheel and headed for the airport.

I checked in the truck at the rental agency and walked across the street to the terminal. I verified my reservation and then quietly sat and thought as I waited for the boarding time. My thoughts were of Melody, Krash, the little Franken girl, and Gray Fox and his family. For a few moments I even thought of Lopez and wondered who he really was. And then for another moment I felt a little sorry for the man.

Finally, the lady at the boarding desk announced the flight for Denver, and I moved out to the tarmac, up the ramp, and into my seat. Denver was just an hour or so away.

After a lengthy layover in Denver, it was onto the plane to Kansas City at about 5:00 p.m. The last couple of hours were the longest, but we finally reached KC International at 7:00 p.m.

As the wheels thumped onto the runway, I was already looking for Melody, even though I was still strapped in my seat. When the seat belt light went out, I rushed as fast as I could to exit the plane. I'm sure I was probably worse than rude as I pushed my way past people to get into the terminal.

The way KCI is set up, I knew Melody would be waiting at the baggage claim carousel.

When I got to the baggage area, I began to scan the crowd, looking for Melody. It was a madhouse of activity, as all the incoming passengers were packed in, jockeying for a position to grab their bags from the carousel. I almost cried as I continued to look for Melody. Outside the crowd, there were very few people present in that area. But as I watched for my bag, I was also looking in all directions in hopes of seeing the woman I loved.

Out of the corner of my eye, I caught a glimpse of a young lady coming out of the ladies' room. I judged her to be about seventeen. She was dressed in a short skirt, a red pullover sweater, knee-length boots, and black designer pantyhose. Her hips were swinging as she continued toward the crowd. And she had a four-inch bubblegum bubble out of her mouth, covering most of her face. Just as she neared me the bubble popped, and I heard, loud enough for everyone to hear: "Hey Mister. Are you looking for a hot date tonight here in KC? My momma thinks I'm at a sleepover, so I got the whole night."

As the entire crowd turned and gawked in my direction, and as I looked for a place to hide, Melody began to laugh as she waved at the crowd and exclaimed, "It's okay, folks—he's my husband returning from a rough business trip in Arizona. And I thought I would give him a little welcome home."

Then she was in my arms, and I thought she was going to smother me. When I was able to break free, I recovered my bag, and we headed for the exit. Behind us I heard loud whistling and applause. As we walked out of the terminal, Melody was gripping my arm when she looked into my face and said, "Teen Angel is a hot little bitch, isn't she?"

I grinned back at her and replied, "Almost as hot as her big sister!"

And then we arrived at the car in the parking lot.

Chapter 32

As I drove to the hotel, Melody was close, and I could hardly breathe. She was talking, but I heard very little of what she said. I hoped it wasn't important, because all I could do was think and dream. Her short skirt bothered me, and her scent was all through my brain. Finally she squeezed my leg and said, "You haven't heard a word I've been saying. I may as well wait until you're satisfied before I try to tell you anything."

She was smiling as she said it, so I didn't think it made her mad or unhappy.

When we arrived at the hotel, and she had my attention for a moment, she once more began to tell me what she was saying in the car.

"I arrived early, so I have already moved into our room. I also ordered room service for 8:30, because I figured you would probably not want to go back out to eat. This way we can play the games any way you like."

I looked at my watch, and it was 7:40. So I suggested, "Why don't we bathe, get into something comfy, and then eat. After that we will not have to worry about being disturbed unless we want to."

"And if we get bored waiting for the food, we can always make up your old man's truck—like we did the last time you were at the canyon—and neck."

"And maybe, a little later, neck in the nude!" I laughed.

We raced to see who could get undressed the quickest. I lost because I did more watching than I did undressing. I knew her age, but she still could play Teen Angel, and I wouldn't be able to tell the difference in their ages. God, how I loved that woman!

We didn't get to neck before dinner, because at almost the moment we got out of the shower and slipped into something comfortable, the food arrived at the door. I had to answer the call, because I was dressed in one of the hotel's bathrobes, while Melody was wearing something dark and transparent. I thought she could have just as well remained undressed. She stayed in the bathroom as I greeted the bellhop.

After he had arranged the food, I gave him a couple of dollars, and he went merrily on his way.

The food was typical hotel cuisine—pricey with just a little taste. But for us, it was filling. And I had more important things on my mind.

Melody finished eating first and disappeared back into the bathroom. I finished eating, gathered the remains, and pushed the food cart out into the hall.

When I finished closing the door, my Sweet Melody came out of the bathroom, wearing...absolutely nothing! She walked to the bed, threw back the coverlets, and made herself comfortable on a pile of pillows. I hit the light switch, dropped my robe, and joined her in the soft surroundings. Over the last two or so years we had become totally acquainted, and our love was able to blot out all the worries of the world, as our love was much more important.

I saw that the lighted clock on the TV showed 2:00 as I closed my eyes and slipped away into that other world of thoughts of pleasure and dreams.

It was past 10:00 before I awakened, and Melody was in the bathroom. I didn't know how long she had been up. Perhaps her getting out of bed was what woke me.

In a few more minutes she walked out of the bath and ran her fingers down my breastbone as I walked by her and into the bathroom. After a shower and other activities, I joined Melody back in the main room. She was dressed and had both our carry-on bags packed. I threw the towel I had wrapped myself in back into the bathroom and quickly dressed. By about 11:00, we were ready to head for Jefferson City. As she lightly kissed my cheek, she said, "We can stop in Columbia about 1:00 or 2:00 and eat breakfast or lunch there."

I agreed, so we got things loaded and moved out onto the highway. Melody sat close beside me, so the road trip was extremely enjoyable. Much more so than with Krash in the seat next to me.

Chapter 33

A little before 2:00 p.m. we arrived in Columbia. By starting home without breakfast, I was beginning to feel the bite of hunger. Melody had been nibbling on some dried fruit she always carried in her car, so she was not as famished as I felt.

I had been to Collier's Steak House a couple of times in the past two years, so I headed off Interstate 70 toward their parking lot on the business loop.

Steak and taters is old country fare, but it sure tastes good when you feel starved. And right then I was beginning to desire two things. First, to be fed, and then to have Melody spend the night with me at the old home place.

After we consumed my steak and her shrimp salad, we headed into the last thirty miles to the City of Jefferson. At 3:30 we drove up to the plateau and home. Melody, when we left Columbia, had volunteered that she wanted to spend the night at my house. It being Saturday, she could get everything straightened out on Sunday and then go back to work on Monday. And I heard her, in no more than a whisper, say, "And we can have one more night to party."

We each had a bowl of canned soup and toast as we watched some TV until about 9:00. Then she asked, with a silly grin on her face, "Do you want me to join you or take the guest room?"

Then she ran as fast as she could down the short hall and disappeared into the master bedroom. I began to kick off my shoes and remove my clothing as I followed her down the hall. It was already dark in the room as I entered the door. I turned off the hall light, and the entire house was dark. Feeling my way to the bed, I slid in under the top sheet and was immediately waylaid in the darkness. But if I had to face a surprise attack, that would be my choice of warfare. After a brutal lip battle, I surrendered to death by sex. Though I did not face execution, I was held prisoner for the next twelve hours. Then, when I regained consciousness, I was forced to eat my last meal before being released. Now even old Krash would agree that bacon, eggs, hash browns, toast, and coffee was not a bad last meal.

Melody and I enjoyed each other's company for the rest of the day, and then she returned to her house to prepare for work on Monday. We made no plans beyond that, because we would be talking to each other by phone daily.

She left a while before sunset, so I was able to walk up to the old bench, sit awhile, and watch the sun drop below the horizon a ways up the Old Muddy.

Just before the sun disappeared completely, I was surprised by the appearance of someone walking out of the scrub brush at the edge of the river bluff. Then I felt both a sense of fear and elation. The figure was that of an old man, almost naked except for an off-white loincloth. He was carrying a hard wood walking stick with a smooth round grip at its upper end. He smiled, waved, and slightly bowed, then faded into darkening shadows of night. As I walked back to the house, it suddenly dawned on me that, until that evening, I had never seen El Buho Viejo smile. As that thought took root in my mind, it caused me to smile also.

That night, as I took my place in my bed, alone, I thought back over the past two weeks or so. I had made new acquaintances and friends. I was able, with the help of a friend—Krash—to make some wrong things right. And, though sometimes I find it unbelievable, I have been befriended by something that I'm not sure really exists. But even that something makes me believe more in "The God" and His teachings. So at that moment, as I felt sleep starting to overtake me, I gave thanks to God for all His grace to this man, Casper Gray, and his friend Josiah Jackson Krash.

Chapter 34

A few days later, as I had just settled back into my routine, the old cell in my pocket reminded me there were scammers out in them there hills. So I looked at the origin of the call, and it was from Gray Fox.

"Hello, you Scamming Redskin, what sad news do you bring this time? I just solved your murder, and now you're back in my yard again."

"Sorry I'm disturbing you, you Scrawny White Eyes. But, I have news I felt you might get a bang out of."

"Great to hear from you Chief; fun aside, how are you?"

"Really good, now that things have quieted down a lot. And thanks again for all your and Krash's help. Without it I would have drowned in my own juice."

"Now give me the wild news you have," I said.

"Casper, I just received a call from Mickey Lopez. After you left, we checked all over the country for any outstanding warrants for the little rat, but no one wanted him. He was a thorn every place he showed up, but he was not really a hardened criminal. And, all we could get him on was being a nuisance and faking a death. And you heard him dispute that charge. He said he never faked his death, we just assumed he had because he dumped some of his old blood that he had drawn and kept for a transfusion in case of an accident. And, he said he had dragged the old chair through it, getting it to the back door to sit on the porch to have a smoke. The knife, he said, got bloody when he cut the plastic bags to dump the blood. Yeah, you remember hearing all that.

"I wanted to throttle the little shit, but in court he would probably have beaten us, and then we would have looked like fools to the public. And you know how politics is—don't ever make a fool of yourself, intentionally. So I turned his little ass loose."

Big Red swallowed a couple of times, and then, in a serious tone, he continued, "And Gray, I felt sorry for the little weasel. He said he only came to Arizona because, before his grandmother died, she told him there was a piece of animal skin in her bible that would make him very rich. After she died, he looked at the animal skin—a piece of finely tanned hide with writing on it that appeared to be a map. He said he followed the map, but all it did was lead him to an empty hole under an old burial box."

I remembered the tale Mickey Mouse had blubbered as Gray Fox was putting him in a cell, but it didn't make much sense. And I also remembered him crying in the cell and saying over and over again, "I just want to go home and see Grandma's grave once more." I felt sorry for the kid also.

"Gray, you remember, he threw the piece of tanned leather at us and said, 'Get rid of this piece of crap, because someone else got the treasure before I got there.' My aunt's husband," and he growled as he said it, "my uncle, is an authority on the early culture here in Arizona, said Lopez must have misinterpreted the writing, because you discovered the treasure was in the woods. But the main reason I called was to tell you the little bastard must know someone, because he told me when he got back to LA, the police came to his house, the one he inherited from his grandmother. He thought they were going to arrest him for something, so he was scared to death again. But they told him a law firm from Silicon Valley had been trying to contact him. It seems, as he said, his grandmother was an easy mark, and evidently many years ago someone coerced her into buying some penny stocks, back when computers first came on the market. And her stocks were worth between 3 and 5 million dollars when she died. And the little skunk is her only living heir. Isn't that a tale?"

A thought quickly rushed through my brain: *Yes, he apparently has an ancestral grandpa who watches over all his people and somehow caused this to happen.* I hoped Lopez would use the money as wisely as his grandfather had protected it.

Then I replied to Gray Fox, "It sounds like Grandma really loved him, and now she has taken care of him in death the way she would have liked to in life."

The chief cleared his throat and then said something I was not expecting. "Oh yes, after you and Krash would not accept the council's gift of some of the coins, they asked me if I would accept some. I did accept one to put in our little ranger's museum at the station, as a memento of this strange, strange case."

Then he quickly continued, "Gray, I need to get back to business here in the canyon, so take care, keep in contact, and let me know when you and the little tour guide are going to tie the knot. Because I may be able to make it to Missouri for the fiesta."

"Chief, back to you on the wishes for a good life, and if a wedding happens, I will want you and Krash as best man and groomsman. Just don't know yet which one of you will be which. Adios amigo, vaya con Dios."

"Give Melody my best, my friend. Adios."

Gray Fox didn't mention it, but I assumed the little Franken girl was doing well in her medical treatment. The Old One took care of her, so I have to believe she was also kin. And in my dream he called her "mi hija"—*my child.*

I returned to the chore I had been involved in before Gray Fox's call. And I allowed my mind to visualize my love in her dazzling state as I daydreamed about our night date, coming tonight.

Chapter 35

Melody enjoyed being a night guest in my house because of various reasons, the main one being, her house was so small, and therefore the bedrooms were small. In my house, most of the rooms are also small for historic reasons. But my master bedroom is a bit larger, and I have a king-size bed.

After almost two and a half weeks apart, becoming reacquainted was an extreme pleasure. And, with two different women in my bed, the love games we played were almost sinful. Melody acted like a mature woman, while Teen Angel was, most of the time, no more than a bubble-gummer. How Melody could play a role such as Teen Angel to such complete perfection was beyond me. I wondered if she was only enjoying reliving her teenage years, and I was giving her the opportunity. Whatever, I enjoyed being her teammate in all the games.

I knew in a while, maybe a week or two, we would return to a state of total maturity. Our lovemaking would become more predictable, but no less enjoyable. Then Melody would lead another tour, and after her return, for a few days, the sex games would once more be wild and unpredictable.

The times I accompanied her on tours, the exotic places we visited would bring on more erotic behavior. I have never been sure which of the situations I enjoyed more—sex in foreign territory or starved sex after a separation. Both kept me feeling young and made Melody irresistible.

But, I had to believe I was smart enough to understand that sex alone would not sustain a marriage. So, for the two years we have been together, I've cultivated Melody's interest in history, sports, hunting, and fishing, plus historical collecting. Her travels while directing tours have widened her scope of geography, politics, and foreign culture. Also, we have established a mutual interest in many other things. However, sex is the spice that keeps our relationship recipe tasty.

As I sat on the old bench and pondered all those things, I enjoyed the comings and goings of the birds and animals as they journeyed across my land and mind.

Then I saw Melody's car as it labored up the drive and found its favorite resting place beside the old barn. I supposed it chose that spot because it was protected from rain, snow, and any other falling weather by the slight overhang of the roof, which also provided shade on hot sunny days. Once more I watched as my Total Beauty left the car with all her necessities for a night bunking party in her hands and over her shoulders. Then she entered the back door of my house, I supposed to drop off her belongings.

As I arose from my seat of comfort, Melody came back out the rear door. "Hey Cass, I've brought lunch and other goodies, if you're interested," she softly shouted.

Lunch sounded tasty, but other goodies sounded even tastier. So I moved on down the slight slope toward the back door. As she started to disappear back through the door, I saw her commence to unfasten certain articles of clothing. I figured she was planning to present the goodies before she served lunch.

As I entered the door, I heard Teen Angel call from the bedroom, "Cassy. If you come on in the bedroom, we can practice the new cheering drills we cheerleaders have been assigned for the Friday night games. I think you will be interested—there are three or four new positions to practice."

New positions? I thought. Now, that invitation sounded extremely interesting! Usually trying to accomplish new positions gave me real satisfaction.

And they did!

Chapter 36

One morning as I approached my old bench to wile away some time and relieve some of the aches and pains that a mature male develops along with wisdom, I noticed in the loose dust between my feet a sparkle of shiny metal. Thinking I had dropped a pull tab from either a soda or a cold beer, I reached down to extract the object from the dust, and a large round gold disk appeared between my fingers. In size it was about the diameter of a US silver dollar. But I immediately recognized gold. I knew it had to be one of the gold coins from the hoard. I didn't rub the dust off, because I knew gold could be scratched by grains of sand. So, I placed it in front of my lips and blew the dust away. Then I saw a date—"1795." As I studied the coin more, I also could read "CAROL IIII. D-G." Then I looked up, and above my head sat the black owl. I immediately knew the source of the coin. He flapped his wings, and I caught a glimpse of a human eye on the tip of his wing. He majestically rose into the air and faded from sight. But the magnificent coin remained in my hand.

For a while I allowed my mind to try to understand what the past few moments meant. I had to believe the coin signified the birth of Miguel Lopez and was a thank-you gift from El Buho. As I stood up, with the intent to return to the house to look at the big coin under a magnifying glass, my cell rang.

"Hey Boss, Krash here. Did you put something in one of my lens filter cases? I found a strange object, and I don't know where it came from."

As Krash continued to rattle my mind, it snapped into gear, and I immediately knew what Krash had found in his filter case. Rudely I broke into his prattle and said, "Let me guess what you found in the filter case. A shiny gold pieces of eight!"

"Damn you, Casper, you did put it in my filter case. But why? You told me not to take a coin out of the hoard because it would make the Old Ghost mad, and then you did it. What a damn fake you are."

"Krash, I didn't put it in your filter case. El Buho did, as a thank-you gift for helping him do what he needed to get done."

Krash almost screamed, "Damn you, Gray, you're lying!"

As he bitched on, I tried to think how I could convince him I was not to blame. Then, I'm sure the Old One placed a thought in my mind. Butting in once more, I asked Krash what caused him to open his lens filter case.

"Something told me to look in there."

"No, someone told you to look in there. What were you doing just before you got the urge to open the filter case?" I asked.

"I was preparing to print a picture of some old dead and gnarled tree branches to try to sell."

"Can you look close at the old twisted branches and see if there is anything in them?"

"Why?"

"Just enlarge a little and check."

There was a pause. And then I heard a very soft "She...it" escape from Krash's mouth.

"He's perched on one of the rotted branches. It's him, and he has one eye closed in a wink."

"Now look again, and he will be gone."

After another moment's pause: "Oh shit, for real! He's gone."

"Krash, he was never there. Remember, you can't take a photo of a ghost. Just thank him for the gift and enjoy owning a piece of El Buho's treasure."

"How did you know what I found?"

Then to tease a little, I said, "And the mint date is 1795."

"How...?"

I explained that I had received the same gift.

Then, Krash also explained, "I thought it had to be you, but I couldn't figure why. You told me not to take anything from the hoard because the Old Fart would take revenge. And seeing what happened to Old Slim Pinn, I didn't want to challenge his power.

But then I thought, if you believed, how could you be dumb enough to try to steal from him?"

Last, I told him I believed we would all be very well rewarded for doing the right thing. Maybe not today, but sometime. Then before the call ended, I told him the tale Gray Fox had told me about Mickey Mouse Lopez.

Krash then said, "Gray, you and I didn't need the money, so the Old One led us to help the less fortunate. That's God's teaching, so maybe he's a messenger from God."

I replied, "Could be," as I bid him good luck and hung up the phone.

Chapter 37

I was beginning to believe that everyone involved in the affair was going to receive a coin from El Buho, but then I received a call from Tama. She sounded excited, but she started the conversation in a calm sort of way. But the longer we exchanged gossip, the higher her voice rose, and finally she blurted, "Casper, you won't believe what has happened."

Then fear caught my mind, and I blurted, "Is the little Franken girl okay?"

"She's great, gaining every day, but Casper, something wonderful has happened to Tom and me."

Then I knew a baby was on the way. And I almost made a fool of myself as she exclaimed, "Tom has an offer to write a book, and the publisher has offered $300,000 as a writer's bonus. And it's all because of you giving him the old leather manuscript to transcribe. It not only located the treasure, but it also located the tiny settlement where El Buho was born and probably buried. He has been doing archeology work there and is finding rare relics of the early period. And what I would have never believed—it's on our property and it's where we most often see El Buho Viejo doing his daily work. Isn't that fantastic?"

I knew what she had just described was her gift from El Buho, and I was very pleased. He had saved her life as a child and now had insured her life for the future. And I believed Tom's book would be a bestseller for years to come. If El Buho had anything to do about it, it would.

I didn't know if Gray Fox had told her about what he had been given by the council and the museum, or how he believed the treasure had been buried in a pine forest under a big rock. She and Tom had to know the truth, because Tom had transcribed the leather message. She probably would not divulge the truth to the chief, because he didn't believe El Buho existed anyway.

As my mind wandered back to her excited talking, I felt extremely happy for her and Tom, and maybe I wasn't far off with my initial thoughts on her excitement. A child might be in their future also.

She finished up her narrative, and then our phone conversation came to a close.

Chapter 38

I was beginning to believe the story of the Old One's treasure was finally coming to an end. With its conclusion, I felt my life would rapidly return to normal, and Melody and I could concentrate on our future. But, El Buho Viejo had one last trick to play.

It all started with a call from Krash. As usual, I was just becoming involved with one of my projects. Melody had expressed a desire for a couple of flower beds to be planted in a sunny open space in front of my house. She had said, "If I become Mrs. Gray and an equal partner in this historic setting, I think there should be some beautiful plant life around the premises."

I decided the stated desire was a veiled command, so I decided to try to please. But before I could get out of the house, my phone rang. When I answered, Krash was on the other end.

"Hey Boss, Krash here."

"Whatsup?" I slurred.

"You won't believe it, but I'm going to do a segment on a nationwide TV news broadcast."

"What's the joke?" I asked.

"No joke, Boss. I've been invited to appear on Cameo Carlile's TV show, *News Is Where You Find It*. She got in touch with Gray Fox to be her guest, but he turned her down. He told her I would be much more interesting and informed than he, so why not have me on? Then she called me, and I said I would have to talk to you, as you and I worked together on the case. Do you want to appear with me?"

I pretended to give it thought for a few moments and then said, "Krash, you tell a better story than I do, and I would have to travel again, right now, when Melody and I are discussing our future. Why don't you do the show and tell the story?"

"Boss, you would trust me to tell the story about the treasure and El Buho all by myself?"

"All I would advise is, be careful what you say about El Buho. Remember how powerful he is."

"Yeah, Boss, you're right. I'll speak in theoretical terms if I mention ghosts or spiritual things at all. Boss, you're sure you don't want to appear with me on her show?"

"Better not—too much happening here right now. But let me know the date of the show, 'cause Melody and I would love to watch. And good luck, Old Buddy."

After our conversation ended, I had a feeling this was one more step in Krash's rise to stardom. Maybe "Krash the Fantastic" was possible after all. As I let my thoughts journey on, I wondered how Old Krazy would conduct himself.

Chapter 39

After getting a call from Krash saying the Cameo Carlile show was to be aired the following Sunday night during prime time, I was caught a little off-balance. Not being a real TV buff, as I grew older the computer took the place of the idiot box. I was not up-to-date as to when various shows were aired. So I knew I had to get prepared for Krash's big day. I didn't even own a satisfactory TV. All I possessed was a tiny little job to watch the news and weather on. Melody said we needed a big set to watch Krash put on his comedy show. She remembered him from our time at the canyon when Pinn was killed. So I rushed to Walmart and bought the biggest set they carried and rushed home to install it in the living room. It was so danged big I was afraid I would have to sit on the porch and look at it through the door. But it worked out pretty well, and I knew I could always give it to one of the neighbors after we watched the Cameo Carlile show get Krashed.

Finally Sunday night rolled around, and Melody and I were prepared for the big entertainment. I had even bought a couple of frozen pizzas for the event. Along with a six-pack of cheap beer, we decided we were more than prepared.

Melody had put the pizzas in the oven and set the timer. We thought a commercial would probably take place about the time the pizzas were ready, so we could grab them and be back for the rest of the show.

At 7:00 p.m., the Cameo Carlile show appeared on the screen. And the screen was so big, when she walked out in front of the camera, I could actually see what she looked like. After a couple of short news presentations—one concerning a woman's attempt to single-handedly save a beached whale, and the second about a man training bees to defend his flower beds from dogs digging in them for field mice—it was time for Krash's segment on "The Treasure of the Grand Canyon."

For about four minutes, we were forced to watch a commercial about treatments for men with ED. Melody giggled and said, "Sure doesn't apply to you." As she laid out the two pizzas and a couple of beers, the commercial was over.

As the spotlight centered on a figure I was not sure I recognized... Krash walked out on stage. He was clean-shaven, and his hair was trimmed and styled to perfection. His dress was a well-cut and fitted suit. His shoes were of the highest quality and shined to reflection. As he continued toward the seating area on stage, he was being introduced by Cameo Carlile.

"Tonight, ladies and gentlemen, we are privileged to have with us, here on stage, Josiah Jackson Krash, renowned nature photographer and sometime sleuth. Over the past weeks he has been involved in a very interesting mystery and search for long-lost treasure at the Grand Canyon of the Colorado. Because of his fearless disregard for most situations and his following of various dangerous adventures, he has acquired the sobriquet of 'Krazy Jack Krash.' Now if you would, help me welcome Mr. Jack Krash."

At that moment Krash seated himself on the sofa, and Ms. Carlile took the moderator's chair. The audience erupted in wild applause. After a minute or two, as the adulation began to quiet, Ms. Carlile continued, "Mr. Krash, did you solve the mystery of the Grand Canyon treasure entirely by yourself?"

"Oh no, Ms. Carlile, there were several others involved, in one way or another. Some were involved with good intentions in their hearts, to help others, and some with the intent to help themselves."

"Mr. Krash, would I be out of line if I asked which group you feel you were associated with?"

"No, Ms. Carlile, not at all. In the beginning I dreamed of buried treasure and great riches. I believe it is an odd individual who would not think that way."

"You seem to sound like you may have changed from that feeling. Am I correct?"

"Yes, after working with a man, Casper Gray, I discovered there were other things in life besides gaining wealth."

"And what are those other things, Mr. Krash?"

"The main thing is gaining self-respect. I learned from Mr.

Gray that self-respect is worth more than gold and silver. Mr. Gray believes in the worth of other people. And now, so do I."

"Mr. Krash, would you continue with your story?" As Krash spoke, pictures and snips of video recordings were played behind him. Pictures of him in his various garbs—the jungle hunter, the detective—and him with his photographic gear, some taped on and some tied to his person. And of course pictures of the treasure. As Krash continued with his story, he spoke in a cultured voice, and I could not envision the man I had been working with. This man, by his presentation and demeanor, was well educated and refined. This man was not Krazy Jack Krash.

"Mr. Gray and I—using clues as they presented themselves, observations, common sense, and the spirits that surrounded us— were able to answer question after question until the mystery was solved."

"Mr. Krash, did I hear you say *spirits*?"

Then I was terribly afraid he was going to mention El Buho, and if he did, perhaps all hell would break loose.

"Yes, remember, we found treasure from over two hundred years ago. Don't you think the spirits of the ones who lost or hid the treasure that long ago were watching us look for it?"

"Did you actually see any spirits or ghosts as you were searching?"

"No, only the screech of birds and the howl of the canyon winds, and perhaps a shadow now and then. But, I would be remiss if I didn't mention Dr. Thomas Dodd and his wife. They were of great help in using their knowledge of Arizona history to answer questions only top scholars in their field could answer. Dr. Dodd is presently finishing a book about the Old Ones of the area, and it will be on the bookshelves in a short time."

As Krash was hawking Dodd's book, he pointed at the camera and continued, "If you want to know more about the Old Ones and their way of life, buy his book."

As Krash stood up to shake Ms. Carlile's hand, he made one more point. "And, if you would like to see the 'Treasure of the Canyon,' visit the Canyon Museum in The Village at the main center of the Grand Canyon of the Colorado, Arizona."

As he walked off stage, Krash waved at the camera, and the audience once more broke into wild applause. With a slice of pizza in her hand, Melody stood up, walked over, and turned off the TV. Then she joined me back on the sofa. After a few minutes of causal talk, we decided to go for a moonlight drive before sneaking off to the master bedroom for a little serious love.

As I drove up old Route 79 along the river, the conversation gradually worked its way around to the subject we had been avoiding for two years. Melody broke the armistice first.

"Casper, we've been together for over two years now. We agreed to get to know each other before we seriously talked of marriage. Do you still want to marry me today as much as you did two years ago?"

"As much and perhaps even more, and now I know exactly what you want out of life, and I want to give it to you, if I can."

Then Teen Angel jumped in and stated, "I graduate in about two weeks, and Momma says if I'm crazy enough to marry a high roller from New York, there ain't much she can do about it."

Teen Angel's last statement caught me a little by surprise. Her character was advancing the pretend graduation by at least a year. But that didn't bother me, because I then knew Melody was finally prepared to make the serious move of marriage.

Then I answered, in my college character, "I didn't get the pro football contract I wished for, but I did learn to scoop manure in college, so I guess I can earn a living. So...let's get the ball rolling."

I pulled off at a wide place in the road and stopped the truck. Melody jumped into my arms and whispered in my ear, "We could go back to the house and consummate the marriage early."

I pushed her back to her side of the truck, turned around, and got back to the house in record time.

Chapter 40

After pulling the truck into the barn, and as Melody and I walked toward the house, I sensed a presence just out of reach. And then in the far distance I heard the lonely hoot of a large Missouri hoot owl, and a feeling of wonder flowed through my being.

After a period of serious lovemaking, Melody said she was ready for sleep, and I pretended by saying I was too. As I laid my hand on the softness of her side, she drifted off to sleep.

I rolled onto my back, and with my hands under the back of my head, I began to drift off into the realm of deep thoughts of El Buho Viejo and what he and his gifts meant to everyone in this little spring fiasco. As I thought, I listed:

First and foremost, he gave life back to Freddie Franken, no matter what his connection was to her. And, I'm sure he will care for her for the rest of her life.

Next, he gave new life to Mickey Lopez.

Third, he assured a great life for Tama Claybasket and her husband, Dr. Thomas Dodd.

Then, he became another step on the ladder to Krash's success and fame.

Fifth, he brought Casper Gray and his love Melody together one summer, and saw them work toward a full life together two summers later.

Sixth, he solved another case for Chief Christjohn Gray Fox, continuing to solidify his position as chief ranger at the Grand Canyon of the Colorado.

And, he assured a boost in tourism money by increasing the holdings of the Canyon Museum.

As I lay there a while longer, a little sadness struck me. El Buho Viejo gave so much, but what did he get for all the gifts he gave?

Then, though I might have been asleep and only dreamed it, I heard a voice—deep and somewhat hollow-sounding—say, in broken English, "Two friends...Owl Gray and the Krazy stealer of souls, with his devil's box."

Chapter 41

After my love's declaration that she was ready to become Mrs. Casper "Spook" Gray, I knew that was my cue to get a move on.

I immediately started making a list of all the necessary things that needed to be done to finally make Sweet Melody my wife.

Together we decided the ceremony would be small, with only minimal invited guests. Of course Krazy Krash, the Old Red Chief Gray Fox, his aunt Tama, and her husband Tom would be on my side of the festivities, along with my neighbor and close friend. On Melody's side would be her good friend Susan and the other bank employees she was close to. Christjohn Gray Fox would be my best man, and Krash would be my groomsman and the official photographer. Susan would be Melody's maid of honor. The ceremony would be held in the side yard of our historic house, near the largest flower bed, as the annual plants would all be in bloom.

I jokingly asked my love if she would be married in her own persona or that of Teen Angel or perhaps a little witch.

Glibly, she replied, "I believe being myself would be the wisest, but the other two will be invited."

I almost immediately contacted Volkens of Chicago and asked if they could produce a very special wedding ring. This time Saulvester replied, "If you are willing to pay the price, we will design and make whatever you desire."

I explained my design as having a medium-size, rectangular, solitaire diamond set in a 14-karat-gold band with a fake filigree design on the outer surface. Within the fake filigree would be hidden the name *Teen Angel*, and on the inside of the band would be a tiny, slightly raised silhouette of a toad.

Saulvester said that in a few days I would receive a drawing of my design, and if it met my desires, the ring would be made and shipped by special delivery. And I was assured it would be completed within fourteen days. I was quoted a price, and I agreed to the terms.

Melody said, "I would like to have a nice wedding gown, but not a white one. I wore a white one in my last wedding, and my man left me. This time I would like to wear something in perhaps a pale green, as it would represent renewal and new life, like plants in springtime."

I decided I would be the one to wear white, as my first marriage was happy and fulfilling, and I felt Lily would be present, and I knew she would be dressed in angel white.

Melody had a custom gown made, and it was beautiful. And I knew with her in it, it would be even more beautiful.

We set a date, and I contacted Krash and Gray Fox, and they both agreed to take part in the ceremony.

Tama and Tom would not be attending, as Tom had a speaking engagement concerning his book, and Tama had just discovered she and Tom were expecting, and she was apprehensive about traveling.

On the sly, Tama called me and explained she and Tom would be sending a tiny, ancient clay bowl that Tom found near El Buho's house remains. Tom believed it was a guard talisman, as it had the eyes and ears design of El Buho, as well as the feather with the eye. She also said, "I believe it was found to be a gift for your family, assuring that the Old One will be with you always." And then she said she called me to explain because she did not know if Melody knew about El Buho. I explained that she did not know, and I was very pleased with the thought and the gift.

Susan agreed to be Melody's maid of honor, and the bank wanted to host a special post-wedding reception in their building's meeting hall.

Krash contacted us and said his gift would be a special, complete photo layout of our wedding: photos of the wedding preparation, the ceremony, and the post-wedding reception. I knew we would not have just a photo layout, we would have a full-sized picture book of our great day.

The wedding ring soon arrived, and I allowed Melody to see it and approve the design. She was happy with my idea, but I had to show her Teen Angel's name in the filigree and the small toad inside the band. She believed the ring was perfect and a real hoot.

At about the same time, Tama and Tom's gift also arrived. I explained that it was very old and the design was considered good luck by the Grand Canyon Havasupai culture. We decided it would have a special place on the fireplace mantel in our historic house.

Chapter 42

One Saturday morning I awakened as the widower Casper Gray, and at the end of the day I was the new groom Casper Gray.

During the ceremony, Lily had her place in the window at such an angle that she could watch the festivities. And for several days prior to the big day, her urn seemed to take on a sparkling shine. Early in the afternoon, the reception was held in the Centrail Bank meeting hall, and most friends and acquaintances were in attendance.

Gray Fox spent the day in full Grand Canyon chief ranger uniform, with all its badges and ribbons.

Krash was decked out in a handmade suit from some fancy Denver tailor. But his trappings included his Japanese camera, and he spent the day pho-tog-er-phating every aspect of Melody's and my nuptials. After the ceremony, when he had a few moments to review some of his work, Krash caught me during a break in my required duties and exclaimed, "Boss, I have a picture or two I can't explain. Would you take a look and tell me what you see?"

He quickly brought up, on the review screen, a frame of Melody and me as I was placing the ring on her finger. There working in the flower garden behind us was an old man showing a huge grin and dressed in a loincloth. El Buho Viejo was actually in two of the pictures.

Krash was shaking like a leaf as he proudly proclaimed, "I got one...I finally got it, the BIG FRAME! I have a picture of a real ghost. I'll be famous, Krash the Great!"

Before Old Krazy could really go nuts, I said, "Hold on a minute!"

I took the camera and stepped out into a crowd of the younger guests, stopped an older teenage girl, and asked her to tell me what she saw in one of the pictures on the review screen.

As she surveyed the frame, she started to give me a strange look. "Mr. Gray, it's you placing the wedding ring on Mrs. Gray's finger."

Then I asked, "What do you think of the new flowers in the flower bed behind us?"

With an even stranger, frowning look, she replied, "On your wedding day, why are you so interested in some dumb flowers? Or are you asking about the big black bird in the old dead tree behind?"

I thanked her for looking at the picture, and then I turned my attention back to Krazy as we stepped away from the girl. "Krash, sadly, you and I are the only ones who can see El Buho in the flesh. He wanted you and me to know he was also here for Melody's and my special day. But, perhaps he will allow his alter ego to remain in a picture for you, even if a wild owl is not that unusual in a forest setting. But, sorry, I can swear you are the greatest, but no one else will know if we have to depend on those two pictures."

Krash's face fell as he replied, "Oh well, we at least know he is real, or was once real, but God still has a place and a job for him to do on His great green earth."

Chapter 43

After a fantastic special day, it was back to the workaday world for Melody and honey do's for the new groom.

Oh yes, there was a honeymoon for the newlyweds. But Melody traveled so much on her job, she asked if we could drive away like we were leaving on a honeymoon and then secretly sneak back to the house and have a few days alone just being us.

After a little thought, I agreed, as we would have many opportunities to go places with the bank tours, and Melody and I would just use one room, instead of two next door to each other.

One morning sometime much later, when I arose a little early before Melody had opened her eyes, I observed the Old Spirit working in our flower bed. I believed he had not noticed me, but he raised his head and gave me a hi sign with a huge smile on his face. Then I remembered the little gray bowl on the mantel, the bowl with the strange dark markings of double V's and circles. El Buho was guarding Owl Gray's family. Forever!

Being a little nosy, later that day I went out to look at the garden work El Buho had been doing in the flower bed.

I noticed some little white blooms that had not been in the bed before. Melody and I had planted several different flowers, but I did not recognize what variety the little white ones were.

A day or so after, Melody and I were walking out to the old bench to sit and look at the river, or for me to just look at her and dream. On our way to the top of the cliff, I pointed out the small white flowers to her and asked if she recognized what they were. She grinned and said, "Yes, some of those were in my bridal bouquet. They're called baby's breath."

Then I asked, "We didn't plant those, did we?"

"No, and I have no idea how they got in there."

We started to walk away, and then I saw something gleaming in the afternoon sun. I reached down into the brown earth among the blossoms and picked up a small, flat gold charm with two figures carved into its surface.

After a brief visual investigation, I saw a very fine rendition of the Virgin Mary and the Christ Child. Immediately the hair on the back of my neck stood straight out from my flesh as I recognized the tiny item from some months in the past. The charm...or one exactly like it...was in the treasure hoard we found at the Grand Canyon.

Then I became aware that Melody was asking if she could see the little treasure. As I turned to hand her the charm, she gave forth with a long, loud burp.

"Oh, excuse me! It's funny, but the past couple of days, I've been burping a lot, and I don't know what's causing it. Do you suppose I should see a doctor?" Then she innocently laughed and asked, "You don't think I might be pregnant, do you?"

A deep-seated, strange feeling invaded my mind as thoughts ran rampant in many directions. Baby's breath, Holy Mother and Child, the Old One with almost a constant smile. Now burping, indicating a stomach issue. *Casper Gray, are you going to be a father at middle age?*

Then, as she handed the little charm back to me, she mused, "Where do you suppose that came from?"

Thinking quickly, I replied, "It appears to be very old. Perhaps it is a piece of trade goods lost by some Native American. It appears they lived on this bluff up until a couple of hundred years or so ago."

As we reached the old bench and made ourselves comfortable, Melody asked, "Cass, did you move the little Havasupai bowl off the mantel and put it next to Lily's urn in the window? It was moved, and I thought you decided it might look nicer there than on the mantel."

I replied, "I just put it there to see how I would feel about it." I knew very well I had not touched it.

Then my thoughts projected to Lily as I silently said, *Lily, we never had a child, and you were not allowed to be a mother. But, it appears you and the Old One will perhaps be guardian angels for a new arrival. And you might be the stepmother of your husband's child.*

Then tears came to my eyes as I whispered, "You are gone, but I will always love you and never forget you."

About the Author

Roger Baker retired from teaching school after twenty-nine years of service.

During his career in education, he used storytelling as a means to enrich his classroom presentations and capture the attention of his students.

He has been spending leisure hours of his retirement with storytelling, now with his pen. He and his wife reside in central Missouri.

Roger has published four other novels: *Two for the Price*, *Death is Sweet Revenge*, *Spirits of Sorrow*, and *The Reverend and the Peacemaker*.

www.ingramcontent.com/pod-product-compliance
Lightning Source LLC
Chambersburg PA
CBHW052024240626
47153CB00006B/1948